Desiring
Bernadette

ALSO BY DANIELLE GRAINGER

THE DENTON HEIGHTS SERIES
Under Her Wing (Book 1):
The Shasti and Madison Story

In Her Cage (Book 2):
The Jaleesa and Tina Story

Within Her Grasp (Book 3):
The Marta and Shanice Story

By Her Command (Book 4)
The Rowena and Minjung Story

THE BERNADETTE SERIES
Wrecking Bernadette (Book One)

(S)mothering Bernadette (Book Two)

Becoming Bernadette (Book Three)

Desiring Bernadette (Book Four)

Loving Bernadette (Book Five)

DESIRING
Bernadette

BOOK FOUR IN THE BERNADETTE SERIES

DANIELLE GRAINGER

Paperback ISBN   978-1-953734-09-9

First Edition 2021

9 8 7 6 5 4 3 2 1

Cover design by Sarah (Forcoverservice)

Published by:
Bibi Books Publishing Company, LLC

Dedication

This work is dedicated to those who practice loving and nurturing BDsM.

Acknowledgments

Big thanks go out to those fans who subtly and not-so-subtly pushed me to continue the series and write from a Domme's perspective. I specifically want to thank Kat, who routinely nudged me to keep writing and who made welcome suggestions. I also want to thank Jiske and Olivia, my awesome Beta readers, who routinely caught those pesky little errors that crept in during my haste to get the story out. Also, I want to lavishly shower love and admiration upon my Kik group of like-minded people who not only help me get the details right but who continue to help me on my life's journey.

Table of Contents

Chapter 1
Points of Pride

I kiss the top of Bernadette's head. She moans sleepily from the beautiful subspace where she is currently flying. My arms that are wrapped around her send the message that she is safe and free to soar. I am unbelievably lucky to have this glorious woman in my life.

"Rikki," Bernadette says after a while. "I need to service you." She sighs contentedly, and her head lolls against my chest.

"Shh, shh, shh," I soothe. "I'm just fine, little bee." I run my fingers over the collar I ceremoniously placed on her neck not that long ago and unclip the leash. "Fly away, my love."

"Mmm," she moans again and snuggles up against me.

My heart is full. She satisfies me in so many ways, and as far as I can tell, I satisfy her needs as well. She has a libido that almost surpasses my own. Almost. Before we officially sleep for the night, I will take her for my own pleasure. Lust hits me deep in my belly. Shit, I could fuck her right now, but no. No, she is still a relative newbie, learning the ways of submission. One of those benefits I offer is allowing her to fly after a flogging.

Bernadette takes to flogging like no other sub I've ever had. And there have been many. She absorbs each stroke intimately. Like most subs, though, she tries to stay strong and not cry out, but I encourage her to. I want her to release whatever is inside. "You must let it out," I keep telling her, and she

1

ultimately gives in. Like this evening. She finally cried out in pain when my rhythmic strokes hit her harder. She knows I will take care of her. She knows I must hit her body, so she gets to the place I want her to go. And she knows that I also need the release of hurting her, the release I feel when inflicting pain on another human. She may not understand my need, I barely do, but it makes me feel strong, in control, and powerful. Yes, it makes me feel like a god watching her take it.

It fascinates me to see her struggle through that in-between stage of trying to be strong and then ultimately succumbing to her own fight-or-flight instincts. She pulls hard against the restraints of the St. Andrew's cross yet accepts each stroke with dignity and poise if there is such a thing during an impact session. Eventually, I reach my own Zen rhythm, an incredibly cathartic headspace for me, and I believe she does as well. Pride fills me as I watch her relax into the pain. She widens her legs, instinctively offering her body to me. Her back arches, silently asking for more. Her cries of pain eventually change to moans of bliss, so at this point, I switch from a four-point to a more intense six-point rhythm. The floggers dancing in my hands become an extension of me.

When her moans stop, and she slumps forward with her mouth open, often drooling, it is time for me to slow my strokes so she can cool down. I stop and let her bask in the pulsing pain, her skin wonderfully red and marked. My fingers make designs on her body, and her moans at my touch are euphoric for both of us. Her moans make my pussy clench and scream for attention. Patience, I tell my body. Her needs are more important right now. We'll get ours—no need to worry.

I then unclip her from the cross and bring her down to the ground, her ankles still tethered. I pull a sheet over us and wrap her in a tight embrace. "I have you," I always tell her. I tell her to fly and that I will watch over her. This evening, she babbled incoherently for a moment and then moaned and grew quiet.

She has never called a safeword during impact play, but this evening, I could tell she was flying so high that she wouldn't have been able to. I am proud of my ability to read her so well, even though she's only been mine for about three months.

Reliving the scene has made me so fucking horny. I know as her Domme, if I flipped her over and fucked the life out of her, she would accept it. Her willingness to submit amazes me. Submissives, in general, amaze me. I could never imagine allowing someone to do to me what I do to them. Ahh, but I can't flip her over right now. I respect her too much. She has earned her flying time and deserves to enjoy it.

Oh, my Bernadette. My submissive. To others, she is Dr. Garneau, a respected professor of mathematics. She is that, yes, but she is also a relative newcomer to the scene, and I must remember that. She has had several disappointing experiences with people who call themselves Dommes. To be fair, Victoria was her last Domme and a respected Domme in our community. She was, anyway, until she pulled that shit with Bernadette. That shit that I'm still trying to clean up. As for the other Dommes in Bernadette's life, they were abusers, especially the one that chained her to a hotel bed for hours and hours against her will, causing the cuff marks on her wrist to scar. That infuriates me. So, this is why I evaluate every move I make with my precious little bee. She is opening up to me so beautifully. I can tell there is something deep inside her that I haven't been able to reach yet. *Give it time*, I hear Aunt Tilda's council in my head. *Let it unfold naturally*. She always told me that when I was a baby Domme trying to rush a new submissive girl.

I tear up at the memory of my great aunt. She was the one who introduced me to BDSM and all it had to offer. She thought I'd follow in her footsteps in the family Dominatrix business, and I have after a fashion. Still, now I only do it professionally as a side gig when time allows. Her boy toys were more than willing to let me practice my fledging flogging, caning, paddling, spanking, and whipping skills on them. Aunt Tilda just wasn't strong enough to satisfy them anymore, she'd said, although she personally kept up the cock and ball torture, something I wanted absolutely nothing to do with. I always let them jerk off afterward, too. I figured if I rewarded them, they'd let me beat them again in the near future. Now I do it for money. Most of the men I service love humiliation, and I make fun of their worthless little dicks. I make them show me that their insignificant worms can actually produce cum. If I let them cum on my boots, then they have to lick it off. It's great for a few bucks, but honestly, it's the power over them that fuels me. As Aunt Tilda knew it would.

This power I have over Bernadette excites me as well but in a different way. She's not playing at this like so many of my former subs who were in it for the temporary thrills. They weren't here for me, not really. I was a fetish dispenser. Eileen especially.

I groan, and Bernadette protests and adjusts against my body. "You're right, little bee. No thinking about the evil ex right now. Or ever again." I stroke her back and kiss the top of her head.

I think she has fallen asleep, and I am ready to doze as well when I feel soft kisses along my wrist.

"I love you, Rikki," Bernadette says. "Thank you for, um…"

"Beating you?"

"Mm hmm," she moans and arches her pelvis. She is horny as well. "Yes, Ma'am. You are wonderful." She trails kisses up my arm and then twists around to kiss my belly, and then moves toward my breasts under my open leather vest. Her lustful eyes look at me, asking permission to touch me there. I answer by putting both hands on the back of her head and pushing her onto my left breast. She moans as she licks my nipple, hardening it. She has definitely learned how to please me. She purses her lips and sucks tenderly.

"Good girl, my Bernadette." I press her head firmly. "Yes, yes." I maneuver her to my right breast, and she makes love to it skillfully. I pull her up and kiss her fully on the lips before my eyes tell her to move down and service me properly. As she kisses her way back down my torso, I unsnap the top of my leather pants and lift my hips. She understands how to peel the leather off me and not break the momentum. We've done this many times since I like to wear leathers during impact play. It gets me in the mood. She tugs the pants off and places them gently out of our way. I have never been one to stop the action by making a sub fold clothes. Who the fuck cares about that?

Bernadette scoops up my left foot in one hand and pulls my toes into her mouth. She begins her exploration. I never taught her this and never knew it was something I might like until she tried it one afternoon while we were watching an old black and white movie. I had commanded her to kneel and lean forward to kiss my feet. She took that further and began making love to my feet. I was putty in her hands, but I never let her know that. I had to stay cool and strong and in charge.

I touch her head, indicating I'd like her to move on. She moves up to my calf and continues to leave a trail of kisses until she pauses to devour my inner thighs. She knows not to move on until I give her the signal. I reach down and grab a handful of her hair. Her hair is relatively short but is just enough for me to grip. "Please me," I command, my voice thick with lust.

She doesn't answer but begins her slow and steady licking and sucking and nibbling of my vulva. I exhale my pleasure, making sure that she hears me. I relax my grip in her hair as she twirls her tongue around my clit slowly, pausing on occasion to suck me rhythmically but oh so gently. She has an amazing touch and admitted to me one time that she loves going down on women. She said it was a privilege to be allowed to touch a woman in this personal and intimate way. I asked her if she wanted me to loan her to other women while I watched, and she didn't answer. I got the feeling she wasn't sure if I was kidding. At some point, I'll ask her again because I was not kidding and already have someone in mind.

I grab her hair again and push her away. "Get the strap-on from the closet. The pink one."

"Mmm," she says with a moan. "Yes, Ma'am." She goes to do my bidding. While she's gone, I take off my vest and gloves and then get us a room-temperature bottle of water. She told me that cold water constricts her throat, so room temperature was better before cock swallowing.

I move to the edge of the bed and command her to put the harness on me. She kneels before me and does so quickly and with sure hands. She occasionally looks up at me, conveying her gratitude. It puffs me up like a peacock. She is one of a kind. I feel a point of pride knowing she is mine.

I hand her the water. "Drink and then please me by swallowing my cock."

"Mmm," she moans again, clearly excited. She takes a few sips of water and then offers me some. I decline but again have a moment of pride. She is so thoughtful. I have never had a sub offer me water or take care of me the way she does. I'm learning, slowly learning, that it is okay for her to take care of me in her own way without me constantly telling her what I want.

She places the bottle of water on the bedside stand and looks up at me from her kneeling position. She reaches up with both hands and then rakes her fingernails lightly down my body. I think this is her way of mentally preparing to do a difficult thing. Once she reaches the phallus, she lifts it with one hand and guides it to her mouth. The other hand wraps around my leg as if to anchor herself. She bobs her head on my pink cock, taking more and more each time. I feel the moment when it hits the back of her throat. Her momentary anxiety dissipates quickly and, on the next stroke, pushes it past the constriction. I let her lead because this is one of *her* points of pride. I've never required subs to deep throat. This is something she wanted to give me.

She looks up, trying to keep eye contact, but it isn't easy at this angle. I give her major points for trying. I gently lace my fingers in her hair, letting her know that I appreciate her efforts. And, shit, there is nothing as hot as watching a beautiful woman on her knees sucking down your cock. At these moments, I wish that pink cock was real and that I could dump my load down her throat.

Her nose bumps into the harness several times, and I tighten the grip in her hair. I finally pull her off me and guide her up and onto the bed facedown. She lifts her ass instinctively and reaches back to spread her cheeks, opening her ass and vagina to me. She learned quickly to offer herself to me. A few punishments when she'd forgotten helped in that regard.

I settle in between her legs and run my cock up and down her slit, making sure I hit her clit. She squeals each time, which tightens my core. It's the power and control I have over her physical body that tightens it. It's the fact that I don't have to ask permission, negotiate, or wait until she is in the mood. Fuck that. She is collared and mine for the taking.

I jam my cock into her sopping wet pussy and jackrabbit my way to a quick orgasm. I don't stop thrusting, though, because she is squirming and will cum soon. I pull out, and she groans her displeasure.

"Ten," I say and take my hands off her. "Nine." Her ass rises off the bed. "Eight." She thrusts back, knowing I won't touch her. "Seven." I move so she can see my face. "Six." She groans as I stroke my slick cock. "Five." She makes eye contact. "Four." Her eyes plead with me. "Three."

"Fuck, Rikki. Fuck," she says.

"Two."

She moans louder.

"One! Cum for me, good girl," I urge. Her body bucks at my words. "Cum now!"

She roars her orgasm, muttering obscenities. "Fuck, fuck, fuck." She writhes on the bed. She holds her breath and then lets it out. "Fuck, Rikki. Oh, my God." She struggles to catch her breath. "You fucking kill me with that voodoo shit."

I chuckle with amusement. My shy and proper college professor sure can have a potty mouth when she cums.

"Oh, oh, oh," Bernadette raises her ass off the bed and moans again. Multiple orgasms seem to be normal for her after a countdown. I watch in utter fascination as she shudders several more times while strong aftershocks possess her body. I swear she's having full-body orgasms.

"Rikki?" she says, opening her eyes desperately trying to find me. "I fucking love you."

"I know," I say and chuckle. "I love you, too, my little bee."

Usually, I would make her undo the straps of my harness, but I do it myself and leap on the bed beside her. I turn her onto her side and spoon her from behind. "I love you, too," I say again. "We both have to work in the morning. Time for sleep."

"Mmm," she moans, already halfway there.

Chapter 2
Big Bertha

I hate when Bernadette has to leave, but since I'm supposed to be the strong one, I wrap my arms around her. It's hard to do that while she's holding her briefcase in one hand and pre-packed lunch in the other, but I manage.

"Will you be a good girl for me today?" I whisper in her ear.

"Yes, Ma'am," Bernadette says with a sigh that makes it sound like she also hates goodbyes.

I pull out of the embrace, grab hold of her chin, and look her directly in the eyes. I already have her attention, so that move wasn't necessary, but I like to possess her. I think she likes it, too. Her breathing changes. She sighs almost imperceptibly, but I hear it. I notice it.

"Text me during your lunch break," I tell her. We've long established this routine, but I like to reinforce it. "If I'm available, I'll call you right back."

"Thank you," she says and then smiles. "Miss Olga has been hinting around that she'd like to meet you."

Bernadette's smile makes me melt. Those dimples are to die for. She is a beautiful woman. Strong, sexy, and relatively independent, but there are parts of her that I have yet to tap into. She has so long hidden her desires from the world that it is taking time to tease them out. But I have patience.

"It's interesting that you call your co-worker 'Miss.'"

She shrugs. "Everyone does."

"She seems important to you," I say, "so we'll figure out a day for me to meet her. At the university, maybe? I'd love to see where you work. And, speaking of work, after your classes, I want a picture of you in the dentist's office."

"For verification that I'm actually there for my appointment?"

"Yes."

"Like when you made me have that checkup at Shasti's office. They took so much blood for testing. Oh, my God. She has a nice setup there. You know I still haven't gotten a bill from her."

I just shrug and think, and you won't get a bill because Victoria took care of that as part of her penance.

"You can trust me, Rikki. Have I ever given you—"

"No," I say, interrupting her. "You have never given me any reason not to trust you. But I've asked you to do it, so you will."

"Okay. I understand." She drops her gaze. "It's because I haven't gone to a dentist in three years, and you think I might chicken out."

"Perhaps," I say. That is part of it. "I just like to know that my property is taken care of, and I also like to know where my property is during the day."

"Property," she echoes back, but I can tell she's murmuring to herself. A small smile creeps up her face. She likes that I think of her as my property. "You're making me wet, Rikki."

"Good," I say and move in to kiss her lips.

She moans, clearly aroused, and then I pull back, reach around, and smack her on her lovely ass. "Have a good day, little bee."

She groans in frustration. "Tease."

"Mm hmm," I say with a laugh. "Time to go. I have to get down to the shop."

"Furnace trouble again," she says. It wasn't a question. "I wish I knew HVAC repair so I could help you. Maybe you should send me to school for that instead of yoga."

I laugh again. "Yoga keeps you supple and strong and oh, so wonderfully flexible for me. But you're stalling. You can't be late for your meeting with Dr. Wainwright."

Her eyes get wide. "Oh, God. I forgot."

"You'll be fine. You read me your syllabus last night before I flogged you. It sounded great. You know your stuff. Now, go." I push her toward the door of my studio apartment.

She looks back at me with a worried expression on her face, and now I regret reminding her of the meeting with her department chair. Ahh, well. She's a tough cookie and passionate about the new course she's developing for the university. So much so that she'll forget all about her nerves once she gets talking about mathematics. Yes, my little bee is a nerd. But now it's time for me to be that HVAC repair person she wants to be.

I put on an old shirt, one that I don't mind getting dirty, and head down the stairs and through my office into the shop. We open at 6 a.m., and I left Bernadette sleeping while I got dressed and stole downstairs at 5:00 to let in my assistant manager, Mark. I helped him open up. Mornings are by far our busiest time—that and when we have events like the darts club on Monday evenings.

"I need to get more events like that," I mutter as I walk into the shop from my connecting office.

I opened the shop five years ago and can generally tell how things are going as soon as I walk in. This morning's eight a.m. vibe is a good one. Although it's cold in here, the line is moving, and my staff seems productively busy. Mark manages them well. I must remember to tell him that.

Mark sees me and smiles. It is a genuine smile. He's been with me for four years and seems to like working here. I think for him, it's more than a job. He has come so far from that young and restless, out-of-control young man that Seamus asked me to take a chance on. He saw the potential in Mark, and it wasn't long before I did as well. He is one of those submissives who simply needs a guiding hand and quick, firm reprimands. Bernadette is like that, also. She learns so quickly.

"I'm going to check out Big Bertha," I tell Mark. "Come back and help me if you get a moment." I want him to know that taking care of the customers and staff is his number one priority. Ahh, but he knows that. I've beaten it into him so many times over the years. Okay, not literally. That's Seamus's job. He likes his boys compliant.

I turn the thermostat up high and then head into the kitchen to greet Marta. She is a Domme I hired when she had fallen on rough times. She works hard and doesn't fight me for top-dog status. I never feel that challenge from her, and I highly respect her for it. She is one of the few who knows I've been struggling financially, and she knows the reasons why, but she never seems anxious or worried about it. She knows I will take care of her and everyone else under my employ to the best of my abilities.

"Big Bertha?" she asks knowingly. She pulls a tray of mini quiches out of the large oven.

"What else?" I say resigned. Perhaps the toolbox I've just pulled out of the supply closet is a clue.

"Good luck."

"Thanks." I laugh and say, "Cover me. I'm going in."

She chuckles, and then her attention is diverted as she instructs my new hire, Kari, how to place the quiches attractively on the serving tray. I hired Kari to replace Brittany, who finally got her passport and flew off to London to be with her Domme. Brittany's Domme will be proud of the progress her young submissive has made in her absence. Somehow, I've become good at brat taming. Who knew?

I pat Marta on the arm and leave them to it, but my heart is full. Marta is a nurturing soul. Her new girlfriend has many medical needs, but neither of them ever complains. They just plow through. I need to convert that empty lot next door into a parking lot with a handicapped spot for them. For the wheelchair. It kills me every time they have to park on the street and then navigate to the shop. If I could only get out from under this shit Eileen has dragged me through.

I open the door to the utility room. It's more like a closet, but whatever. The furnace is not running. I turned the thermostat up in the shop before coming back here, and the furnace should be on or at least trying to kick on. I flick the switch off and remove the top panel. Mark comes in, and I move over to show him what I'm doing.

"Let's see what happens when I switch the old girl back on." I flick the switch, and Big Bertha bursts into life. The flames are lit and burning nicely. I know not to high-five Mark yet, and he knows it, too. True to form, Big Bertha is not interested in working this morning and shuts off. Like me, she is weary. Unlike me, she needs to be retired and replaced. But I try not to say that out loud because she may decide to take me up on it.

"Dirty flame sensor?" Mark suggests and picks out the quarter-inch socket and a wire brush from the toolbox.

"Most likely. Let's try it." I turn the power off again.

He undoes the screw and pulls out the flame sensor. "Hoo-ee," he says, revealing his Wyoming upbringing. "That is one dirty sensor." He cleans it up with the wire brush, reinstalls it, and I flick the power back on.

"Fingers crossed." I flick the switch. Bertha bursts into life, but this time stays on. We wait an entire minute and then dare to high five each other. "If this happens again, I'll clean the burners, too."

"I can do it right now, Ma'am."

"No, you head back in. I'll close her up."

"Are you sure, Ma'am?" He picks up the top panel and is ready to reinstall it.

I take it from him. "I've got it, Mark. You've been helpful. I will tell your Sir how much I appreciate you and how proud I am of your growth."

His face softens, and he gushes, "Oh, thank you, Ma'am. Thank you."

"No, no, no," I stop him from kneeling. "Go on back to the shop. You're a good boy."

He squeals his pleasure at my words, bows to me, and then takes three steps backward before turning and heading out. That's one of Seamus's high protocol requirements – never turn your back on a Dominant if you can help it.

I put the furnace back together and give her a pat before washing up in Marta's sink.

"Out, out, out," she commands me good naturedly.

"Okay, okay, Mistress," I say sarcastically and turn to go. "Board meeting on Sunday?"

She nods. "I may need your girl's help getting Shanice's wheelchair up the front steps."

"Will do. I'm glad Bernadette is finally going to meet Shanice."

"Me, too," Marta says. Her tone tells me that she likes Bernadette. She's told me how much calmer I am now that Bernadette is in my life. She says Bernadette is good for me.

"Tell Shanice that Miss Riri is looking forward to seeing her."

"Oh, I will. She loves you, Rikki," Marta says with a smile.

"You have your hands full, Marta. She is an adorable little. Does she need any more coloring books? Or crayons? Colored pencils?"

"God, no." Marta rolls her eyes. "Thanks for asking. What I really need is a wheelchair-accessible van with hand controls so Shanice can be more independent." Marta's smile is grim but then turns into a scowl. "What you can do for me, Boss, is get out of my kitchen."

"Taskmaster," I mutter, loud enough for her to hear. She snaps a dirty dishtowel at me, and I dart out of the way. "I'm going. I'm going."

I put the toolbox back in the supply closet and head into the main shop. I pause in the doorway when I hear Mark reprimanding Kari. Her back is to me.

"I asked you to bus those tables, Kari." Mark pulls himself up to his full six-foot height.

"Whatever," she says and pulls out her phone, making no move to bus tables. "She's in the back. I'll get to it in a minute."

The 'she' is apparently referring to me. I don't interfere because I want to see how Mark handles her.

"This shop works on a strict and defined hierarchy, Kari. You know that. Miss Rikki took a chance on you when Miss Jaleesa asked her to. She didn't have to, you know."

This seems to quiet Kari momentarily until she opens her mouth again. "But Miss Jaleesa isn't here either, now, is she? And who the fuck are you, anyway? You're just one of Seamus's fucktoys acting all high and mighty like you're my Dom or something. Fuck that." She waves her hand dismissively.

My eyes open themselves wide. Jaleesa calls me a brat tamer, but shit, this one may be unsalvageable. I motion with my eyes for Mark to back away and that I'll handle it. I walk up behind Kari and say, "Turn around."

She visibly stiffens but does as I ask.

"Mark told you to bus the tables?"

"Yeah, so?"

My soul takes an inner breath. "And you didn't."

"I was getting around to it." She challenges me with her eyes.

Oh, honey, I think. There is no way in heaven or earth that you will win this one. "Is bussing tables beneath you?"

"No, it's just disgusting. People's saliva all over—"

"Wear gloves," I say matter-of-factly.

"I have a latex allergy," she counters.

I usually don't barter with subs or employees like this, but I am amused, and interacting in this manner helps me understand exactly what kind of brat she is. Obstinate and entitled, for sure. A pillow princess, perhaps? Her Domme's little precious jewel? She's in for a very rude awakening as my employee and as Jaleesa's new sub, if that's what she thinks. As far as I know, she's still under consideration with Jaleesa, and I guess you could say she has the same status with me as her employer.

"They're latex-free," I say simply.

She has no response to that and says, "I was going on my break now, anyway." Without being dismissed, she turns away from me.

"My office, please," I say in the gentlest of tones, but I hear some of my staff gasp. Going into Miss Rikki's office is worse than being sent to the Principal's office.

Once inside, I motion for her to kneel, but she resists and says, "You're not my Domme," and folds her arms across her chest.

"Kneel," I say again calmly.

She lets loose a bratty sigh of irritation and frustration yet slowly goes down to her knees. Obstinately, she doesn't lower her eyes subserviently. She's obeying but is letting me know that I haven't won this battle yet. But I will.

"Miss Jaleesa said you had potential," I begin, and she rolls her eyes. I move so fast that she recoils in fear. My face is now inches from hers. "You've been here five days, and I've yet to see it. Why is that?"

She swallows hard and shrugs.

"Answer me," I say sternly.

"I don't know, Ma'am." She looks down.

"I am this close," I hold my thumb and index finger a half-inch apart, "to firing you and telling Miss Jaleesa you're a washout."

"No, Ma'am," she pleads. "Oh, please, no, no, no."

"You're done here for the day."

"No, Ma'am. Please," she whines and falls forward as if to kiss my feet. I back up so she cannot reach me.

Undeterred, I say, "I will expect you here tomorrow at five a.m. with a completely different attitude."

"Oh, Ma'am." She sighs, dejected. She knows she is in trouble but seems resigned to her fate.

"Miss Jaleesa will be getting a full report from me within the hour."

She groans.

"Head directly to her hair salon and nowhere else. I am so disappointed in you, Kari. I hope you can do better." I pull out my phone to text Jaleesa. "I'm not sure you can."

"Oh, I can. I can," she assures me, but I'm not buying right now. "I'll go out and bus those tables now. And, and I'll do anything you and Mark tell me to. Oh, God, don't send me to her. She's going to punish me. Oh, God, I just earned my way out of that basement cage."

"Go hang up your apron, apologize to Mark, and get out of my sight." I turn my back on her, the ultimate insult to a sub.

"Yes, Ma'am," she says, utterly defeated. "I'm sorry that I'm such an asshole."

I bite down a laugh but stay silent. As soon as my office door closes, I shake my head. "Big Bertha might be easier to fix than you are, Kari." With a sigh, I text Jaleesa.

> RIKKI: She's heading your way. It's not a good day for your new brat. Call me when you get a chance.
>
> JALEESA: Did she get herself fired?
>
> RIKKI: Not yet.

The phone rings in my hand. It's Jaleesa. Wow, the Domme hotline is quick this morning.

Chapter 3
My Submissive

It has been a wonderful Saturday. I haven't felt this fulfilled in a long time. Kari came in this morning with a newish attitude and seemed much more manageable. I did, however, notice that she took her breaks standing up. Jaleesa must have made her ass sore as hell as a punishment. Even Lydia, my other assistant manager, commented on it. I know Kari is far from a model employee, but Mark started out much the same way.

Bernadette came by earlier than expected and helped out in the shop. She likes working with Marta in the kitchen. I should feel slighted because Marta always throws me out, but she welcomes Bernadette with open arms. Maybe sending her to Marta for punishments in the nude after we closed helped form their bond. That's the amazing thing about our community—we are like a village, always looking out for and helping each other.

A hand comes to rest on my thigh as I drive us home from Shasti and Madison's place. The hand lightly strokes my leg, and I allow it. Bernadette is feeling frisky, but I'm going to make her work for it.

"I'm proud of you," I say.

"Why?"

"Your dentist visit this week," I say coolly. "No cavities." The hand continues to caress my leg. "And your compliance in sending me a picture. That shows me you're a good girl."

"Mmm," she says in response.

"Did you enjoy movie night at Shasti and Madison's?" I ask, still not acknowledging her hand.

"Mm hmm," she says. "I'd never seen 'The Secretary' before."

"It's a classic." I turn onto Market Street. "Famous actors and a fairly decent plot."

"When the boss hung her typos on the wall, was that to humiliate her?"

"Yes," I say, "and she loved it. I think she made some of those typos on purpose just to get his attention."

"Yeah," Bernadette said pensively, and the hand stops rubbing my thigh. "I don't like humiliation. It just ..."

"I know, little bee. That's a hard limit for you and not one I am going to push."

"Thank you, Ma'am." She leans closer to me. Her hand trails up and down my thigh, finding its way to my inner thigh. She keeps getting dangerously close to the apex between my legs.

She's turning me on, but I don't want her to know, so I deflect the situation some more. "Did you see Madison's punishment station right there in the dining room?"

"Oh, yes," she purrs, and this surprises me. Maybe this is what has her turned on. "The 'Bad Girl' sign. The chains. Does Madison get chained there a lot? And for how long? Does Shasti leave her there for long periods?"

"Not too long, I don't think. Long enough to make her point. And, yes, she gets chained up often enough." I wonder if my own submissive would like a punishment corner. I hadn't considered it because of her recent experience with a sadist Domme that forced her into bondage, leaving her both physically and mentally scarred. "Shasti has her hands full with Madison's ADHD and says the chained time-outs help. Hopefully, Madison is learning some lessons."

"Does Shasti beat her?"

"No."

"Why don't you beat me when I do something wrong?"

I love her questions. She is always thinking and wondering, and the fact that she feels safe enough to ask is refreshing. "I learned early on never to hit in anger. Impact play is just that—play. It is intense, and I always want you to feel good during our sessions together. I want it to be mutually pleasurable."

"Mm hmm," Bernadette murmurs. Her hand goes back to my thigh and cups me between my legs in an incredibly bold move. She rubs me up and down, putting pressure on my clit. I could swat her hand away for being so forward and impertinent, but I know that she's exploring her boundaries. And she knows beyond a shadow of a doubt that she is not getting away with anything. She knows that I am *allowing* her to touch me this way. Her other hand snakes its way under my shirt and rubs my stomach for a while. And then it goes higher toward my breasts. Honestly, why I'm allowing this is beyond me. I just … like it.

I am breathing hard when I pull the Subaru down the alley behind the coffee shop. I park. Her hands then move aggressively over my body. If she's not careful, I'm going to take her right here in the car. My hands are shaking, I am that turned on, but I manage to twist the key and turn the car off smoothly. She applies pressure to my mons, and I grab her hand. I pull her arm back. She cries out, not in pain, but at the surprise of it. I throw her arm away from me as if disgusted and get out of the car. I go around and open the passenger door. The lust in her eyes fuels me as I grab the collar of her jacket and yank her out. I slam the door shut and drag her to the side door of my office. She stumbles behind me but keeps her balance. I throw her against the brick wall. She grunts, but her jacket absorbs most of the force. I unlock the door swiftly, jerk her into my office, and then lock the door behind me.

"On your knees, you bad girl."

She drops to her knees in front of me.

I hang up my coat and order her to take off hers. How I am this calm and cool is beyond me. It's that inner calm every Domme has somewhere inside. I have not ordered her to keep her eyes down, and she watches my every move. I reach down slowly and grab a nice handful of her hair. I tug. "Up." I practically drag her up the stairs by her hair until she finds her footing. Her hands are on mine, trying to lessen the pull on her scalp. Once inside the apartment, I shove her against the wall. I am on her in seconds, bruising her lips with mine, pressing her back against the wall, jamming my thigh between hers. I pull back, and her eyes are full blown lust mixed with fear.

I grab both sides of her button-down blouse and pull. It takes me three tries, but I am rewarded when the buttons pop off and clatter to the floor. She gasps. No matter. I bought the damn shirt; I'll buy her another and probably do the same thing to it.

I grab her by the throat with one hand and kiss her like I'm starved. Breathplay is one of her hard limits, so I don't press hard, just enough for her to know that I am in control. With my other hand, I unbutton her pants and thrust my hand inside. She is pantyless this evening at my request.

"Rikki, take me," she pleads into my mouth. "Please, Rikki. I beg you."

I yank off her shirt and then pull down her khakis. Her pussy is glistening. She is wet.

"Take off your shoes and get those pants off," I order her.

She fumbles mightily but finally does as instructed. She is completely naked. I am completely clothed. This is a fetish for both of us, we've discovered. I grab her shoulder and spin her around so she's facing the wall. I press her against that wall, and she turns her face to the side, her cheek and shoulder absorbing all the force. I reach around her hip and rub my fingers through her sopping wet pussy. I circle her clit, causing her to buck her body against my hand. God, she is so wet. I thrust two fingers inside and then stop and grab her by the mons, the heel of my hand against her mound. I pull, and she has no choice but to follow me. I push her on my bed. Ahh, too bad the fresh sheets she put on this morning are about to get ruined.

I don't need the lube, but I get it anyway.

She arches her pelvis and bucks. "Fuck me, Rikki. Please." She draws out the last word. "I'm so ready for you, Ma'am."

I swat her breasts three times in succession. It's not a punishment; it's a message. A message that says, I am in charge and will proceed any way I want to. We haven't moved on to face slapping. Not yet, anyway. That takes time to develop.

I nestle between her legs and plunge two fingers inside her again. I pump slowly.

"Oh, yes, Rikki. Yes."

I add a third finger. "I'm going to make you scream, Bernadette." Oh, yes, this is going to happen tonight. I have been waiting for the right opportunity. I pump her pussy, and she arches toward me. She moans with every push. She is close to cumming, but she's not quite there yet. My pinky finger joins the other three.

She humps my fingers, but I need her to stop if I'm going to get them all in. I reach up and smack her breasts again. "Stop moving. Lay still."

She groans and bucks once more. I should smack her for it, but I think it was involuntary.

I pump my four fingers inside, spreading them as much as I can. I squirt lube on my thumb, my knuckles, and the back of my hand. I tuck my thumb in my palm and push.

"Oh, Rikki," she says. She understands what is happening. I could ask for her color, but she will tell me if she needs to pause or stop altogether.

I push in and out, gaining a little ground each time until my knuckles finally breach her entrance. I push forward slowly. My entire hand is now inside her.

"Ahh," she moans in the highest pitch I think I've ever heard from her. "Rikki. Oh, my God."

I look down and wish I could take a picture for her. Her body has swallowed my hand. My clit pulses at the sight. Shit, I could cum from this myself. I twist my hand ever so slightly, knowing my knuckles are grazing her g-spot. Her body clenches as her pussy spasms once. I don't make a fist inside but keep my hand in that arched state with my thumb tucked. I stay still until she catches her breath. I twist, and she spasms again. My movements seem huge to her, but they are slight, and they are enough.

"Enjoy it, Bernadette. Cum anytime," I say to her softly. I can tell that she is caught somewhere in subspace and sexual arousal. Not that these are mutually exclusive. I lean down carefully and lick the only thing I can reach—her clit.

Her pelvis rises off the bed, and I follow her. I have no choice. I twist my hand gently and lick her hard and distended clit. I get a bit of lube in my mouth, but who the fuck cares? The orgasm of the century is about to happen.

Her low growl is something I've never heard before. It comes from the center of the earth, and she erupts in a howl. Her pussy spasms against my hand, so I still it, but not my lips or tongue. It's hard to stay latched on while she bucks her orgasm, but I stay the course. She lowers her pelvis, and I twist my hand again, ever so slightly.

"Oh, fuck, Rikki," she cries and cums again. My hand is getting oh so deviously devoured by her pussy again.

One more orgasm later, as I try to extricate my hand, Bernadette is out for the count. A puddle of cum follows my hand, and the sheets are soaked. So, what else is new? My baby cums gloriously for me every time. I get up quietly and wash my hands. I relieve my bladder and am amazed at how wet I am. I briefly consider flicking my clit to get off but decide against it. It never hurts to abstain every once in a while. It keeps you hungry for it, I reason. I grab a towel to place under her because I don't want her to sleep in her own spendings.

When I come out of the bathroom, I am shocked to see her sitting up, drinking water. "Come to bed," she says. It almost sounds like a command. But I do as she asks since, well, I was heading there anyway. I take my time, though, and spread the towel over the wet spot.

I climb onto the bed from the foot and lay on top of her. I hold my weight on my arms but insinuate my legs between what has to be her tender pussy. I know that my hand was cramping there at the end, but I'll never tell her that I was uncomfortable. I reach down and kiss her lips sweetly. A few afterglow caresses, and I'll spoon her tightly as we fall asleep.

She has other ideas. Her strong arms go around my back, and she flips us both over. She is now on top. "What are you—"

My words are cut off by her hand covering my mouth. "Trust," she whispers simply. She wags a finger at me and settles her weight on my hips. What in the world does she think she's doing?

She removes her hand from my mouth and takes hold of both of my wrists. She raises them up and over my head. She holds them there, knowing I can throw her off at any time, and there will be hell to pay. While she has me "captured," she leans down and kisses my lips tenderly, softly. I am appalled at myself when I mewl into her mouth, betraying my need. I feel her smile against my lips. I am caught. Her exhale tells me that she knows I am a willing participant in her little game now.

She holds my arms over my head with one hand and reaches down with the other to caress the one breast that she is not lying on. I whimper my arousal. Oh, God, have I lost all control? Her hand reaches lower and dips into the well between my legs. She grunts her approval and then maneuvers my hands to grasp the headboard bars, one in each hand. She silently indicates that I am to keep them up there. And I do. For some reason, I do. I think my Bernadette has her own voodoo magic and is using it on me right now.

She moves down my body, trailing kisses as she goes. I squirm when she licks my collarbone. Am I suddenly ticklish there? What the hell? She moves lower and worships my breasts for a while and then kisses my hip bones, one after the other. She licks my mons but does not move lower with her lips. Her fingers part my labia. It's as if she is examining me. Maybe she is. She runs one finger slowly through my folds. I arch my hips. Oh, God, I have lost all control. I will not beg. I will not. No way.

She circles that one finger just inside my vaginal entrance. Oh, God, I want her inside me. But she doesn't go in. A frustrated moan escapes my lips. I might as well turn in my Domme hat right now. Oh, my God.

I'm sure she is smiling, but I can't tell. She lifts my right leg and slides her body underneath. She is sideways to me now. What is she doing? My calf comes to rest on the back of her neck. I adjust so some of the weight falls on her back. Her left arm reaches around my leg and over my clit while the fingers on her right hand plunge inside me. I involuntarily raise my hips. Her left hand splits the hood over my clit, and I feel her warm exhale over the tender spot. I moan helplessly. She is in control, and she knows it.

Her left shoulder pushes my leg back even further. Maybe I need those yoga classes, too. I have never been eaten out sideways like this. Her right hand pistons slowly inside me. Her tongue finds my clit, and I jump. My pussy clenches in pre-orgasm. She stops all motion and turns her head to look at me with a mischievous grin.

Oh, no, no, no. I will not beg.

She brazenly continues to meet my gaze, her eyes never wavering. All movement has ceased. Oh, God, I feel like one of her students being reprimanded. That look is withering my resolve. We are at a standstill. My hands continue to grip the headboard bars over my head submissively. My pelvis arches without my permission. It doesn't care that I am trying to hold my ground. It wants her to pleasure me.

She raises an eyebrow, and I whimper. Yes, I fucking whimpered. I close my eyes, and her fingers tighten painfully on my thigh. This is her signal that I am not getting out of this so easily and that I need to open my eyes. I open them and mouth the word, "Please."

She doesn't move. She is not impressed. Okay, fine. "Please, Bernadette. Please, touch me, baby. I need to cum. Please get me there."

She smiles in victory and then pulls her fingers through my labia and plunges inside again. Her tongue hits my clit, and she is taking no prisoners. My ass rises off the bed as my core tightens deep inside. I tilt my head back as the tide recedes, hangs momentarily, and then rushes back like a fucking tsunami.

I screech my orgasm and buck my hips as she pumps me furiously. Her left hand buzzes my clit. When I moan my last moan and sigh contentedly, she stops her motions as well.

She kisses my mons and wiggles her way out from under my leg. She crawls up my body and pulls my arms down slowly. Oh, God, they are sore from being in one position for so long.

She kisses me deeply and then pulls me to her. My head rests on her chest, and she cradles me close, stroking my head. My God, she is giving me aftercare. No submissive in my history of submissives has ever done that.

"I don't know whether to punish you," I tell her, "or give you a reward."

"Punish me in the morning, Ma'am," she says sleepily.

Ahh, there she is. My submissive girl is back, although I think she was here all along.

Chapter 4
The Board Meeting

I sneak a glance at Bernadette in the passenger seat. I'm proud of the submissive she is becoming, and I'm confident she'll do well at her first real community event. As for me, this is the first time I've had a submissive of my own to bring in a while. Since Eileen. It is kind of a getting-back-on-the-horse moment for me. And, thankfully, Bernadette is *not* anything like Eileen – good riddance.

"You look good," I say to her as I park in one of the designated spots behind the private gates at Rowena's house.

"Thank you," she says and tugs on her skintight V-neck t-shirt, which shows her cleavage oh so nicely. Her yoga pants hug her body wonderfully, and I can't wait to rub my hands over her ass again at some point this afternoon. Maybe I'll steal her away to the back restroom before the board meeting. "I feel so exposed," she says. "Almost naked."

"You're *not* naked," I say with a chuckle. "But some of them inside might be, so be thankful I'm not going to make you strip down when we get in there."

Her jaw falls open in shock. Obviously, the possibility of having to be naked at the event had never occurred to her.

"You're a sexy, attractive woman, Bernadette. It's about time you realized it. And besides, I want to show you off." I stroke one of the welts on her thighs. I gave her a short session with the cane this morning for two reasons. One, to remind her who she belongs to, and two, so she has ownership marks to show off to the other subs. And, okay, fine, the third reason is so the other Dommes will have visual proof that I have complete control over her. Not that I have to prove anything to anybody, of course, but there will be a lot of welts and bruises on display today, I am absolutely sure.

I don't want the other Dommes thinking I'm getting soft or something. It's a good thing no one witnessed Bernadette's little power-grabbing routine last night. They would question my Domme status for sure.

Speaking of which, another reason I'm making Bernadette wear provocative clothing today is as a punishment for topping from the bottom. She admitted that she's not used to clothes that reveal or accentuate so much of her body. The new bras I purchased for her lift her breasts invitingly. Her cleavage is making my mouth water, and that's precisely the point. Subs constantly compare themselves against each other. Who's got the sexiest body? Sexiest outfit? Who's Domme is the best? Who's got more welts and bruises, and so on and so on. Even though this is only a Denton Heights BDSM Women's Board meeting, it is still a community event, and I want Bernadette to feel like she fits in.

She knows not to get out of the car until I open the door for her. Yes, I like controlling things, controlling her. Yes, I get off on it, but it also gives her structure, something I've come to realize she needs. She likes order. She has me trained to bring my shoes up to the apartment instead of throwing them in the ever-growing pile on the stair landing. The same goes for all my jackets and coats and sweaters. Now there's room for her jacket, a detail I hadn't considered. And it takes a little more time, but separating the laundry into colors and whites *and* placing them in actual hampers has made her extremely happy. All of that need for order fits right in with my need to control. Ours is a match made in BDSM heaven.

I open the passenger door and command her with a hand gesture to swivel in the seat. I don't like subs to put on and take off their own collars. In my mind, it makes it seem as if they have control over that part of their lives. They do not. I reach in and buckle on her leather commitment collar. It covers up her day collar – a thin, washable, stretchy choker that she is required to wear in public. It's perfect for showering, and that's why I picked it.

I snap on the leash, and she looks up at me. There is fear in her eyes. No, fear is too strong a word. Apprehension, maybe? Nerves? I give her my best reassuring smile and decide to give her my speech right here while she sits in the car. "You represent me, Bernadette. In everything you do and everything you say. Please remember that."

"Yes, Ma'am," she says.

Ahh, she is feeling submissive. When she calls me Ma'am, that's always the first clue. Good. She needs to understand her place.

"You will address every Domme by Miss. Miss Rowena, Miss Shasti, Miss Jaleesa, unless they specifically tell you otherwise. Ma'am or Daddy is also fine, except Daddy Vic won't be here today, so never mind the Daddy thing."

"Daddy Vic?" Her eyes grow large at the mention of her most recent ex.

"She's on the board, yes, but is, uh, on a short leave of absence right now."

"I understand." She relaxes visibly. "But, Ma'am, I've never called Shasti by her title Miss."

"Yes, I know. That has been an oversight on my part. Subs always address Dommes by their titles. So that will begin today. Understood?"

"Of course, Ma'am." Her tone is pensive. I can tell she is wondering what crazy world she has found herself in.

"Obviously," I continue, "Miss Shasti and Madison will be here, and I want you to take care of Madison. You know, keep an eye on her. She can get hyper and out of control, especially when overstimulated. I'm sure Miss Shasti would appreciate your attention to Madison while we're in the Dommes' board meeting."

"Yes, Ma'am," Bernadette says. "Rikki?"

"Yes, little bee?"

"Should I call you *Miss* Rikki?"

"Do you want to?"

She searches my eyes as if trying to find the correct answer there. "I believe I should, Ma'am."

"That doesn't answer my question."

She lifts her chin and says, "I want to. To show respect. To show you that I understand my place, although I'm still learning what that is. And I'm not sure what came over me last night. I wasn't trying to take your place. I'm not a Domme. It just welled up inside me, and I acted on it."

"It's okay, little bee," I say, soothing her anxiety. "Just don't expect that to happen often." I bop her gently on the nose with the tip of my index finger.

She sighs nervously and says, "When I met you, you introduced yourself as 'Rikki.' And now that's how I think of you. I'm afraid I'll have a hard time saying 'Miss Rikki.' Does that make sense?"

I cup her chin and then kiss her forehead chastely. "Yes, it makes sense, and yes, you may continue to call me by my name, little bee. Thank you for being honest about that. You always show me respect, so there is no need to force something like that on you."

"Thank you, Ma'am," she says and visibly relaxes. "What will I be doing when you're in the board meeting?"

"Miss Rowena set up a flexibility class for all the subs. I believe you all will be learning submissive poses. You know some, but here's a good chance to practice them. Now, aren't you glad I put you in yoga pants and a t-shirt this morning?"

She nods but doesn't respond verbally. And that's okay. I don't always require a verbal response. She's nervous. I tug on her leash, and we head toward the front porch steps.

The front door opens, and one of Rowena's new subs ushers us in. She is a strikingly tall, dark-haired woman who looks to be in her late twenties. As expected, she is entirely nude, except for the nipple clamps attached to a labia clamp below. Bernadette is doing her best not to react. The woman takes our coats, and I notice she has a black eye. That's one of the hard limits our group has agreed upon. No striking near the eyes. It's too dangerous. Rowena will be asked about that, and she knows it. Rowena is rough with her subs, but she doesn't usually cross that line. There's always a first time. We've already reprimanded one Domme for unsafe play, and I don't feel like punishing another today, but I will if I have to.

The dark-haired sub takes three steps back and then turns to bring us into the living room. Evenly spaced cane marks mark the backs of her thighs. Yes, Rowena always wins the marking category among us Dommes. The sub's anal plug is a red heart, and I am positive that it is a vibrating plug and that Rowena has the remote control.

"Professor," Madison screeches and runs over to Bernadette.

"Hi, kiddo." Bernadette allows Madison to hug her.

"Hi, Miss Rikki," Madison says to me, her face blushing a deep red, probably because she's never seen her former teacher's cleavage exposed like this.

"Young Madison," I reprimand. "Get on your knees, please."

She does so and hangs her head.

"Who do you always greet first?"

"I'm sorry, Miss Rikki. 'Always greet a Domme before greeting her sub,'" she quotes from rote memory. She leans forward and kisses my boots repeatedly. I place a hand on her head and motion for her to sit back up.

"Go get one," I say.

"Yes, Ma'am," Madison says, defeated. I do my best to hide my smile as she goes to a table and retrieves a small red ribbon that says, "I disrespected a Domme."

"Turn." I twirl my finger in a circle and then clip the ribbon to the back of her collar. "What do you say?"

"Thank you for reprimanding me, Miss Rikki," Madison says with her head hung low.

"Would you please introduce Bernadette to some of the other subs? She doesn't know many."

"Yes, Ma'am." Madison reaches for Bernadette's hand.

"Oh, I see that Marta and Shanice are already here," I say to Madison. "Did you help with the wheelchair?"

"No, Ma'am," Madison said. "Miss Marta asked me to watch Jaleesa's subs. Dana and Tina do it. Just in case I'm ever asked to help. Ready, dip, pull. That's how it goes, Miss Rikki. Did you know that?"

"I did not," I say with a smile. I am also amused that Madison is still holding Bernadette's hand. Bernadette looks so scared that she doesn't seem to notice or care. "Okay, you two. Go on."

Bernadette looks at me, and I nod that it's okay for her to go. She exhales nervously, but I know she will be okay. She will get a lot of attention today, being my new sub. But it will be both good and bad attention. Subs can be awfully competitive with each other. So can Dommes, I have to admit.

As is customary, I seek out our hostess and greet her before greeting any other Dommes. Rowena is seated in a high winged back chair as if it is a throne.

"Thank you for having us, Rowena," I say to the stout brunette. Her long-term submissive, Minjung, kneels nude by her side, eyes down. Her long dark hair sits in a bun on top of her head. She turns her palms up when I approach. This is a sign of respect for me. She is signaling that I am her superior and that she will obey anything I ask of her. I squat down in front of her and lift her chin. She looks up at me. "You are a good and faithful sub to your Mistress, Minjung." I reach out with one hand, alternately teasing one nipple and then the other until they harden. Touching another Domme's submissive is typically taboo. No one, and I mean no one, will touch Bernadette without my explicit permission. Rowena, however, has expressed that she would like us to touch and fondle Minjung regularly, only in her presence, of course. Rowena says this helps reinforce the idea to Minjung that her body is not her own and is simply a vessel for others' pleasure. "Quite responsive," I say to Rowena.

"Indeed," Rowena says. "You may borrow her should you need Minjung to show your girl etiquette and manners."

Ahh, typical passive-aggressive Rowena. "Thank you," I say and then smile. "I will keep that in mind." She is in a button-pushy mood this afternoon, and I know why. Everyone, except Bernadette, knows why.

It isn't long before Rowena announces that the subs are to head to the closed-in back patio for their submissive positions class. I am pleased that Bernadette seems to have taken to Marta's little, Shanice, and is wheeling her toward the class. I smile as Madison tags along, chattering happily as usual. Once they are settled, we Dommes move to the dining room to start our quarterly spring meeting.

Everyone finds a seat, but I remain standing at the head of the table and tap the ceremonial gavel on its companion base. The gavel is handed down from lead Domme to lead Domme and kept for the entire three-year term. Rowena is chomping at the bit to take over, but I have another seven months to go.

"This quarterly spring meeting of the Denton Heights BDSM Women's Collective will now come to order." Our group and the men's group have agreed to follow Robert's Rules of Order. Early on, we realized that a room full of Dominants would go nowhere without order.

I sit down and call roll so it can be officially entered in the meeting minutes by our secretary Marta. I read the agenda from my notes. It is agreed upon and put into the record. Marta reads the minutes from our last meeting, which are also accepted into the record.

We only have six board members today since Victoria has been temporarily suspended from community interactions and events. I just have to hope that any votes that come up don't end up in a tie since we have an even number. From my seat at the head of the table, I say, "Our biggest agenda item is our high protocol masquerade ball Memorial Day weekend." There is a mixed bag of emotions at the table. Some groan because we have experienced how much work it is to organize and pull off such a big event, while others cheer because it is the event of the season. The Holiday party next December will be my last high protocol event as lead Domme, and then Rowena will take over in January. I'm ready for someone else to take the gavel, especially now that I have a new submissive to look after, but then again, I'm not sure I trust Rowena with it.

I settle in as Jaleesa discusses this year's venue. She says she has already booked and sent in the deposit for the former fire station on the edge of town. Thank goodness for Jaleesa. She is a no-nonsense, get-things-done kind of woman. Hayley, the decorating chair, discusses her plans and mentions that she needs more volunteers. I volunteer Bernadette, but I'm sure I will be volunteering right alongside her. Hayley also mentions that she has yet to reach out to the men's group, and Rowena recommends contacting Seamus. He is the lead Dom of the men's group and is more than willing to get his group moving. His and Jaleesa's subs alone could get the venue decorated in a couple of hours.

"That's good to hear," I say, and we move on to other details like music, catering, ticket sales, and BDSM demonstrations.

"I assume you'll be delighting us with your whipping skills, Rikki?" Rowena asks.

I always detect sarcastic undertones in her voice, and today is no exception. I ignore whatever message she is trying to send and say, "Yes, of course. Thank you for having me." Hey, kill them with kindness, right?

Once all the masquerade ball business is concluded to my satisfaction, we move on.

Shasti raises her hand. I recognize her with a nod, and she says, "I move that we discuss the obvious black eye of the submissive named Alyssa, AKA Pet Number Two."

Jaleesa seconds the motion, and all eyes turn to Rowena.

"I knew somebody was going to bring that up," she says with a sigh. "If you looked carefully, you saw that the bruise is old and yellowing. She got it from her old Dom, who is a mean and vindictive top. He treated her like a slave, although she never signed up to be one. She's contracted to me for a couple of months until she figures out what she wants to do."

Heads nod, and Shasti moves to accept the explanation and pursues no further action. The motion is accepted unanimously. We do, indeed, police each other. It is a system that has worked well over the years. Aunt Tilda always said that the vanillas didn't understand our lifestyle and we should refrain from bringing them in if at all possible.

Without waiting for me to recognize her, Rowena blurts, "I move that we reconsider our actions relative to the Victoria situation."

"I second," Hayley says quickly. I note Rowena's subtle nod to Hayley.

Jaleesa groans loudly, but I am cool and get the conversation going. We need to wrap up this meeting because my stomach is growling, and I need sustenance. Rowena always provides a good spread after the meetings.

Rowena leads with an accusation. "Rikki, you dominate the other Dommes. You have your little clique of faithfuls who do whatever you say." Her sweeping gesture includes Shasti, Jaleesa, and Marta.

My eyebrows are trying to raise themselves to the roof, but as Aunt Tilda always told me, you have to focus on the matter at hand and *not* on the personalities. In Rowena's case, this is extremely difficult. And I've come to believe that positions of power need self-control. That is the only way to keep the peace and keep control of a situation. I also feel that I get respect from others because of it.

"You're all too quick to judge," Rowena adds.

Keeping the sarcasm out of my voice, I say, "What say you in the matter of this board's actions relative to Victoria?" Out of the corner of my eye, I see Jaleesa visibly relax. Marta's grin almost makes me smile, but I squelch it.

"You four voted to suspend Victoria from board decisions and community events for three months, but you had no shred of evidence. In fact," Rowena says smugly, "it would seem as if our dear lead Domme maneuvered things to obtain and own Victoria's sub. That is really low. Even for you, Rikki."

Shasti lays a hand on my arm and says, "I'm glad you brought up the suspension, Rowena, because I was about to. More evidence has come in. A friend of mine in the hospital lab analyzed the packet of supplements Bernadette handed over to me at my request. And for the record, I am referring to the supplements the Domme Victoria gave to the submissive Bernadette without telling her what was in it."

"She agreed to take it," Rowena bellows.

I am about to call order, but Shasti continues calmly. "The results are shocking. The supplement contained both Metoclopramide and Aripiprazole, an antipsychotic drug used to treat psychotic depression, among other things. One of the side effects of this concoction can be spontaneous lactation. Other side effects include symptoms of Parkinson's disease, suicidal thoughts, depression, uncontrolled muscle spasms, and impaired speech. Withdrawal from this drug can cause permanent neurological disturbances as well." She passes the printout of the results around the table.

"So," Jaleesa jumps in, "although Bernadette took the supplements willingly, she did *not* know what was in them. Granted, that was stupid on her part, but Victoria knowingly put another person's life and health at risk."

"Bernadette was fortunate," Shasti continues. "Her blood tests and physical and neurological exams came back normal. Practically perfect, you might say." A relieved murmur goes around the table. "And for the record, Victoria voluntarily paid for the medical tests." The approval continues.

Hayley raises her hand. I recognize her to speak. "Maybe Victoria didn't know about all the side effects."

"She should have," Marta blurts. My eyebrows raise in surprise. Marta doesn't typically say much at our board meetings. "Dominants have a responsibility to their submissives. We are responsible for their well-being. If she didn't know about the side effects, she damn well should have researched it." Marta smacks the table with her open palm, causing just about everyone to jump, myself included.

Jaleesa picks up the mantle. "A Domme has *influence* over her submissive. A Master has *authority* and makes any and every decision they want on her behalf. Victoria has never claimed to be a Master. She did not have full authority to do whatever the hell she wanted to this submissive. Not that I think giving someone unknown drugs is right in the first place."

Listening to my friends defend the decision to reprimand Victoria reminds me of an Isaac Newton quote. "Tact is the art of making a point without making an enemy." My hope is that we break through Rowena's protective instincts toward her friend and help her understand how truly dangerous Victoria's actions were.

Rowena's body language is subtle, but I see that she is caving. Downcast eyes one time, pulling at her sweater, a soft resigned sigh. At least she'll be able to tell her good friend that she tried to get the decision overturned.

"I ask permission to withdraw the motion," Rowena says.

Everyone at the table seconds, and I say, "Granted." I ask if there is any unfinished business, but I hope there isn't because I am officially hungry.

Just as I bang my gavel to end the meeting, Bernadette appears in the doorway, a stricken expression on her face.

"What is it?" I say, standing up.

She looks past me to Shasti, who bolts out of her chair and rushes past us both.

Chapter 5
Appetizer

Shasti sends us home, saying our nervous energy isn't helping. It is late Sunday evening, and I still need answers. I remain positively furious as I pace around my apartment. Bernadette cowers on her knees in the corner where I sent her. I grab the box of rice, rip off the top, and dump the entire contents on the hardwood floor.

"Put them back in the box. One grain at a time." I throw the now-empty box in front of her, scattering some of the rice.

"Yes, Ma'am," she says, her voice hitching with tears. She wipes at her eyes, trying to clear them, and then leans down to begin her task.

"I'm going to ask you again." I pull over a chair and sit. I take my thousandth deep breath since the incident. "Where were you when it happened?"

Bernadette sighs. It is a frustrated sigh. "I told you. I was right there. The instructor gave us a short break, and I was talking to Shanice about her computer job."

"And where was Madison?"

"Right there in the room. We were all in the room. Even the instructor was there." Bernadette picks up another grain of rice and throws it forcefully into the box. That attitude is going to have consequences if she doesn't check it.

"You were supposed to be watching her," I accuse.

"I *was* watching her," Bernadette says and smashes her palm on the floor.

I leap to my feet and grab her by the collar, forcing her to look up at me. My heart clenches at the fear in her eyes. "Stop with the attitude and tell me what happened." I push her away, and she takes a gasping breath as she goes back to her task.

"I'm sorry, Ma'am." She picks up a single grain. "I'm just as upset as you are. We all are."

"I'm running out of patience."

"I told you already. I told Shasti. I told everyone."

"Tell me again."

"I didn't think much of it when Rowena's new girl, Alyssa, gave Madison a gummy bear. I briefly thought that Shasti wouldn't like Madison to eat sweets, but it was only one. The only one that I witnessed, Ma'am. I promise. I didn't fuss with her about it. It seemed like a small thing."

"She may have eaten more," I muse out loud. "You're sure it was Alyssa who gave it to her?"

"Yes," Bernadette says without looking up.

"But they weren't ordinary gummy bears, were they?" I ask, the defeat clear in my voice.

"Ma'am, I didn't know that. I don't know what edible marijuana looks like. I don't do drugs."

I inhale deeply.

"Ma'am?" she says.

"Yes?"

"What did I do wrong? I'm sorry that Madison is having a bad reaction, and I hope she'll be okay, but please tell me what I did wrong so that I can understand." Bernadette continues to pick up the rice grain by grain. She has accepted the punishment I gave her.

"When you accepted my collar," I say evenly, "I promised I would take care of you. Part of that is punishing you when I feel you could have done better." Bernadette remains quiet, but I can tell that she is listening, so I continue. "And that's just it. You could have done better. That little girl is suffering because you didn't watch out for her like I asked you to."

Bernadette starts crying earnestly and puts one hand over her eyes as if to hide.

"Fuck," I say to the universe. I am a monster. I am punishing her for something she had absolutely no control over. I bolt off my seat and sit on the scattered rice to pull her into my arms. "C'mere, little bee." I kiss the top of her head and rock her. "I'm so sorry. It wasn't your fault. This was your first event, and I shouldn't have asked you to watch over Madison."

"No, I—"

"Shh, shh, shh," I interrupt. "You couldn't have known they were edibles. It was—" I swallow my pride and say, "It was wrong of me to punish you. I might not have known they were edibles, either. I would have made her spit out the candy, though."

"I'm not a Domme," Bernadette pleads. "I didn't feel I had the authority to make her do that. It was just one. I mean, I just saw her eat one."

"Did Alyssa offer the gummies to anyone else?"

"Yes. To everyone."

"Everyone?" I ask. "Even you and Shanice?"

"Yes, Ma'am. We both said, 'No, thank you.' Alyssa even offered some to the instructor."

"And you all refused?"

"No, one of Jaleesa's subs took one. I don't know her name. The Black girl with the super short haircut."

"Dana. Okay, I understand." I kiss her head and squeeze her tight. I send Jaleesa a quick text so she'll know. She gets back to me quickly. "Ahh, Jaleesa says Dana started having a bad trip when they got home."

"Oh, no," Bernadette says and starts crying again.

"I'm glad you didn't take one," I say and squeeze her tight.

"I'm not allowed sweets without your consent."

"And that makes you a very good girl." Bernadette snuggles into me, sniffling. "Once Madison recovers, we'll sit down with Shasti to determine how much authority you can have over Madison. How does that sound?"

"Needed."

"Hmm?"

"It sounds like something that is needed," she clarifies.

"Ahh, yes."

"Ma'am, will Madison be okay? I mean, she seemed to calm down when we got her home, and Shasti chained her to the wall."

"I know it seemed cruel to chain her, but oddly enough, restraints for Madison represent safety and caring, so that makes sense. Shasti says Madison should be okay once the drugs leave her system. She said the gummies probably had a high concentration of THC compounded by the fact that Madison hadn't eaten much that morning."

"Is that why Shasti made her eat a roll?"

"Yes, to slow down the effects."

"Rikki, I was so scared. She was freaking out about the room spinning. She lost her balance and fell. She said the floor was tilting. I thought she was goofing around at first. She wanted to know if we were on a ship. I thought she was having a seizure or something. Oh, God, that's when I ran to get you."

"You did the right thing, Professor."

"No, no, no. Do not call me that right now."

"Oh? Why not?"

"I don't deserve it. I messed up. Just keep me under your thumb, Ma'am."

She needs to feel her submissiveness. She needs my authority. I squeeze her to let her know that I understand.

"Okay," I say, "I think we both messed up a little today. Let's get this damn rice back in the box." I pat her on the side, and she leans over to continue the task. I join her and pick up a grain. She makes a noise of surprise but doesn't protest.

We work in silence for a while. Except for my aching knees, picking up rice grains is kind of Zen.

"You touched that girl," Bernadette says after a while.

"What girl?"

"Minjung."

"I did," I say but offer no explanation.

"That made me jealous, Ma'am."

"It shouldn't."

"It did."

Hmm, she's pressing it. Okay, this must really bother her. "It's not that I wanted to; it's just that Rowena expects us to."

"Oh," she says succinctly.

"Do you expect the other Dommes to touch me?"

"Oh, no. Only if I invite them to."

"Do I get a say?" Bernadette doesn't look at me and continues to pick up the rice grains.

"Yes." I like that she thinks about these things and is brave enough to ask questions.

"I have questions."

"Go."

"Do you, um, want to share me with someone?" Bernadette clears her throat, plainly uncomfortable asking. "You mentioned that once."

"Do you *want* to be shared?"

"That wasn't my question," she says impertinently.

"Watch that tone," I reprimand.

"I'm sorry, Ma'am." She takes a big breath. "Only if you'll be there. Like the whole time. And only if this is something you also want because if you don't want this, then I'm okay."

"I saw you watching someone today. And I've seen you watch her at the coffee shop. Especially on darts night."

Bernadette stiffens for a moment. "I'm sorry, Ma'am. I didn't mean to dishonor you."

Hmm, she isn't denying it. "You don't want to replace me, do you?"

"No, no, no, no, no, Ma'am." She leans down to kiss my hands that are busy picking up rice. "Oh, God, no. Never. I love you. Please forget I brought it up, Ma'am."

"No. This intrigues me. I'll feel her out about it."

"Please don't say it was my idea. Please, Ma'am," Bernadette pleads. "And she won't have time, anyway. Just forget the whole thing."

I lean back, pull out my phone, and send the text. An affirmative answer comes back quickly, and I show Bernadette.

"Oh, Ma'am," she groans. "What have I put in motion?"

"Once things settle down after gummy-gate, I'll negotiate terms with her."

"You make it sound like a business arrangement."

"It kind of is. There are lots of things to be agreed on. Your safety is paramount."

"Thank you, Ma'am."

I sit back and say, "Fuck this. I'm getting the broom."

~~~

The Monday evening darts tournament is well underway with a capacity crowd. "C'mon, Bernadette," I encourage as she steps up to the line to throw. She seems to be a bit off today. I don't think either of us got much sleep worrying about Madison, and she was up at 4:30 a.m. making coffee for me, even though I don't require her to get up with me so early.

"Yes," I shout with the crowd when Bernadette scored on her opponent with a bullseye. Her poise and confidence are through the roof when she's playing. I wish she would have that kind of confidence in all aspects of her life.

Bernadette blushes as her girl crush high-fives her. I think I'm handling this the right way. Open and honest communication is key to a healthy relationship. As long as she and her crush understand that Bernadette belongs to me and that it is *my* collar she wears, all is good.

My eyes open wide when I see something I should not see. "Bag, please," I hold my hand out to Lydia, one of my assistant managers. Within seconds, a small black plastic bag is in it. I march through the darts crowd and get in the face of an early twenty-something young man wearing a black t-shirt one size too small.

He gives me a "what the fuck" look and backs up. I move back into his personal space and say loud enough for the crowd to hear. "Who owns this puppy?" The group grows quiet, and all play stops.

"Oh, uh, he's a friend of mine, Ma'am," one of the young Doms that Seamus is mentoring steps forward.

"Does he know the rules about alcohol in my establishment?" I keep my eyes on the young offender. My face is inches from his daring him to roll his eyes so I can throw his ass out on the sidewalk. I breathe into his ear, "You got caught, puppy. Best to own up to it. If the wrong person had seen you, all of this goes away. I lose my business. These people lose their hangout, you're ousted from the community, and *you* end up turning tricks on the streets of Cincinnati because no respectable community will have you."

Fear floods his eyes. "I'm sorry."

"Sorry, what?"

"Ma'am," he amends. "I'm sorry, Ma'am."

"Better." I step back. I hold out the black bag. "Put that pint in this bag. You can pick it up from Lydia on the way out. It will be labeled 'puppy.'" He does as I request.

I turn from him. He is dismissed wordlessly, and I fix my gaze on the friend that claimed him. "Tell me why I shouldn't throw you both out of here."

He stumbles over his words and apologizes six ways from Sunday, saying it'll never happen again, Ma'am, and on and on.

"See that it doesn't." I shoot Seamus a serious glance as if to say, 'He's your responsibility, friend.' Seamus nods. Message received and understood.

The tournament gets back underway, and I head over to Lydia with the bag and give her the labeling instructions. She chuckles and says, "Way to handle the newbie, Boss." She shakes her head and adds, "They think they can get away with anything." Lydia, like Mark, is hardworking and faithful. She's a bisexual switch with a recent string of bad relationships as a submissive with Doms and Dommes alike. I keep telling her to flick that switch and explore her Domme side. We'll see what happens.

My heart leaps when the door to the shop opens and in walk Madison and Shasti. Madison throws her coat on a hook and practically jumps into my outstretched arms.

"Thank you for taking care of me yesterday, Miss Rikki. I almost died."

I squeeze her back and pat her head. "But you look very much alive today." Her cheeks are pink, and her eyes are bright. "Feeling better, are you?"

"Oh, yes," she says with a dramatic sigh. "Mistress stayed up all night with me. Miss Rikki, I love her so much, and I told her I was sorry I ate candy when I wasn't allowed. And now I have to apologize to everyone. But you know what?"

"What?"

"That candy really sucked."

The crowd chuckles. Madison jumps at the sound and then greets Seamus and the other Dommes and Doms. She then hugs Bernadette.

"You okay, kiddo?" Bernadette squeezes Madison back.

Madison steps out of the hug, brushing away her tears. "It wasn't your fault, Professor. Mistress said you were supposed to watch me, but she said no one could have known they weren't candy gummies." She whispers, "That girl was stupid to do that to me."

"I agree," Bernadette says. "I'm glad you're okay now. No aftereffects?"

Madison shook her head. "The boat is steady now." She holds her arms out to her sides. "Rock solid. But I got to stay home from school today anyway."

The group laughs around her.

"I am never ever doing drugs ever," Madison says. "Except maybe coffee."

"Madison is back," someone in the crowd announces, and a collective cheer erupts.

Shasti clears her throat and says, "Rowena assures me that her new sub is under lock and key and is being dealt with. Harshly."

"Good," I say, and the crowd chimes their agreement.

Seamus rounds up the darts players to continue the tournament. Before Bernadette turns to head back, I whisper in her ear, "The moment the tournament is over, say your goodbyes, go into my office, strip, and then kneel."

"Yes, Ma'am," she says, a slightly hungry look in her eyes.

Excellent. I like to keep her hungry.

When the tournament finishes, the crowd clears out reasonably quickly. I think most of us are tired after worrying about one of our resident *littles*. I usher out the last employee, lock the doors, and turn off the lights.

I step into my office, and there, with her head down and hands turning upright on her bare thighs, is the beautiful woman who agreed to wear my collar. Sometimes I can't believe she's mine. "Eyes up, please."

Bernadette lifts her head and smiles. "Permission to speak, Ma'am?"

"Of course."

"When you reprimanded that young buck in there earlier, that turned me on."

She likes seeing my authority in action. Good to know. We talk for a few moments about how relieved we both are that Madison seems to be okay.

Someone raps five times on the outside side door.

"Come in," I say. Bernadette's eyes grow wide in fright. "Eyes down," I command her.

My visitor comes in, locks the door behind her, and hangs her coat up. She grunts appreciatively at the morsel I have presented for her. "Very nice," she says warmly.

"Domme Rikki," my guest says, "this pet belongs to you and will remain yours. I will respect any and all ground rules and limits you set for her."

"Domme Jaleesa," I respond ritually. "I accept your words. You may direct my submissive as you please."

"Greet our guest, please," I instruct Bernadette.

"Good evening, Miss Jaleesa," Bernadette says, her eyes still down, her palms still up. There is a nervous lilt to her voice.

"Good evening, pet," Jaleesa says back. I lean back against my desk, excited to see what will happen next. "Stand, pet. Inspection pose," Jaleesa says quietly.

Bernadette looks up at me as if waiting for me to okay it.

"Obey Domme Jaleesa, Bernadette." My voice is stern.

Bernadette stands and places her hands behind her head and spreads her legs a bit wider than shoulder-width apart. Her chest rises and falls quickly. She is both nervous and turned on at the same time. She looks at me again, and I see that her eyes are a deep, lusty blue. God, I love this woman. At the moment, my prevailing emotion is pride. I do, however, detect a small kernel of jealousy. I am the one who put this whole scene in motion, though, and I must have faith that Bernadette will remember who owns her.

Jaleesa takes her time looking Bernadette over from head to toe and back again. She makes appreciative noises as she does so. She finally looks Bernadette in the eyes. "You are a beautiful woman, Bernadette."

Bernadette doesn't respond, and Jaleesa looks back at me with questioning eyes.

"Bernadette is trained to only answer direct questions during high protocol moments like this," I say.

"Ahh," Jaleesa says.

Bernadette gulps visibly. She is blushing furiously from her chest to the roots of her hair.

Jaleesa steps forward and cups my girl's breasts. "Nice and firm." The nipples harden without stimulation. "Great response, Rikki. I didn't even touch the nipples." She squeezes one while watching Bernadette's reaction. Bernadette grunts slightly and trembles. She is now looking Jaleesa right in the eye. Some Domme's don't like that, but it's up to Jaleesa to correct her or not. She doesn't.

"Is it all right that I touch you, Bernadette?" Jaleesa asks huskily. She is as turned on as I am, and I'm only watching.

"Yes, Ma'am. It's okay."

Jaleesa tweaks Bernadette's other nipple, and Bernadette shudders again as the pain turns pleasurable. I've seen it happen so many times that I know what she's feeling. "Your reactions are enticing, pet." She strokes Bernadette's face, and Bernadette leans into it affectionately. Jaleesa lets out an approving grunt. "Yes, yes, you've got yourself a good girl here, don't you, Rikki?"

"Mmm. I do, indeed," I say.

Jaleesa's hand strays down Bernadette's torso, making Bernadette squirm. She is turned on. Jaleesa stops her progress and grabs Bernadette loosely by the chin. "You need to stop moving while I'm inspecting you, pet. It's bad form and is making your owner look bad."

Bernadette swallows hard and nods.

"She's quiet," Jaleesa says. "I like that." Jaleesa's hand continues its slow descent down Bernadette's body until it reaches her mons. Jaleesa squats and taps Bernadette's inner thighs. Bernadette separates her legs further. "There we go," Jaleesa muses. She runs a finger through Bernadette's labia, and Bernadette's mouth drops open. "Delightful aroma. She is very aroused, Rikki."

I don't respond, but I knew my little bee would be wet. I puff with pride at my submissive. She is performing well.

Jaleesa purposely misses Bernadette's clit and runs a solitary finger through the slick folds before plunging inside. Bernadette arches her pelvis toward her benefactor.

"Mmm. Beautiful response," Jaleesa murmurs. After what must have felt like forever to Bernadette, Jaleesa splits the hood over her clit, making Bernadette gasp. Her clit is long and distended. "Nice big clitty," Jaleesa says, clearly impressed. "Top grade, Rikki. Jesus." She blows gently on Bernadette's clit.

"Ma'am," Bernadette whimpers.

Jaleesa ignores the whimper and stands. She presses her body against Bernadette, backing her up against the wall. Bernadette cries out in clear lust. Jaleesa reaches down and cups Bernadette's sex. Her middle finger runs circles over Bernadette's clit.

"I've inspected you," Jaleesa whispers into Bernadette's ear, "and I like what I see. And now you're going to cum for me." She presses her lips against Bernadette's, who hungrily sucks the probing tongue. Bernadette's arms wrap themselves around the woman kissing her. That green glob of jealousy spikes, but I tame it quickly. This was my idea, I remind myself.

Bernadette moans into Jaleesa's mouth as the hand stimulates her. Bernadette's moans increase in frequency and pitch. She bucks against Jaleesa's hand. "Cum, little pet. Soak my fingers. You'll lick them clean."

I recognize the sound of Bernadette's moans. She is right there, ready to cum. Bernadette searches for me over Jaleesa's shoulder. She finds my eyes and keeps my gaze. I nod and say, "Cum for her, my good girl. Cum now."

"Oh, God," she growls and moans, her release cumming all over Jaleesa's probing fingers. She thrusts against Jaleesa's still-moving hand. "Fuck, Miss—" Her moans of passion are pure ecstasy to my ears.

Jaleesa's fingers stop moving, and she cups Bernadette's sex while searing her with another kiss. She brings her fingers up and fucks Bernadette's mouth with them. Bernadette raises her head and takes the fingers deep without gagging. I can see her tongue licking the fingers when she can.

"She is fucking impressive, Rikki. Most subs gag at this point." Jaleesa looks back at me, eyebrows raised.

I nod, proud of my girl.

Jaleesa removes her hand from Bernadette's mouth and kisses her one last time. She leans in and whispers, "Thank you, pet. That was nice to experience. When I step back, you are to drop to your knees and thank me. When I leave, you are to present yourself in pleasure pose to your Domme, who is probably as wet as I am."

I nod when she turns to see my response.

Bernadette drops to her knees at the appointed moment and then leans forward to kiss the hand Jaleesa offers. "Thank you, Miss Jaleesa. Thank you. You are a generous Domme. Thank you for spending time with me." That would have been good enough for both Jaleesa and me, but Bernadette lowers herself further and kisses Jaleesa's boots repeatedly. "Ma'am, may I service you? May I please you somehow?"

"Oh, yes, you may," Jaleesa says. "But not tonight. I have to let a few pets out of their cages at home. I believe you sucking me off is part of the plan for Friday night, my pet." She pulls Bernadette back up into a kneeling position and traces Bernadette's lips with a finger. "These lips and that tongue will be pleasing me Friday while I hold your head in place." She sucks air through her teeth, clearly turned on. "Would you like that, pet?"

"Oh, yes, Ma'am. Yes, I would. Thank you."

"You like eating pussy, do you?" Jaleesa asks in disbelief.

"Very much, Ma'am."

"I believe her," Jaleesa says, sounding impressed.

Bernadette licks her lips as if on cue, making us both laugh. Jaleesa kisses Bernadette on the lips one more time and then retrieves her coat.

"You're a good girl, little pet. Be good for your Domme. Remember what I told you to do when I leave."

"Yes, Ma'am." Bernadette sits up taller.

Jaleesa turns toward me and says, "Yep, she's everything you said and more. Thank you, Domme Rikki, for this unexpected appetizer tonight. I'll see you Friday for the main course."

As soon as the door clicks shut, Bernadette sticks her tongue out in pleasure-ready pose. My adrenaline surges. My pants are already unzipped. We are not going to make it upstairs.

Chapter 6
Make Your Domme Proud

The four days leading up to this Friday evening's festivities were hard on Bernadette. Okay, they were hard on me, too, because we didn't get to see each other. I made her go directly home after work each day and pack boxes for her move on Sunday. She was not allowed to orgasm or touch herself at all.

Her ex is moving out today. Tomorrow, we are going to inspect the house and do some cleaning. She doesn't know it, but I hired a company to do what's called a "move-in clean," where they wipe down everything inside and out—cabinets, refrigerator, appliances. They do the floors, ceilings, and walls. It is a total cleansing. Once they're finished, Shanice, Marta's *little*, arranged for a healer to come in and sage the space clean spiritually. We'll stay back at Bernadette's apartment on Saturday night and then move everything into the house on Sunday morning. I told her I'd arrange everything for the move. And I have. Jaleesa's subs will be ready with a moving truck and their strong bodies to move Bernadette's meager furniture and storage unit contents. They won't be paid monetarily, but Jaleesa and I will make sure they are rewarded well.

"Big day tomorrow," I say to her. "Even bigger day on Sunday." She doesn't respond. I am basically talking to myself because I put noise-canceling headphones on her ears, which means she cannot hear me. She is also blindfolded and gagged. She cannot see or speak, either. Her wrists, ankles, and collar are chained to bolted brackets I had Mark install one afternoon this week. Bernadette seemed intrigued by Madison's punishment corner, so I installed one for her, although maybe it's more for me because I am getting turned on observing my nude submissive sensory-deprived and helpless. The chains clinking against each other are tangible bonds of obedience and fuel my ardor. Bernadette is nude and I am in my robe, cinched at the waist.

A soft but rapid knock on the apartment door signals the start of the scene.

I open the door, put a finger to my lips, and point to Bernadette in the corner.

Jaleesa grunts her satisfaction. "You are a fucking Dommes' Domme, Rikki Carmichael. Son of a bitch. Look at her arranged on a platter for us."

Bernadette senses my proximity when I come near and lifts her head. I take off the headphones and signal to Jaleesa.

"Domme Rikki," she says, and Bernadette jumps. She is nervous. Good. Jaleesa chuckles and starts again. "Domme Rikki, this lusciously displayed pet belongs to you and will remain yours. I respect any and all ground rules and limits you set for her."

"Domme Jaleesa," I respond ritually. "I accept your words. You may direct my submissive as you please after she greets you."

"Greet this Domme, please," I instruct Bernadette.

Bernadette is gagged and cannot speak, so instead, she reaches around with her hands until she finds Jaleesa's boots. She lays her forehead down on the leather and makes a sound that is a mixture of whimpering and purring. Jaleesa raises an eyebrow at me. She is pleased, as am I.

"Sit up, pet," Jaleesa commands, and Bernadette does as commanded. "Kneel. Open." Bernadette works around her chains and kneels with her legs wide open. "I do love a glistening cunt," Jaleesa comments. She looks at me and says, "Might we unchain her? I'd like her to undress me."

"Excellent," I say and undo all the locks. My little bee has progressed from Velcro restraints to metal chains with locks, and I am beyond proud of the trust that shows me. She rubs at the places the bonds have dug in a bit.

Jaleesa gestures for me to remove the blindfold. I am absolutely okay with her leading. We've only done this kind of thing once before when I was a guest Domme in her basement dungeon. In essence, I am repaying her kindness to me when I was struggling after Eileen's betrayal and sudden departure.

Bernadette blinks as the light in the apartment assaults her eyes.

Jaleesa reaches down and cups Bernadette's chin lightly but firmly. "Will you make your Domme proud this evening, pet?"

Bernadette nods and mumbles something behind her gag.

"Take my instructions without question?"

Bernadette nods again and tries to rub her cheek on Jaleesa's hand. Is she acting like a pet, or does she just want affection from her crush? A little of both, maybe? Jaleesa allows it and strokes my girl's cheek. She shoots me a grin as if to say I am one lucky dog to have a sub like Bernadette. Don't I know it. I clip the leash on her collar and hand the leash to Jaleesa, who nods her acceptance. This tells me she understands the gift I have just given her.

"Stoplight system for safewords?"

Bernadette nods.

"Stand, pet," Jaleesa says and tugs up on the leash. "Undress me."

With shaking hands, Bernadette unfastens the buttons on Jaleesa's shirt, pulls it off, and then folds it carefully. She steps in close, almost touching Jaleesa, reaches around, and unhooks the lacy bra. She gently pulls it off and looks down on Jaleesa's full breasts. And, I will admit, they are impressive. Large dark areolas, sturdy nipples already hard. Bernadette hesitates in her task as she takes in the sight. She slowly raises her eyes and meets Jaleesa's gaze as if asking permission.

Jaleesa seems to understand my girl's need and removes the ball gag. She offers Bernadette a breast for sucking. Bernadette moans her appreciation and kisses her benefactor's breast, and then licks and sucks until Jaleesa moans her arousal. I am supposedly passive as I watch the events unfolding before me, but my libido is not. Watching my submissive service another Domme is exciting me to no end.

Jaleesa moves things along, and soon, her boots, socks, pants, and panties have joined the rest of her clothing. I hand her a red silk kimono that she slips on before sitting in one of my living room chairs. She commands Bernadette to get down on all fours in front of her. Jaleesa scoots forward in the chair and places a pillow behind her back. She opens her robe and tugs on the leash, pulling Bernadette between her open legs.

Bernadette looks back at me, her eyes asking permission. The invisible bonds of obedience are clearly strong. I nod once. I like that she wants me to approve. That strokes my ego along with my libido.

"Crawl over here and please me, pet," Jaleesa commands. "I will accept nothing but your best."

Bernadette crawls closer and nudges Jaleesa's legs farther apart with her shoulders. She needs room to work. I bite my lip at this bold move, but Jaleesa seems unaffected and hands Bernadette a dental dam for protection. While Bernadette gets to work, I get up and pull out two harnesses. One is for me right now, and one will be for Jaleesa later. I strap on the harness, wistful that Bernadette is unavailable to do it for me. Wow, I have become one lazy Domme. I wiggle my fingers over the selection of dildoes and decide on a medium-sized one.

Jaleesa nods her approval, and I move in behind my busy girl and grab her by the hips. She makes a noise of surprise but doesn't stop stimulating Jaleesa. Jaleesa is getting turned on by my girl's attention, that is obvious. I put the tip of the dildo at the entrance to Bernadette's vagina. She moans her approval.

"Fuck, yes, girl," Jaleesa says and grabs the back of Bernadette's head. She bucks her pelvis over Bernadette's lips and tongue. She stops and says, "Yes, yes, yes. Suck that clit. Yessss." She sucks air through her teeth, a clear sign that she is close to cumming.

I enter Bernadette slowly. She doesn't react because she is busy pleasing our guest. I push until I hit her cervix. I grip her hips firmly and pull back out again slowly. I want my girl to feel all kinds of sensations and begin a series of medium-speed strokes. I am surprised that Jaleesa didn't put any nipple clamps on her or warm her up with a flogging. That's okay. The night is young.

"Fucking suck that clit, you fucking slut," Jaleesa hisses.

Bernadette moans in clear arousal at Jaleesa's harsh words. Her reaction surprises me.

Jaleesa says, "Looks like your good little girl likes a little degradation." I shrug in a manner that tells Jaleesa to go for it. I am as surprised as she is by this revelation.

"It's a good thing your owner lets you service people, slave," Jaleesa says. "You're no good for anything else."

Bernadette lifts her head as a pre-orgasmic wave hits her. I know this because I have a hard time thrusting as her pussy clenches.

"She had you chained to the goddamned wall so anyone could use you," Jaleesa continues. She lifts Bernadette's head by her hair. "Isn't that right, slut?"

"Yes, Ma'am," Bernadette says, her voice thick with lust.

Jaleesa taps Bernadette on the cheek with the flat of her hand. "Tell me who's a slut."

"I am a slut, Ma'am," Bernadette says. She thrusts her ass back at me. She wants me to fuck her harder and deeper.

"We should have chained you down at the board meeting and let the Dommes have their way with you," Jaleesa says, "Isn't that right, Domme Rikki?"

I don't answer her because degradation is not my thing, and I won't do that to Bernadette, although she seems to like it from Jaleesa.

"Use that talent, slut." Jaleesa shoves Bernadette's face in between her legs. "Make me cum in your mouth."

It isn't long before Jaleesa smothers Bernadette's face with her release. I continue to fuck Bernadette slowly as they both recover. It isn't long before Jaleesa grabs Bernadette by the hair again and taps her face. "Look at my cum all over your face, slut. You'll leave that on to show your Domme your one useful skill." She grunts her power and then says, "So much for the dental dam. Oh, well. Now you can lick me clean, cum junky."

Bernadette arches her back at the insult and starts to shake. I increase my thrusts, and Jaleesa picks up on what's happening. She continues to degrade Bernadette, and it isn't long before Bernadette breathlessly calls out, "Rikki, please. I can't see you."

"Ten," I stop thrusting. "Nine," I pull out. "Eight."

"Rikki," she pleads.

"Seven." She moans, frustrated. "Six." I move behind Jaleesa's chair. "Five." She locks eyes with me. "Four." Her breathing heaves. "Three."

"Fuck, Rikki. Fuck."

"Two." Bernadette glances at Jaleesa and then back at me.

"One. Cum for me, my good girl. Cum now!"

Bernadette's mouth opens wide, and she becomes rigid. It's like watching the tide recede, and then her orgasm hits her. She writhes and shakes wildly, screeching her release. "Rikki, I love you," she sputters and then arches her back as another orgasm hits. She is a wonder to behold.

"This is some kind of magic," Jaleesa says in awe.

Bernadette falls to the floor and kisses Jaleesa's feet repeatedly. "Thank you, Miss. Thank you."

Jaleesa looks at me like she simply cannot believe what she has just witnessed. Her eyes tell me that I will have to reveal my Domme secrets about this parlor trick. She pulls Bernadette up gently and coaxes her onto her lap. Bernadette puts her arms around Jaleesa's neck, and they kiss passionately. My arousal surges at the sight of Bernadette's pale white skin juxtaposed against Jaleesa's dark, my faithful submissive in the arms of my faithful friend. I take a mental snapshot of the scene. It's sexy as hell.

Bernadette lays her head on Jaleesa's shoulder, and they cuddle for a while. I clean the dildo and hand out bottles of water all around, making sure Bernadette's is at room temperature. She knows why.

After we've rested sufficiently and used the facilities, Bernadette is instructed to get the flogger and her favorite crop. She does so and kneels in front of Jaleesa. She holds the items out in front of her with both hands as a submissive offering. Her head is bowed.

I gesture for Jaleesa to take them. It's only fitting that my guest gets the first crack at beating my submissive. Jaleesa and I are both sporting harnesses with dildoes now. There is no doubt what will be coming next in this scenario of ours.

I hand Bernadette a foil-wrapped condom.

"Put it on me, slut," Jaleesa says.

Bernadette gasps. Jaleesa's words excite her. Bernadette puts the condom in her mouth and crawls over to the phallus protruding from Jaleesa's harness. She lifts the phallus with one hand, looks Jaleesa in the eye, and then wraps her arm around Jaleesa's leg for support. Still making eye contact, Bernadette reaches up and rakes her fingernails gently down Jaleesa's torso. She breaks eye contact to focus on her task ahead. She pushes forward. The condom unrolls over the bulbous head. She pulls back and then pushes forward again, gaining more ground. I know she is finding her groove, finding a way to open her throat to take the entire phallus in. She pulls back and pushes steadily forward until the whole thing is embedded in her mouth and throat. She pushes her nose against Jaleesa's harness and then pulls back and takes a breath. She deepthroats several more times before Jaleesa pulls out completely.

"Where the fuck did you find this talented cocksucker, Domme Rikki?" Jaleesa asks. "How do you … You need to give classes on this shit. And why do you only keep one sub at a time? I've never understood that. You could have a fucking harem, woman."

I just smile and say, "Bernadette is all I need."

Bernadette's head is bowed, but I see her relieved smile.

"Wipe that fucking grin off your face," Jaleesa barks, startling both me and Bernadette. She yanks Bernadette up by her leash and then marches her over to the St. Andrew's cross. She smashes Bernadette roughly against it, her back to the cross. Jaleesa smacks Bernadette across the breasts several times without explanation. She spins her around, and I help her strap my girl to the cross face first. Restraining her in this manner is for her safety. She can't suddenly turn or try to block the blows with her hands. That could seriously hurt her and cause permanent damage. She's also told me that being restrained makes her feel secure as if she doesn't have a choice anyway, so why fight it?

Jaleesa warms up Bernadette's ass, back, and thighs gently with light blows from the flogger. I already knew she would, but I am pleased to see that she carefully avoids the kidneys and spine and never once wraps the tails around Bernadette's shoulders. I am also pleased that Bernadette stops fighting the pain quickly and lets herself take it in. Jaleesa senses this shift and increases her intensity. She has a steady rhythm that mesmerizes me. She has a half-dozen submissives, and that must keep her flogging routine in shape.

Without warning, Jaleesa drops the flogger and picks up the crop. There is no warmup this time, and she whacks my girl several times in succession. Bernadette's cries seem to fuel Jaleesa, and she increases her pace and locations. Jaleesa presses her body up against Bernadette's naked form, her raw skin. Bernadette moans in both pleasure and pain. A few welts are swelling up prominently from the crop strikes.

Bernadette cries out again when Jaleesa impales her on the dildo. Jaleesa thrusts wildly. Bernadette's cries turn to passion quickly. Jaleesa fumbles for my girl's clit and rubs furiously. She reaches her release before Bernadette even gets close. Bernadette is gracious and doesn't groan at the missed orgasm opportunity. She understands that our guest's pleasure is paramount.

Jaleesa stumbles back into a chair to catch her breath and recover.

"You did so well, little bee," I whisper in Bernadette's ear.

"Please touch me, Ma'am," she pleads.

I gently stroke her warm ass with my hand and then reach over for my faux rabbit fur. I lovingly rub the red areas, and she practically purrs. Abruptly, though, I ditch the fur and spread her ass cheeks wide apart. "Ma'am," she says sharply. This was not the kind of touching she wanted from me. She groans as I lube up her rosebud. She always laughs when I call it that. It's what Aunt Tilda called it, and the name stuck. I move a gloved finger inside her, and she thrusts her ass toward me. Yes, she likes her anal rewards, that's for sure. One finger becomes two. I work them around and then lube up the anal plug that will stretch her.

"That is fucking hot," Jaleesa says.

I nod my agreement and fill her with the plug. Bernadette sighs her contentment at the intrusion. I unchain her and help her lie down on her side on the mat in front of Jaleesa's chair. "Rest, little bee," I tell her.

"Seriously, Rikki," Jaleesa says, "you could make money selling your techniques. Jee-zus."

My heart clenches. Does she know about my financial trouble? Only Marta, Shasti, and Victoria know. Did one of them betray my trust?

"Use this pet here as a model." Jaleesa prods the prone Bernadette gently with her toe.

No, no, I don't think she knows anything. She's just impressed with what I've been able to do with Bernadette, my very willing partner.

Bernadette stirs and sits up. I hold a water bottle to her lips, and she drinks her fill. "May I service you, Ma'am," she says to me. I kiss her on the lips and say, "You're a good girl for offering, but I think we have other things in mind."

Jaleesa pulls Bernadette up and then pulls the used condom off her dildo. She hands Bernadette a fresh condom and watches in fascination as my girl deepthroats her a second time. Jaleesa maneuvers Bernadette onto all fours and nods at me to enter her from behind. I do and begin a slow fuck in rhythm to Jaleesa's thrusts in Bernadette's mouth. Jaleesa has a nice approach. She starts with gentle strokes in my girl's mouth and then grabs Bernadette's head, signaling that she's going in deep. I follow suit and also ram my cock inside her. With the butt plug inserted, Bernadette must be feeling stuffed.

Like a champion, Bernadette keeps her throat open and loose to take Jaleesa's strokes. Jaleesa eventually slows down and then stops. She motions for me to pull out and then maneuvers Bernadette onto her lap, impaled on the dildo, of course. She lifts Bernadette up with her strong arms and plunges her down hard and fast. My girl's breasts bounce with every thrust. "Take over, pet," Jaleesa demands in a husky voice. Bernadette has one leg on the floor and the other tucked on the chair. She rides Jaleesa expertly while Jaleesa plays with her bouncing breasts.

Jaleesa motions for me to join them and halts Bernadette's motions. She pulls Bernadette to her, effectively lifting her ass for my easy access. I straddle Jaleesa's legs. Using a bit of lube, I pull out the plug with a twisting motion and then generously lube up my cock. I press the head against her tiny hole. She gasps. Jaleesa is buried to the hilt in her vagina. Yes, my girl will be full, indeed.

I press on, and the pressure on the front end of the dildo presses against my clit gloriously on the back end. I push in gently and finally break through the ring of muscles. God, she is tight with her pussy filled like that. I pull out slightly and then thrust in deeper. I continue in this slow fashion while Bernadette moans in pleasure. "Rikki, I'm going to cum." She cries out as a pre-orgasmic wave hits her. I smack her ass. "You don't get to cum until I say so."

"Yes, Ma'am," she says clearly in orgasmic agony.

I continue my thrusting, and then Jaleesa joins in counter rhythm. When I thrust in, she pulls out, and vice versa. Jaleesa and I latch on to each other's gaze and feed on our collective power. She changes her rhythm to match mine—Bernadette squeals between us.

"Squeal all you want, fucktoy. You're not done until we say you're done." Jaleesa's words make Bernadette groan in frustration.

Something changes on Jaleesa's face, and I can tell that she's ready to cum again. I pull out slowly and let her ram her cock into my girl. She jams in three times in succession and then cums. She holds her breath and then exhales forcefully. "Oh, yes," she says and pumps Bernadette a few more times. She pets my girl's head. "I like having you impaled on my cock. Do you like that, toy?"

"Yes, Ma'am," Bernadette says. There are tears in her eyes.

Oh, shit, did we hurt her between us? Jaleesa sees it, too, and pulls Bernadette off the phallus and into her lap.

"Are you hurt?" Jaleesa asks and brushes the tears away.

Bernadette shakes her head. I visibly relax and move so she can see me.

"Tell me," Jaleesa's voice is stern. It's exactly what I would have said and the way I would have said it.

She snuggles into Jaleesa's shoulder.

"Bernadette," I say sternly.

"I just … it's …" she sighs and says, "I just feel loved. That's all."

Jaleesa chuckles gently. "You are something else, little pet." She kisses the top of Bernadette's head and then rocks her. Bernadette closes her eyes and seems to doze. There has been a lot of physical and emotional stimulation on my little bee today.

"Are you sure I can't convince you to come back and do Tina with me again?" Jaleesa asks me.

I shake my head. "Bernadette's all I need." I point to the girl she's cuddling in her lap.

"Rikki?" Bernadette murmurs. "You can do Tina."

I burst out laughing. "Thank you for your permission, little bee. That would be something you and I discuss with Jaleesa and Tina."

Jaleesa groans. "I never got a single clamp on you, pet." She smacks Bernadette playfully on one ass cheek.

"Next time," I offer.

"Yes, please, Ma'ams," Bernadette says drowsily.

After a few more minutes, Jaleesa rouses Bernadette off her lap, cleans up in the bathroom, and takes her leave after kissing Bernadette sensuously one last time.

After Jaleesa leaves, Bernadette insists on servicing me. Who am I to refuse this beautiful, passionate woman? We head to the bed after I cum, and I pull her close, spooning her from behind. We should clean up, but I am exhausted, and my eyes are already closing.

"Thank you for that, Rikki," Bernadette says sleepily. "I love you."

"I love you, too, sweetie. You made me immensely proud this evening."

"Mmm," is her only reply. She is asleep before I can finish laughing.

Chapter 7
Safe with Me

E arly Sunday morning, I pull the Subaru up the long tree-lined drive to Bernadette's three-story farmhouse that sits on a secluded five acres. The back of my car is filled to the brim with boxes. One day, I'll ask her how she could afford the place on a college professor's salary. Money is not an easy topic for me, though, so that conversation may never happen.

Bernadette makes a surprised noise of disbelief. There are more than a dozen people in her yard.

"I told you our community looks out for each other."

"You said that, but I didn't realize," Bernadette says. "I thought it would only be Jaleesa's subs and the moving truck today. God, they were so helpful getting the stuff out of the apartment and down three flights. I feel bad."

"They live to help," I tell her. And it's true. Jaleesa only accepts subs with a giving nature. That's why her taking on Kari has perplexed me.

Bernadette leans over for a kiss, which I gladly give. "I love you," she says. There are tears in her eyes. "You are the best thing that's happened to me. Ever."

My heart swells. "I love you, too, little bee." I kiss the back of her hand, which I am somehow holding but didn't realize I was. "Big breath now. This is all about you today." She groans. She hates attention.

"Okay, you lovebirds," Jaleesa says, tapping the hood of my car, "let's get this party started."

I get out of the driver's seat and walk around to let my little bee out.

"Very chivalrous," Jaleesa says, clearly impressed.

I simply nod and offer Bernadette my hand. I've dressed her comfortably but provocatively today. I admit it. I am showing her off again. The yoga classes I've made her attend at the university have made her stronger and much more flexible. She has a toned look to her that she has taken great pride in. In fact, she signed up for a strength training class over the summer.

I gather everyone near the porch and lay the ground rules. The biggest ground rule is that Bernadette is in charge. What she says goes. She blanches when I say that and is clearly nervous when I ask her to assign tasks.

"It's just like teaching a class," I tell her quietly. "Think of them as your students."

She clears her throat and says, "Well, the furniture should have the first priority in order to empty the truck. Then the truck has to go to the storage unit on Kirkland." She turns to me and says, "I guess I'll need to go with them?"

I nod and shrug. "That makes the most sense."

"Meanwhile," she addresses the crowd again, "the smaller boxes from Miss Rikki's car and the truck should go to the designated rooms. The boxes are labeled. If you're not sure where a room is, ask Miss Rikki.me, Miss Shasti, or Madison. They've all had the tour." She looks at me, her eyes searching mine to see if she's forgotten anything. "Oh, there are sodas and waters in the refrigerator if you get thirsty. Help yourselves. I have pizzas coming in around noon as a big thank you." She looks at me again. "Umm, okay, that's it, I guess. Oh, wait," she says, frantically waving her hands. "Would you all please wipe your feet before going in?" She grimaces, but her smile is so endearing that everyone chuckles.

"Off you go," I add when no one moves. They head to the car and the truck, Jaleesa taking charge of her subs and the furniture.

I pull Bernadette into a quick hug. "You did well." I kiss the top of her head.

She takes a big breath and lets it out slowly. "Thank you. I'm not great at public speaking."

I can't help but laugh. "You speak for a living, little bee-ee." I make the word 'bee' into two syllables.

She rolls her eyes and scoffs. "I'm a bit of a contradiction, aren't I?"

"And," I say, "you referred to me as Miss Rikki."

"In front of the subs and *littles*," she said. "That's how they refer to you, so I thought—Was that wrong?"

"Nope. It was perfect." I pat her on the butt and say, "Now, you need to grab light boxes and be visible to help people find rooms. Shasti said she would start unpacking the kitchen, but you may want to check in with her on occasion."

"Yes, Ma'am." Bernadette takes one step down the porch steps and stops, looking lost for a moment. She turns back to me and says, "Thank you. For everything." I nod and follow her to my car to empty it of boxes.

The moving of boxes and furniture goes smoothly, except for one scraped Madison knee and subsequent bandaging by her Domme. Madison's limping is endearing and garners a ton of sympathy from everyone. At one point, Jaleesa picks her up in a fireman's carry and gives all the Dommes free shots at spanking her. Madison's giggles help keep the hard work light.

At first, Bernadette seems nervous about going to the storage unit without me, but I reassure her I would take care of things here at the house and that Jaleesa will direct things. Is she nervous about being alone with Jaleesa without me? No, I don't think that's it. It's more that she doesn't want to be in charge. If I know my friend Jaleesa, Bernadette needn't worry about that. Jaleesa is in her early forties and has been a Domme and "in-charge" since her twenties. I'm satisfied that Bernadette will be fine. She needs to get out of her head more.

Once the truck heads out for the storage unit, I commission the more tech-minded subs to hook up Bernadette's electronics and internet equipment. The rest, I ask to arrange furniture and not to worry about getting it wrong because we can always rearrange it later. While they are doing that, Shasti and I take an unguided tour of the house, scoping out the best place to put a dungeon. She thought the third-floor dormer space would be perfect, but I point out the low roofline. It would be difficult to get my whip flying correctly, the whip that Bernadette has not yet met. Shasti agrees, and when we get to the basement, our eyes light up. There is some clutter in the corner, but it is a finished basement with good lighting, and Shasti points out that it would be cooler than the dormer in the summer. The only other option would be to knock down walls on the second floor between two bedrooms. We stop our mental destruction of Bernadette's house and head back upstairs to her bedroom. It isn't long before we hear them return.

"Thanks for the help, Kari," Bernadette says. "This one goes in the living room." I hear them both grunt and then laugh. They must be carrying something heavy. Something large clunks on the floor, and then they both exhale loudly.

"Is Rikki moving in with you?" Kari blurts.

"*Miss* Rikki?" Bernadette says, emphasizing the word Miss. She is clearly setting boundaries with Jaleesa's new sub.

"Yeah, whatever," Kari says. Only a pop of bubble gum would have completed that statement.

Shasti and I exchange a look. We are both wide-eyed at Kari's impertinence, although I am not surprised. I take a step toward the stairs to intervene, but Shasti puts a hand out to stop me. "Let's see what happens." Ahh, ever the Mommy Domme, she likes subs to learn and grow from their own experiences instead of always being saved by a Domme. That is incredibly hard for me, but I see the wisdom in it.

"Here, sit," Bernadette says. "Look, I'm kind of new on the scene and don't know a hell of a lot, but I do know that the foundation of our community is respect, you know? And referring to someone by their title shows respect."

"She thinks she's all high and mighty," Kari says. "Pushing people around all the time."

Bernadette doesn't respond immediately, probably because she's choking on Kari's words like I am. "Actually, neither of those things are true. She doesn't think she's all 'high and mighty,' and she doesn't 'push people around.' She has a domineering personality, yes. She likes to be in control. But that's what makes her special, Kari. She is special to me, so please remember that when you speak to me about my owner. And she's more than my owner. She's my Dominant, my teacher, my confidante. She's my girlfriend." There is a momentary pause, and then Bernadette asks, "Tell me, Kari, why do you think she pushes you around?"

"She just does."

"Unfairly?"

"Kind of."

"How?" Bernadette asks in a genuinely inquisitive tone.

There is a long silence, and I'm beginning to wonder if Shasti and I should make ourselves known by clomping down the stairs loudly. Shasti must have sensed my unease, so she uses hand gestures to tell me to chill and let Bernadette handle it.

"Is she unfair to you at work?" Bernadette pursues.

"Well, no, I guess not," Kari says. "I mean, she just watches me a lot."

"Why does she watch you?"

"Because I fuck up so much, I guess."

"What do you consider to be a fuck up?" Bernadette asks.

"I don't know," Kari mumbles.

"She makes you work hard, doesn't she?"

"Yeah."

"But she also insists you do things correctly and efficiently?"

"Yeah, all of that."

"And she praises you when you do well?"

"Are you watching me?" Kari asks accusingly.

Bernadette laughs. "Not at all. That is who Rikki is. A fair but firm Dominant. This is how she treats me, too, and I don't think of her as 'high and mighty.' I think of her as strong and knowledgeable. And I'm grateful for every correction and punishment she gives me because it makes me a better person with a better understanding of things."

There was more silence until Kari says, "That makes sense, Miss Bernadette."

Shasti's eyes bug out. She mouths to me, "She called her 'Miss.'"

"I heard it," I whisper. Wow. Look what my girl did. She got a tried-and-true brat to show respect.

"Miss Bernadette?" Kari says.

"Yes, Kari?"

"Are you going to be one of Jaleesa's subs now? Like, are you going to have two Dommes because that would be kind of epic."

"Oh, uh, no, Kari. Where did you get that idea?" The question clearly throws Bernadette.

"Tina said that Miss Rikki loaned you to Miss Jaleesa Friday night."

"Ahh," Bernadette says, clearly stalling to figure out how to respond. I'm curious to hear what she's going to say. "Miss Rikki *shared* me with Miss Jaleesa. And, no, I'm not going to become one of Miss Jaleesa's subs. Miss Rikki is my Domme. Friday night's scene was a gift to me from her. It was wonderful, but I don't think it's going to be a regular thing."

"Oh, okay," Kari says. "That's cool."

I feel Shasti staring at me. I turn and shrug sheepishly. Apparently, news of the Friday night threesome hadn't made it to all corners of our community. Shasti smacks me on the arm and shakes her head. She is smiling, though, so I know she's not upset with me.

It's time to head downstairs. "So that back room gets the perfect afternoon sunlight," I say loudly.

"Oh, yes. I agree," Shasti says. "That's the best room for her office."

We get to the bottom of the stairs and see Kari and Bernadette sitting on the floor near the coffee table they must have just brought in.

Bernadette leaps to her feet, runs over to me, and whispers, "I love you." Her arms wrap themselves around me.

"I love you, too, and I am keeping you," I answer back and pull her into a kiss that deepens with every passing moment. I finally pull away first, breathless. I feel my face flush when I realize that Kari, Shasti, and even Madison have been staring at us.

"Get a room, you two," Jaleesa yells from the front door. "You've got seven thousand to choose from." Her gesture indicates the large house. Everyone chuckles, breaking the embarrassing moment.

"Miss," Kari says, running over to Jaleesa, "may I help you with that box?"

Jaleesa looks as surprised by her sub's offer as the rest of us are. "Yes, you may, Kari. Thank you." She unloads the box into her sub's outstretched arms and then pats her on the ass playfully as she walks away. Kari turns and smiles back coquettishly at her Domme.

"Hmm," Jaleesa muses out loud once Kari is out of earshot. "Is it opposite day?"

~~~

Once everyone except Shasti and Madison are gone, we plop in the newly arranged living room with the coffees Bernadette made, decaf for Madison, of course.

"I have something—" Madison starts to say.

"Your house is beautiful, Professor," Shasti interrupts. "Thank you for letting us be a part of your move."

"No, thank you, Ma'am," Bernadette says. "You were both a tremendous help."

"Can I please—" Madison tries again.

"You have a massive plot of land to mow," Shasti adds. "Madison will help."

"I will?" Madison says, her eyes bugging out. Shasti tilts her head in such a way that Madison changes the punctuation of her sentence. "I will. But now can I—" She stops talking as if she knew her Mistress would interrupt her.

We all laugh at her surprised expression when that didn't happen.

"Go on," Shasti says.

"I think there should be—"

"I apologize for the bad coffee," Bernadette interrupts. "My coffee pot, apparently, needs to be 'tossed immediately.'" She uses air quotes and bugs her eyes at me.

"Gahhhhh," Madison groans and falls on the floor in frustration, her arms spread out to her sides.

We laugh again, and Bernadette says, "I couldn't resist, kiddo. Go on. What have you been dying to say for the last half hour?"

Madison sits up. She purses her lips and says, "I don't remember."

We all groan.

"Wait, wait, wait," she says urgently. "I remember, Professor. Is Miss Rikki going to put in a punishment corner for you? And where will the dungeon be?"

"I, I," Bernadette stammers, "I hadn't thought about any of those things."

"Dr. Garneau," Madison says, aghast, "you have this big giant house. You have to have a dungeon or a play area or something. Don't you?" She looks from Bernadette to me and then to her Mistress as if the entire world suddenly makes no sense.

"Yes," Bernadette says with more conviction, "I suppose I do need to think of these things, don't I? Thank you for reminding me."

Madison puffs up and then says, "Mistress, can I have some cookies?"

Everyone laughs, and then we have a brief but serious discussion about Bernadette's expected role with Madison. It's collectively decided that Madison should continue to think of Bernadette as her professor, and she should obey anything Bernadette asks of her. Madison is to refer to Bernadette as 'professor' or 'Miss Bernadette.' She readily agrees and apologizes again for eating stupid gummies when she wasn't supposed to eat sweets. Bernadette also seems satisfied with her newly defined role. That settled, Shasti and Madison take their leave, Madison with a cookie in hand, and I am finally alone with my girl.

"Oh, God, I could sleep right here in the living room," Bernadette says as she locks the front door. "I assume you're staying here tonight?"

"Is that an invitation?" I ask, sidling up next to her.

"Yes, yes, yes. Please don't leave me alone." She lays her head on my chest.

I wrap my arms around her and squeeze her tight. "I would like nothing more, *Miss* Bernadette."

She pulls her head back and narrows her eyes at me. "What are you getting at?"

"You were wonderful with Kari this afternoon."

"Oh, no. You overheard. Rikki, I'm sorry she spoke about you like that. You weren't supposed to hear any of it."

"I already knew how she felt, Bernadette. And my overhearing was accidental, I promise." I put my hand in the air as if taking an oath. "You were so calm with her."

"I was hopping mad by what she said. But I'm a lover, not a fighter, so I stayed calm."

"Lover?" I say and pull her toward the stairs.

"Wait," she says. "Let me check my school bag and set up the coffee pot before we go upstairs."

"That coffee pot—"

"I know. I know," she says and waves me away. "I'll get a new one soon."

Within minutes she is satisfied that she is all set to make a speedy exit in the morning. I've already notified Lydia that she'll be opening the shop without me. She is capable and intelligent and should do fine. Bernadette keeps insisting that I need to trust my managers more, and I make a vow to do just that. Trust is sometimes challenging for me. I've been burned before.

We drag our tired selves up the stairs and down the hall to the large master bedroom.

"Whoa," Bernadette says and stops so abruptly that I bump into her. "Who made my bed?" She rushes over and smooths out the new comforter.

"Who gave me this?"

"A gift from Marta and Shanice," I say. "They couldn't be here today but wanted to contribute."

Bernadette turns toward me, her eyes filled with tears. "That is so sweet. I will have to thank them first thing tomorrow." She pulls back the comforter and runs her hands over the soft microfiber sheets. "Who made the bed?"

"Shasti and I did."

Bernadette picks up her beloved Pooh bear stuffie. "Miss Shasti saw him, I suppose?"

I nod.

"I'm so embarrassed."

I chuckle. "Don't be. She, of all people, understands. I do, too. You're not a *little*, Bernadette, but you look for things that nurture and comfort you. We were coming down the stairs after making your bed when we overheard you and Kari talking."

"Oh, no," Bernadette cries. "Shasti heard, too?"

I nod.

"Ahh, so she now knows about Friday and Miss Jaleesa. Oh, God. Now she knows what a ho I am." She grimaces at me. "Seriously, does Shasti think I'm a slut?" There is genuine contrite in her voice.

"Absolutely not," I say. "I think she champions a woman new to the scene asking for what she wants and experiencing it. I think the same thing and applaud you."

Bernadette, in spite of herself, yawns big.

"All right, little bee," I say, "we've had a big day today."

Bernadette smiles, yawns again, and then apologizes.

"C'mon," I say. "Let's get showered and hit the bed."

She puts her Pooh bear down, and I undress her. I push her gently toward the bathroom in the master suite. I follow behind, shedding my clothes as I do. It's a wonderfully large bathroom with an overlarge clawfoot tub underneath the window. I foresee many fun times in that tub, but not tonight. We're both too tired.

I reach past Bernadette and turn on the water. When it's the right temperature, I enter first and pull her behind me. I open a new purple scrubby and pour almond-scented body wash on it. I've discovered that my girl likes almond-scented things, so I hope she likes this. Her eyes open wide at the small presents I've provided, and she gushes how much she loves everything. She protests when I begin washing her but soon relaxes into my touch. She's quickly learned in our relationship not to challenge me when I've made up my mind.

When I've finished washing her body, I wash her hair gently, rinse, and then apply conditioner. While her hair is conditioning, I hand her a brand new green scrubby, and she washes my body. I don't let her linger anywhere fun, and she groans her disapproval but accepts it.

I rinse her hair and mine and then push her back against the tile wall. "I adore you, Bernadette. My smart, way smarter than me, wonderful woman." My lips silence her reply, and I kiss her passionately. She moans into my mouth, and I know it's time.

I slowly kiss my way down her body. I don't linger too long in any one place until I am finally at the apex. She tenses, and I ask, "Do you want me to stop, little bee?" I hear the husky quality of my voice. I didn't realize how turned on she's made me.

She doesn't answer verbally. Instead, she reaches down and pulls my head closer to her pussy. That's my girl. Three months ago, she never would have done anything like that. She is growing. And I love it.

I touch my lips to her slick folds tenderly. My kiss turns into a full-on feast. I sense her relax as I make love to her. I pull her lips apart with my fingers and thrust my tongue inside. I then circle her clit with my hardened tongue until she bucks her hips. I suckle and circle and thrust. Her musky scent has aroused me mightily, but I will receive no relief this evening. No, this is about my girl and her pleasure. She is wet against my tongue. The low moan deep in her throat lets me know she is close. She holds my head against her as if to say, "Right there. Right there. Right there." So, I keep doing what I'm doing, and it isn't long before she's screeching my name and bucking against my face.

Afterward, I clean and dry us both and then lay her down in the new sheets. I curl up behind her, make sure she is clutching her Pooh bear, and silently let her know that I've got her and that she is safe with me as she begins this new phase of her life.

Chapter 8
The Owner and the Owned

The morning rush at the coffee shop is pretty much over by the time I get there. Lydia and the crew seem to have handled things well. It's a short distance from Bernadette's house and is closer than her apartment. I went back to sleep in her bed after she kissed me goodbye and headed to the university. I don't know if it was the new sheets, the warm woman I'd woken up to, or what, but I was feeling the most relaxed and content I'd felt in an exceptionally long time.

One significant detail I had forgotten about was clothes for Monday morning, so I ended up rooting around Bernadette's semi-unpacked closet for something clean to put on. I look for the skirts and "girly blouses" that Victoria made her buy but then remembered that she'd donated them to the women's shelter, so those were out. I found nothing but men's button-down shirts. Her dress slacks were a size too big for me, and even those were menswear. At least she had a fashionable belt that allowed me to cinch the pants at the waist so they wouldn't fall down.

I originally had intended to head straight up to my apartment and change, but I decide to wear what I have on into the coffee shop. I kind of like it because it feels like I've got my little bee wrapped around my entire body.

"Uh, Boss," Lydia says when I walk into the shop, "this is a new look for you."

I laugh. "No kidding. I feel like a menswear model."

"A hot one, if I might say." She waggles her eyebrows and then takes three steps back before turning to address an employee's frustration with one of the espresso machines. I sigh. That particular machine needs to be replaced. So does the furnace, and I don't even want to think about the central air conditioning system. Mark and I have managed to keep it going, but spring is here, and summer will hit soon. Selling coffee with no a/c is not a good combination.

Before my financial woes can take over my headspace, I check in on Marta in the kitchen. She is whistling, which means she is in a particularly good mood.

Before I can ask, Marta says, "She finally let me use needles." She whips out her phone and shows me a few pics of precisely placed needles.

"Whoa," I say, impressed. "How did she like it?" The shiny silver needles against Shanice's dark skin look artful, albeit painful.

"Uh, we didn't stop fucking until two in the morning."

"You are one impressive Domme, Marta," I say with a laugh.

"And you are looking kind of butch today, Boss." Marta gestures to my outfit. "A little role reversal? Please don't tell me you made Bernadette wear a skirt to teach in. I felt so bad for her when Victoria forced that fifties household kink on her. Bernadette was miserable."

"Victoria tried to make her femme, which she isn't," I say. "And, no, I'm not forcing her to wear skirts. I just forgot to bring clothes for this morning."

"Any discussion about moving in together? That would solve the whole packing a bag for every sleepover."

Kari walks in with a tray of dirty dishes, and Marta gestures for her to sort the garbage from the cups and plates.

I don't want to talk about my private life in front of Kari, so I say, "I need to get to the bills. We'll talk later."

Marta winks and then thunders, "Would you please get out of my kitchen, Boss?" She snaps a clean towel at me.

I laugh, shake my head, and do just that.

As I sit in my office sorting which bills will get paid this month and which can wait a little longer, I think about my girl's obvious masculine traits. Her masculine walk. That short hair that Jaleesa convinced her to grow a bit longer. The new hairstyle totally suits her because Jaleesa is a genius when it comes to those things. But the lack of variety in her wardrobe has me upset. There is an opportunity for growth here, and I am going to help her. I don't mind her wearing menswear, but I want them tailored to fit her body. Her clothes are comfortable, she says, so she doesn't care how they fit. But I do. She represents me. I need to take her to Robert's shop.

I open the banking app on my laptop and sigh. The last time I'd been in Robert's shop was with Victoria. She and I used to be good friends. There we were, mid-twenties, baby Dommes. We learned together and bounced ideas off of each other. We even shared the same subs to practice our fledgling Domme skills on. Although, seriously, I have to give Aunt Tilda's boys a lot of the credit for putting up with my fumbling and bumbling attempts at Dominance, especially with impact play. I'd make them tell me how it felt, not just physically but emotionally and mentally as well. Victoria and I even practiced impact on each other. She has a heavy hand but has good instincts, and I knew she would be a good Domme. Even Aunt Tilda thought so.

I well up with tears as I finished paying the electric bill. It's not the bills that have me choked up, although that's reason enough. No, thinking about all that Aunt Tilda did for me has me emotional. She knew I would take to the Domme life. She'd had an "inkling," she'd told me. She'd heard stories from my grandmother, her sister, how I'd play pirate, tie up the neighborhood kids, and poke them with sticks pretending to make them walk the plank. And then later, after I'd moved here and lived with her, she had that awful stroke. The memories of that horrible night only come in flashes now. At least I don't relive it on a regular basis anymore—the paramedics putting her on the stretcher, her confusion in the hospital, the death rattle in her lungs, and then the stillness when she passed.

Her affairs were in good order, so I took over her house seamlessly. I also had a dozen or so slave contracts to contend with, but I had to set them all free. During this time, I sought comfort from Victoria but got little. Emotions aren't her thing, and we grew apart. Thank goodness the new doctor in town gave me comfort. She'd recently joined the community and was looking for a *little*. She'd asked for Aunt Tilda's help, but *littles* and pets weren't Aunt Tilda's specialty. Aunt Tilda mentored young Dr. Shasti Balakrishnan in the art of gentle, loving Dominance. Aunt Tilda used to call me, Victoria, and Shasti her treasures – Tilda's Treasures.

I smile when I remember Aunt Tilda at community events. She was the belle of the ball, always. She knew everyone in the community, and I distinctly remember how the stoic Shasti melted into a shy mountain of nerves when Aunt Tilda arranged a somewhat private meeting with the newbie *little* named Madison. Shasti was so nervous, but Madison took to her like a puppy, finding her forever home. It was one of Aunt Tilda's best matches.

I was envious of what Shasti and Madison seemed to have and of the unconditional blessing Aunt Tilda had put on the pairing. I thought I would get the same treatment when I wooed and finally landed Eileen. But I didn't. Aunt Tilda told me on more than one occasion that Eileen was trouble and that Eileen was going to break my heart. The one and only good thing about Aunt Tilda's passing was that she didn't have to witness how right she was. I'm still trying to dig myself out from under Eileen's betrayal and its aftermath.

I finish paying the bills I can afford and shove the rest to the side. One day, I'm going to organize these piles, but that day is not today. I ignore the letter from the lawyers about the lien they so generously would like to place on my business. Yes, I know I should call my own lawyer about it and get advice, but that phone call can wait one more day.

There is, however, a certain phone call I've decided to make, even though I didn't think things would ever come down to this again. Desperate times call for desperate measures, I reason and pull up Mistress Dominque's contact information. Our conversation is short and to the point. And, yes, she can always use me. How's tomorrow night, she asks? Perfect, I tell her.

Bernadette's lunchtime text comes in right on schedule. She is quite punctual about things like this. She enjoys order, and so do I, with the exception of my desk. Shasti showed me the alphabetized spice rack with all the labels facing out that Bernadette had arranged at some point yesterday during the move.

I call Bernadette immediately, and before she can say hello, I say, "I'm picking you up after school, taking you shopping, and then out to dinner at the Indigo Café."

"Where it all started," she purrs. "What about darts?"

"We'll be back at the shop in plenty of time."

"Do you want to meet Miss Olga this afternoon?"

"Yes," I say simply.

"I'll arrange it if she's available."

We chat for another few minutes, and I can't help smiling at the fact that my wonderfully compliant submissive didn't once ask me what kind of shopping we would be doing. Aunt Tilda would say that shows trust and obedience. You can't have one without the other, she always said.

~~~

I find the mathematics building easily using Bernadette's precise directions and am impressed with its five stories. I wonder why in the world so many people have an interest in this brain-draining subject. Ahh, it may not be my kink, but these people have a right to theirs, I think wryly.

As much as I enjoyed wearing Bernadette's clothes this morning, I changed into something more me before heading out. I smooth down my three-quarter sleeve v-neck blouse and head into the building. I smell the coffee in the lobby and am appalled by the slovenly appearance of the baristas. They should be ashamed. "Tuck in that shirt," I mutter as I take a seat and text my girl that I am here.

I hear her before I see her.

"Will I see you during office hours tomorrow, Jamal?" She asks from somewhere around the corner. I don't hear the student's reply, but then I hear someone call to her.

"Dr. Garneau, I wanted to tell you. Marty, Eashon, and I are taking your new course this summer."

"That's fantastic, Bianca," Bernadette says. "I'm looking forward to having you as official students instead of all of you jammed in my office for impromptu study sessions."

"We owe you more cookies, don't we?" the student asks.

Bernadette laughs. "No, no, no. I'm not allowed sweets anymore, but thank you anyway."

I grin at her subtlety. The student has no idea the meaning behind the words. When my Bernadette finally turns the corner, she takes my breath away. She is stunning. She is in her environment and positively thriving.

Her face lights up when she sees me. "Rikki," she says, her voice filled with joy. She hugs me and gives me a sweet peck on the lips.

"That was a wonderful greeting, sweetie."

"Let me take you to meet Miss Olga right away," she says. "And then we can go back up to my office to get my things. Oh, I should show you the lecture hall first. That's where I teach."

She is excited to show me this part of her life. And I am curious to see it. We step inside the lecture hall, and I am intimidated by its size. There are at least a hundred seats, but she tells me that the university tries to cap each section at fifty. I tell her that, still, fifty is impressive, and I simply cannot picture my attention-avoiding submissive commanding a room full of that many people. According to her former student Madison, she commands it well.

After the lecture hall, she takes me to the mathematics department offices. I see the administrative assistant's name on the door in the reception area, and my suspicions are confirmed. Bernadette opens the door, and before she can make introductions, Miss Olga is out of her chair and wagging her finger at me before pulling me into a hug.

"Rikki Carmichael, I thought it might be you." She nods her head toward Bernadette. "This one has been mooning over you for months now. I had a feeling she wasn't saying R-I-C-K-Y." She spells out the letters. "I had a strong feeling it was that baby Domme I'd met at Mistress Matilda's place all those years ago by the name of R-I-K-K-I."

"You two know each other?" Bernadette's jaw drops open in disbelief.

Miss Olga lowers her voice and says, "Rikki's Aunt Matilda and I go way back." She winks at Bernadette, and I nod to corroborate the story.

Bernadette sits down in the closest chair and murmurs. "Oh, my God." She rubs her collar with two fingers.

"I was ecstatic the day she came in with that day collar, Rikki. She was riding on cloud nine. And that's when I knew for sure it was you."

I laugh and ask about her husband, Doug. "How is our favorite fox?"

"He is a very happy canine."

"He takes that very seriously if I remember."

"It's cathartic for him," Miss Olga says. "And I encourage it. He is a very compliant little subbie when I let him out to play."

I bust out laughing at Bernadette's shocked expression.

"You're catching flies there, little bee," I say to her.

"It's just," she swallows hard, "a lot."

"You always wondered why you called me Miss Olga, didn't you?"

"Yes, Ma'am."

"I wasn't sure, but I felt your submissive nature. And I knew it would give you comfort to call me Miss Olga."

"It did," Bernadette says. "Still does."

"Later, not right now," Miss Olga says to Bernadette, "I want the full story about those scars." She points to the oh-so-obvious restraint scars on Bernadette's wrists.

"Yes, Ma'am," Bernadette says and stands up. She seems shaky, so I wrap my arm around her waist, giving her a quick squeeze for reassurance.

We talk for a few more minutes and then say our goodbyes. Miss Olga says she will see me at the masquerade ball at the end of May.

Bernadette is a walking zombie as we make our way to the second floor. She insists on taking the stairs, and once we get to the top, I realize how *in* shape she is and how *out* of shape I am. But I try not to let it show.

For the second time since I arrived in the building, I am appalled. Her office clearly looks like an afterthought. It seriously looks like a janitor's closet with a desk jammed inside. I bite my lip and tuck away my fury for another time. For now, I decide to soak in all that is my girl. Her office is immaculate and uncluttered. The floor-to-ceiling bookshelf is jammed with books, but they are orderly and neat. Even her desk is perfectly arranged. The pencil holder and stapler are angled just so. The laptop computer is perfectly aligned with the desktop calendar. And it's obvious that she didn't just clean up for me. When she opens a drawer to pull out her keys, they are laid out in a spot specifically designed for them.

"Sweetie, I am so impressed with all of this." I gesticulate wildly.

She laughs and says, "This is my home away from home." She grabs her briefcase and tosses her laptop inside, not that she's going to have a chance to use it tonight. I have other plans for her that involve the start of our quest to christen every single room in her house. The shower got christened last night, and I still have yet to pick out the room she cums in tonight.

"Are we shopping or eating first?" she asks as we head back down the same three flights. Going down is so much easier than going up.

"Shopping. We have to build up an appetite." I hold every single door open for her on the way to my car. "I'll drive you to school tomorrow morning, okay? You can leave your car right here."

She is okay with that and holds my hand all the way to Menswear Inc. on Kirkland Boulevard. "Oh," she says. "You're taking me clothes shopping.

For some reason, I thought we were going to buy a coffee pot."

"Actually, I already know the coffee system I want you to have. I'll order it tomorrow," I say.

"Ma'am?"

Uh-oh, she went straight to submissive mode. "Yes, little bee?"

"Would it be okay if you sent me the link? You shouldn't have to pay for my stuff."

I smile at my girl. She is entirely unlike anyone I've ever been with. "If that's what you want."

She nods, a smile lighting her face, her dimples deep. Sometimes, it doesn't take much to get that smile to come out. "But you'll definitely pick it out, right?" she asks. "Because that part is beyond me."

"I will. Already have."

I pull into the nearly empty parking lot, and Bernadette says, "Oh, no. Is the store closed on Mondays?"

I wink at her. "Not for us. Robert is waiting inside."

The front door is locked, but Robert is there within seconds.

"My beautiful Rikki," he says as we exchange air kisses. "Come in. Come in." He looks immaculate in his perfectly fitted suit, his broad shoulders intimidating. His strong features give him that Dom's Dom look, which he kind of is. He is in his mid-to-late-fifties and has been in the life for a long time. I've known him for at least a decade, maybe longer.

He doesn't acknowledge Bernadette, but I didn't expect him to. Robert is from the old school, where subs and slaves are barely seen and heard. Bernadette makes a small noise at his perceived rudeness but follows us silently to the private tailoring room in the back of the store.

"Strip," he says to Bernadette.

She doesn't move and looks at me. "Just to your panties and bra, little bee. He needs to measure you for fit."

"Yes, Ma'am," she says. Good, she is in submissive mode. I hadn't thought about our visit with Robert this evening in terms of D/s, but this will be a good experience for her to see how it feels to be objectified. Robert will not abuse Bernadette, but he will also not treat her as an equal.

Robert and I chat about the happenings on the men's side of the community as he measures Bernadette's waist, hips, inseam, thighs, arms, shoulders, neck, neck to waist, and bust. He is thorough in everything he does. I can barely keep up with the players as he talks about the men's group. It is ever-changing. My only real contact with the men's side is through Seamus and Mark and the men who come into the coffee shop. The spring masquerade ball and the December holiday party bring us together twice a year, but there are always many new faces. I wonder if that is something Seamus and I need to discuss – having more mixed events together like the darts league.

"I would like for her to have masculine clothes that accentuate her female body," I say when he asks me what I want for her. He never asks her what she wants, nor do I. He nods his understanding. "Some will be for work. She's a teacher, so we can't plunge the neckline too far. But some are for her to feel sexy and for me to enjoy her, uh, assets, if you know what I mean."

"I do," he says to me. "Walk for me," he directs Bernadette, but she looks confused. He points and says, "Go to the far wall, turn and pause, and then come back. Go, go, go," he says. The irritation in his voice is quite evident.

She looks at me, and I nod. Her face is tinged pink, and she is clearly uncomfortable but is behaving admirably. She will definitely be rewarded for her excellent behavior later. We both watch her walk away, and I am mesmerized. Her walk is strong and confident. She turns, pauses, and walks back. Her head is down, her eyes watching her feet. Oh, not so confident now.

"Head up," Robert commands. "Shoulders back." She does as he asks. "She is sloppy, Rikki. Her posture is terrible. I'm surprised at you." Now it's my turn to feel embarrassed.

"It's not something we've worked on, Robert," I say to him calmly.

"Best get that done by the masquerade ball, I'd say."

Bernadette stands in front of us. Her arms folded in front of her body.

"Inspection," Robert says, and Bernadette snaps into the pose. She clasps her hands behind her head and spreads her legs apart, but not overly so. Her eyes dart at me with a pleading look. I give her a reassuring nod that all is okay, and she seems to relax a micron.

He reaches around, cups her buttocks, and then runs a hand over them as if smoothing her boi shorts. He runs his hands up the sides of her body from her knees, up her thighs, over her hips and waist. It's as if his hands are memorizing my girl's body. He turns her and does the same to her front and back, pausing at her breasts. Finally, he cups them over her bra and then lifts them.

"She needs better hardware," he says matter-of-factly. He is obviously referring to her bra. She has better bras but isn't wearing one of them today. I should have thought about that. "These boyish panties are fine." He rubs his palm over her ass again. Bernadette swallows hard, betraying her discomfort.

Robert notices. "Is she not trained to be touched, Rikki?"

"Limited," I say.

"She is clearly not a slave. A submissive, then? A modern submissive with a working mind of her own?" That last is asked in a slightly derisive tone.

"It's the modern way, Robert," I say. I am not going to get into an old-school, new-school debate with him this afternoon. Another time, perhaps, but not here and not now.

He nods, clearly disapproving. "Get dressed," he tells her and leads me over to his computer with a large display. While Bernadette dresses, facing away from us, he scrolls through the options. I pick out both dress and casual outfits, pants, shirts, suits. Robert suggests sweater vests since she is a teacher. He has an exceptionally good eye and seems to understand his clients. I also select some shorts and summer attire for her. As we look over the options, a strange feeling overcomes me. It is one of hope. I hope that my relationship with Bernadette is the real deal. I see myself taking Bernadette to Provincetown, Massachusetts, in the summer and walking the quaint sea town. I'm in a sundress, and she's in one of these short outfits I'm picking out for her. I see us in a cabin in Asheville, North Carolina, with a sweater around her shoulders as we hike a pine-filled forest. Or maybe a day trip to the art museum in Cincinnati, the zoo, or even a baseball game. She likes baseball.

I look up, and Bernadette catches my eye. I signal for her to kneel beside my chair. She does so without protest. I tousle her hair and tell her she's a good girl. She lays her head against my thigh, and I pet her head lazily.

"And this for the masquerade ball?" Robert points to an ensemble that will look positively amazing on my little bee and will complement my dress perfectly. We discuss a few more details, and he says, "I'll write all this up and include the photos so you remember. Send me back your final decisions." He clears his throat and adds, "Sometimes client's eyes are bigger than their wallets, so to speak."

His remark hits me right in the solar plexus. What the hell am I doing? I can't afford any of this. My desire to help my little bee made me forget that I do not have deep pockets or any pockets at all. She'll offer to pay, but this is my idea. I can't let her.

Calmly and cooly, I thank Robert and instruct Bernadette to thank him as well. He merely grunts at her, which is actually kind of rude. Robert is about to lock the door behind us when I see an older man leading a twenty-something man up to the shop. Robert greets the older man but not the younger one. I smile. Mondays must be kink day at the men's shop.

I pull the car onto the main road and immediately apologize to Bernadette. "I made a mistake, little bee. I should have prepared you for Robert. I can move smoothly between expectations in the vanilla world and ours, but you're new to this. You did extremely well in there, though. You looked to me for guidance, which was the right thing to do."

She is quiet, obviously trying to figure out how to respond, so I prompt her. "How did you feel about our visit with Robert?"

She lowers her head and picks at a thumbnail. I let her take as much time as she needs to collect her thoughts. "I didn't like his hands all over me, and he was a little rude, Ma'am. But I'm grateful you took care of everything. I would not have been able to do that."

"Thank you for your honesty," I say. "He wasn't trying to cop a feel by running his hands over you. That's just how he works. I've seen him do that before." I don't tell her it was Victoria. No, she doesn't need that name brought up right now. I do, however, explain some of the old-school ways of thinking to her and point out there are still many people in our community with this mindset.

"I'm glad you aren't one of those, Ma'am. I would not make a good slave. I've been told that I would not."

"You are most definitely not my slave. And I am not cut out to be a slave owner, either."

I find a parking spot in front of the Indigo Café, and we cheer our good luck. Ahh, there's her smile. I could live for that smile alone.

"And sweetie?" I say.

"Yes?"

"Even though we may throw around the words owned or owner or property – I heard you refer to me as your owner yesterday – it doesn't mean that I own you. Wearing my collar signifies that you've agreed to be in a power exchange relationship with me, but you are your own person." I reach over and run my fingers along the stretchy day collar she wears.

"Power exchange," she says, "means you take charge of things like you did with Robert?"

"Exactly, little bee. Exactly." I chuck her chin. I go around the passenger side and open her door. "Oh, hey, did I tell you that you'll be giving a demonstration at the masquerade ball?"

She falls back in her seat, slack-jawed, her face in shock.

"C'mon, little bee." I reach my hand in to help her up. "I'll tell you all about it at dinner."

Chapter 9
Settle Yourself

Following dinner at the Indigo Café and then the darts tourney, I finally have Bernadette all to myself. She is draped over my lap as I sit on the couch in her living room. Her clothes are in a pile on the floor. I rub my hands over her slightly pink ass. I lift my hand and smack her again. She clutches but doesn't cry out. Her breathing is heavy as she absorbs the pain. My girl does like pain, and we both like the intimacy of a late-evening spanking.

I smack her again, and she grunts, but after a moment, her legs widen ever-so-slightly. I'm not even sure she's conscious that she does this. It signals to me that she has become aroused and that the pain is turning to pleasure.

"This is your reward, little bee," I say and smack her three times in succession.

She grunts with each smack and then says, "Beating me is a reward?" She laughs, probably to let me know that she is teasing.

"Oh, yes," I say. "You were such a good girl back there with Robert. And later at darts, when one of Seamus's boys beat you that one round – you were so gracious. You congratulated him on his smart play. You impressed everyone, including me, with your sincere sportsmanship."

"Thank you, Ma'am," she says.

"Yes, such a good girl," I mutter as I rub her warm and pulsing ass.

"Oh, Ma'am," she says with a moan, lifting her hips off my lap.

"We're not even close to being done, little bee." I nudge her off my lap and into a standing position. "Inspection."

She strikes the pose, and I reach between her legs. As expected, she is wet. I want to fall to my knees and taste her, but I want this evening to last.

"Lay down on the couch, face up." She does so, and I place a pillow underneath her to raise her pussy off the couch. I look her right in the eye and show her my hand. She has no clue what I'm about to do. I smack her pussy lightly. She jumps but doesn't guard or protest. I smack her again and again. I get into a rhythm, and in no time, I've smacked her at least fifty times. At some point during my assault, she tilted her pelvis toward me, her eager body asking for more. Her legs had spread further apart as well, and that's how I knew she liked it.

"I won't see you tomorrow," I say. She starts to ask why but I ignore her. "Or Wednesday or Thursday. And since I won't see you, I have assignments for you. One of them will be to smack your own pussy one hundred times and then text me how that feels."

"It feels amazing. I'm so turned on, but I don't understand why I can't see you."

"Look at this place," I gesture to the boxes stacked like sentinels watching over us. "You have to unpack. You have final exams to finish writing and submit. You also have to work on your lesson plans for the new course. Am I right?"

"Yes, Ma'am."

"I'm giving you the gift of time."

"You're busy," she says glumly, not fully accepting my explanation. "You have things you need to do."

"Aww, little bee. There is nothing I'd like more in the whole world than to be with you every night," I say. She is more insightful than I realized. I hate not being completely honest with her, especially because I insist on it as a foundation for any relationship, but some things are best kept under wraps. She'd probably leave me if she knew I was broke and close to losing everything.

"Hey, where'd you go?" she asks.

I narrow my eyes and lie. "Get up, and I'll show you." I point to a spot on the wall and instruct her to stand facing it with her palms flat. "Walk your feet back a little. Yes, that's it."

"Are you going to frisk me?" She looks back at me over her shoulder.

"Nope." I show her the medium butt plug and then apply lube to it. She reaches back and spreads her cheeks as I've trained her. I douse a little lube between her spread cheeks. She moans in both pleasure and frustration as I torture her with the plug – inserting the head and then taking it out. Inserting its full width but then sliding it almost out. Ultimately, I thrust it inside with a twist. Her relieved sigh makes me chuckle.

Next, I show her the belt I have in my hand. She takes a deep breath and lets it out slowly and carefully. I allow her this preparation time, mainly because she hasn't yet met this particular implement of impact. I flick my wrist, and the belt smacks her back. She yelps in surprise, but I can tell she's ready for more. I keep the same level of intensity for a few more hits, and when I see her relax into it, I pick up the speed and intensity. I keep going for about fifty lashes and then pause. Her back is nice and red now, matching the color of her beautiful ass.

"Stand up fully." She does, and I hand her the belt.

It is about an inch wide and sixteen inches long. The end is shaped into a v-point. The other end has been carefully wrapped in red duct tape. "Is this homemade?" she asks.

"Yes. Madison made it and gave it to me for Christmas. She told me that I could use it on my next sub. She said I should show my next sub how to use it, too."

"Me?" Bernadette says, thoroughly confused. "I'm not a sadist, Ma'am. I don't want to hit you with this. Or with anything."

I laugh. "Well, that's good because I don't want you to hit me, either. You're going to hit yourself."

I laugh at her surprised expression and then mimic what I want her to do. She grips the red taped handle with her right hand and flicks the belt over her shoulder, making a direct hit with her reddened back. Her eyes pop open wide. "Oh, that's nice." She hits herself again. "I never knew doing this to myself could feel so good."

"And you will when I command you to over the next three days."

She hits herself again.

"Try bending over and hitting your buttocks." She misfires the first few times, and we laugh at her ineptness. She tries again and then seems to get the hang of it.

I take the belt from her and put it on the coffee table. I ask her to stay in the bent-over position. I smack one of her breasts with my hand several times and delight when they swing back and forth. I reach over her body, and even though the angle isn't great, smack the other breast. I pop it five times, making sure I get her nipple as often as I can. That move kind of hurt my hand, but she is writhing in pleasure, so it was well worth it.

"This, too?" she asks breathlessly. "Do it to myself, I mean?"

"Yes," I say. "Try it."

She hits herself a couple of times and looks up at me for approval.

"That's it, sweetie," I say and sit on the couch. "Come here. Kneel."

She kneels in front of me, and I love the way she looks up at me with so much trust in her eyes.

"You'll need this pain to settle yourself while you're all alone in this big house."

"Mmm," she says as if she hadn't thought about being alone.

"There will be rules while we're apart. No touching yourself unless I've given you permission."

"Check," she says.

"And if I allow you to touch yourself, which I may not, you can edge but not orgasm. I will be terribly upset with my little bee if she cums when I'm not here."

She looks up at me with such adoration that I gush arousal. Oh, yes, those lovely pouty lips of hers will be pleasing me soon. I just have to pick which room. Probably this one since it's the closest.

"Ma'am," she says shyly, "I am afraid to cum without you present. *You* are the giver of my pleasure. You've told me that many times. It would be shameful if I disobeyed you."

She is genuinely upset at the thought of displeasing me. Wow. Many subs say words to this effect, but they never mean them, not really. They're just words in a script for the role they're playing. Bernadette believes her words, I can tell.

My breathing deepens. Oh, yes. It's time. "Undress me," I say simply. She takes off my shoes, then my dress socks. She stands and looks me in the eye as she unbuttons my blouse. It is the sexiest thing in the world to have a woman do that. It's even sexier when my Bernadette does it. Her gaze is intense, but she breaks it when she pulls my shirt off. My pants are next, followed by my underclothes. I snap the leash on her collar and let it dangle from her neck while I throw the portable mat on the living room floor.

I lay on my back and open my legs. "You know what to do." I tug on her leash. She gets on her knees and works slowly at first. I like my subs to look me in the eye now and then as they're going down on me. Her intense gaze finds mine, and I involuntarily raise my pelvis toward her. I tug her toward her goal.

"Faster, sub," I say to objectify her. Although she liked the degradation from Jaleesa, she did not like the objectification from Robert. Maybe because he is male. "Yes, this sub is a talented little pussy licker," I say to the room.

She moans her approval at my words, and it isn't long before she makes me cum, bucking and writhing on the mat. She licks me clean until I tell her to kneel. "Good girl," I say, a little breathless. She sits up taller. She is proud that she pleased me.

I stand up and then command her to lay face down on the mat with her legs spread and ass tilted up, ready to receive. "On my knees, Ma'am?" she asks, and I like that she seeks clarification. Communication is vital in any relationship, but even more so in BDSM relationships.

"No," I say. "All of you on the mat. Ass tilted up. Yes, that's it. Just lay there for a little while. I want you ready to receive me when I get back." I leave the room, pretending to need water from the kitchen. Well, actually, water is a good idea, so I grab two from the relatively empty refrigerator. I am purposely making Bernadette wait in that position. I want her body to feel that familiar ache of arousal for a while. In the meanwhile, I put on my strap-on. This one doesn't hit my clit at all, it's not designed to, but that's okay because she just satisfied me, oh so nicely already.

I love the fact that there's a door in the kitchen leading out to the back patio. She doesn't have a grill yet, but I can envision summer get-togethers here where our friends can be themselves and not worry about prying eyes from the neighbors. And the large country kitchen is a dream. There aren't as many boxes in here, thanks to Shasti. A vision of Thanksgiving dinner comes to mind. Bernadette and I are sitting at the massive table with Shasti and Madison, Marta and Shanice, and Jaleesa and Tina. Who knows? Maybe more. It would be perfect. I don't know what it is about Bernadette's big ole farmhouse, but it seems to calm me in ways I haven't been calm in years.

Once five minutes are up, I quietly sneak up on her. "How are you feeling?"

She jumps when I speak. "On display," she says. "For anyone to see and use."

"Oh?"

"It feels sexy, Ma'am."

"Ahh, I hoped it would. I may ask you to go to sleep this way at some point during our three-day hiatus."

"Ma'am," Bernadette says and reaches back to spread her cheeks, "will you fuck me now? Please? I, I need some relief. Please, Ma'am?"

Her need is intoxicating. I command her to her knees and enter her vagina slowly with my strap-on. The butt plug is filling her up, and I will remove it soon to fuck her there, but for now, it's all about the full feeling.

I grip her hips for leverage and get into a lovely rhythm. Yes, it is lovely, indeed. Her soft moans fill the space wonderfully. I rub her back and say, "You like this."

"Oh, yes, Ma'am," she says, almost purring. She is not passive while I'm fucking her. She pushes back against me, wanting more. Her head lolls as she succumbs to her passion.

"Down on your elbows."

I slow my thrusts and then pull out. She groans, but it is a temporary groan, if there is such a thing. She knows what's next. I reach for the bottle of lube and lace some around the butt plug. I twist and pull it out gently. She lies still until it's out, and then her pelvis arches and she blows out a sigh. My girl loves all things anal. Yes, she does.

"Take this like a good girl now," I say and press my lubed-up cock at the entrance to her tiny hole, as she calls it. I push, and her ass accepts me peacefully. I slide all the way in and wait for her to finish her gasping breath. I pull out and take another slow ride into her body. Fucking her this way arouses my power centers, and the fact that she loves anal makes it even better.

She thrusts back against me again, and her breathing changes. She is getting close but won't orgasm unless we count down or I touch her. I reach underneath and find her wonderfully wet center. Her clit is large and distended. She jumps when I touch her. She might be too sensitive right now. I distract her by running my fingers through her labia and then entering her vagina. My fingers can't get very deep at this angle, but that's okay because she is becoming lost in sensation. I can tell by her head tilt. She trusts me absolutely. The most sadistic thing I could do right now is pull out and deny her the orgasm, but I'm not feeling that. My little bee needs her reward for dealing so well with Robert this afternoon.

When I sense she's ready, I go back to her clit.

"Yes," she murmurs from outer space.

I circle her nub slowly and in time with my thrusting. Her moans match my rhythm. I increase the pace, and her upper body falls as if she doesn't have the strength to hold herself up anymore.

I could have her touch herself, but I want her to associate these good feels with me, with my fingers, with my occupation of her body. She has been the sole proprietor of her own pleasure for far too long. I am the giver of pleasure for her now.

I puff up like a peacock and say, "Cum for me, my good girl. My sweet, obedient sub. Cum hard for me."

I'm glad the neighbors are so far away because she screeches her orgasm with a string of expletives, but as long as my name is in there, I am okay with it.

"Fuck, Rikki," she says as I pull out. Her pelvis is still rocking even though I'm not touching her anymore. "I love you."

"I love you, too, little bee." I lay on the mat and pull her onto her back. I kiss her passionately and then pull her head onto my chest.

She rests for a few minutes, but her night is not done. Oh, no. That bed upstairs is the same bed she used to fuck her ex in. It is time to begin erasing those memories. Eventually, that bed will be replaced—once I can afford it.

She doesn't know it yet, but she is going to learn how to rim me properly. First, she'll clean me thoroughly in the master bathroom, and then I'll get on the bed on all fours. I'll probably lower myself to my elbows so she has a better angle. I'll tell her to kiss and lick my inner thighs. Before introducing her to my perineum, I'll have her apply the tiniest bit of lube to a dental dam to hold it in place. I want this to be a pleasurable experience for both of us, so I don't want her ick-factor taking over. Dental dam in place, she'll focus her attention on my perineum, the oft-overlooked spot between my rosebud and my vagina. Once I'm primed, I'll instruct her to lick my rosebud like she's licking an ice cream cone, licking up and down and then side to side. I'll suggest she

84

alternate between a flat, relaxed tongue and a stiff one. I'll let her decide. I want to enjoy the sensations, not critique her every move. And then, if she doesn't go for it first, I'll suggest she stiffen her tongue, making it into a tiny phallus and penetrate me gently. She'll be okay because the dental dam will make it alright.

I turn Bernadette to her other side, and she mumbles her disapproval until I spoon her. I undulate my hips against her backside as I think about how I'm going to touch my clit and make myself cum while her tongue is in my ass. "Time to go upstairs and please me again, Bernadette."

"Mmm?" She clears the sleepiness out of her throat and sits up. "Oh, yes. Yes, Ma'am."

"It's time for the teacher to become the student," I say cryptically and follow her nude body up the stairs.

~~~

When I step into the shop at 9 a.m., Tuesday morning, Lydia reports that they handled the morning rush just fine without me. There was only one minor crisis involving a late employee, and I am relieved to hear that it wasn't Kari. I refuse to feel guilty about being at Bernadette's this morning when I really should have been here. Still, Bernadette has pointed out on more than one occasion that I pay my assistant managers a good salary, and it's okay if they earn it. She is wise, my little bee.

Satisfied that the shop is running smoothly, I greet Marta, who snaps me out of her kitchen and then head to my dreaded office. I plop down in my chair, trying not to reminisce about the mind-blowing full-body orgasm Bernadette gave me on her bed. As I washed her body in the shower afterward, she declared that she wants to "do rimming" on me again. I have never had a lover so invested and eager to please me. Hmm, lover. I just thought of her as my lover, not my sub. That's interesting.

No, no. I have to stop this thought train. I have work to do here—phone calls to make. Comparing Bernadette to my past subs is counterproductive. I get up and retrieve a bottled water from my mini-fridge and make the easier phone call first.

Oh, good, it goes right to voice mail. "Hey, Mistress Dominique, it's

Mistress Rikki. I'll be there by 6:30 this evening to set up." I don't know what else to say but add, "You asked how I wanted payment, and I guess I'll just take your check as usual. All right, call if you need anything. Oh, I'll bring my own whips, but I assume it's okay if I use your other implements of impact. If not, let me know. Okay, see you tonight."

I click the button to end my message and let out a long, slow sigh. I genuinely don't want to work at her dungeon again, but it pays well, and I need the money. I should use it to fix the air conditioner or the espresso machine, but I'm going to outfit my girl instead.

A sharp knock sounds on my door. That can only be one person. Am I ready for this confrontation? I stand up and smile. Yes, I'm always ready.

"Hello, Victoria," I say, gesturing for her to come in. In true Victoria form, she sits in my office chair, forcing me to sit on the physically lower couch. As usual, she is immaculately dressed, wearing flattering black dress pants, severe pointed-toe leather boots, and her signature form-fitting button-down shirt. "What brings you here?" I ask.

She is holding a cup of coffee in her hands, obviously just purchased. "It's not a crime to buy coffee, is it?"

"Of course not," I say. Typically, I'd offer to reimburse her, but I'm not in the mood. I'm also used to leading conversations, but I'm not in the mood for that, either.

"Robert called me," she says simply and takes a sip of coffee.

"Oh?" I'm not giving her anything, mainly because I don't know what she's after.

"That could have been me, you know," she says and looks down at her cup.

This move surprises the shit out of me. Strong, emotionless Victoria is showing vulnerability. How unlike her.

"It could have been you doing what?" I ask. "Outfitting Bernadette with tailored menswear?"

"Yeah." She looks up at me, attempting a look of defiance but not pulling it off.

I look at her in disbelief. "Vic, you were outfitting her in skirts and femme blouses."

She looks down again. "Yeah, I know. I don't, uh, begrudge you, you know."

"For what?"

"Stealing Bernadette from me," she says and looks up, flicking a lock of hair off her forehead.

This false statement could have sent me into a tailspin, but I don't let it. "We'll go ahead and disagree on your choice of words."

She plunks the cup on my desk and then leans forward, her elbows resting on her thighs, her hands between her knees, fingers touching. "She fits you, Rikki."

"I know."

"After my first night with her, I could tell that it wasn't going to last long," she says. "She wanted more from me than I could ever give. Don't get me wrong, she liked the sex. Fuck, so did I, but that's all it was. And if she has one fault, it's that she might be too submissive for my tastes. I like them with a little more fighting spirit."

She looks up at me, and I simply nod that I heard her, but I don't say a word. She came here for more than this confession.

"And, I promise," she says, sitting up quickly, "I had no idea that shit was in those supplements I gave her. The dude I got them from said it would help with lactation, but, fuck, I'm usually more careful." She looks me right in the eyes and pleads, "C'mon, you know I'm a stickler for safe sex, and I'm a big giver of aftercare."

"You are," I agree. "Aunt Tilda beat that into both of our thick skulls, didn't she? But you also didn't tell Bernadette that you were trying to get her to lactate. That's a serious personal decision. It's her body, and she has a right to decide what happens to it. And who knows, Vic? She may have said that she'd try it. You didn't give her that chance."

"I know. I need to apologize to her. I'm so stupid," Victoria spats. "I could have hurt her. She's a good person. I'm glad you were the one that got her, Rik."

I nod. "I can arrange a time for the two of you to talk if that's what you want."

She nods. "Thanks, but I need another favor. I, uh, met someone. Someone who I think might matter."

"Seriously?" I say. "I'm genuinely happy for you, Vic."

"Thanks. I haven't acted on it yet because, well, you know, the ban and all. I mean, I don't think I have ever in my life spent time getting to know a sub like this before. Just talking and sharing stories? It's like, wow."

I take a deep breath. I want to tell her that's precisely what I had been doing with Bernadette before she swooped in and stole her out from under me. But I don't.

"Listen," she says, "I don't resent the three-month ban from community activities. I really don't. It gave me time to figure out where my priorities are and to get some of my shit together."

"Getting shit together is always a good thing," I say, and we both chuckle. Ahh, there's my friend.

"Rowena is so pissed by what I did. She told me she defended me but maybe shouldn't have. She gave me a hot earful after the board meeting the other day. Holy crap. That woman can curse."

I smile at the truth in her last statement but wonder why she's here. Why is she extending this olive branch? "What did you want to ask me?"

"My banning is finished next week. Well before the masquerade ball."

"By design," I interject.

"Cool. If all goes well, I will have a new sub, and I want to bring her. But I don't want everybody looking at her or me like we're a couple of pariahs."

"Who's your potential new sub?" I ask, cringing inside because I think I know the answer.

"Alyssa, Rowena's temporary sub."

I nod. Suspicion confirmed. "Can you handle her, Vic?"

"So far, so good. We've had supervised visits, so nothing has happened yet. Rowena wants it known that I am abiding by the board's decision by not participating in BDSM activities. So, I'm just hanging out at Rowena's. A lot. I, uh, heard about the edible gummies incident."

"That was scary stuff, Vic. Madison tripped out and not in a good way. And Jaleesa's sub Dana, too, although mildly."

"Rowena disciplined Alyssa for that, and I honestly believe she learned her lesson. I read the apology notes she sent to Shasti and Madison. And the other ones she sent to Jaleesa and Dana. The notes were articulate and seemed remorseful."

"Just be careful, my friend."

She looks down at her shoes, and when she looks up, there is a sheen of tears in her eyes. "After what I did, you can still call me 'friend?'"

"Of course, Vic. We've been through a lot of shit together, haven't we?"

"Yeah," she laughs and wipes the tears from her eyes.

"How's Aunt Tilda's torture equipment?" I ask her.

"Holding up great. I'm glad I could buy that stuff from you after the idiot did what she did."

"She who shall not be named," I say with a laugh and then stand up. She stands as well. "I will do what I can to spread messages of forgiveness toward you and your potential new sub."

"Thanks, Rik. I appreciate it."

"Trust will have to be earned all over again, Vic."

"I know. And I'm sorry."

"For what?"

"I had no clue that you liked Bernadette. Otherwise, the code of Dommes would have been in effect, and I would have stayed away." She rolls her eyes. "Shasti gave me an earful about that after I took Bernadette home that first night. I should have apologized to you then, but things were already in motion."

"I understand. I acted slowly."

I open the office door, and suddenly, all the employees, including Marta, scurry around looking ultra-busy.

"She suits you," Victoria says. "She's good for you."

"Thanks. I think so, too."

Victoria heads out the main door of the shop, and Marta is in my office instantly.

"What was that all about?" Marta asks, wide-eyed.

"It's all good," I say, giving her the briefest overview, ending with my decision to grant Victoria and her new potential sub forgiveness and the benefit of the doubt. Marta will probably call Shasti within minutes, and soon enough, Jaleesa and her subs will know. But that is by design.

And for Victoria's sake, this had better not turn around and bite me in the ass.

Chapter 10
The Picnic

Thankfully, there are no cars in this remote section of the park as we pull up in the Subaru. I want some badly needed alone time with my girl. I park and then load up Bernadette with our picnic basket of food and the blanket while I grab the cooler of beverages and my frisbee. I haven't played frisbee in ages, but it is a fun way to get exercise. And this gorgeous, unseasonably warm Saturday afternoon is perfect for a picnic and some activity with my girl. My three exceptionally long nights at Mistress Dominique's dungeon showed me how out of shape I have become, partly because of the winter and partly because I'm in love with that beautiful and smart woman carrying my lunch and have gotten lazy.

"This was such a great idea, Rikki," Bernadette says as we head down the barely discernible trail through the woods.

"I missed you," I say. "I thought we needed some time away from our responsibilities."

"I love picnics." She takes a big breath in, enjoying the cool air. Her gaze darts toward a tall pine. She points and says, "Cardinal."

"Oh, cool." The red cardinal looks like a Christmas ornament on the pine tree.

"I've always liked birds," she says as she picks her way down the leafy path. "I should do more bird watching. My mom always ..." She stops talking mid-sentence, obviously choked up over a sudden memory.

My hands are full. Otherwise, I would hug her. "I know, sweetie," I say. "Sometimes things remind me of my mom, too."

"Yeah," is all she says. She needs a moment, so I leave her be.

We walk on for another five minutes or so until we finally come to the stream. It is so inviting, but April is the wrong month for swimming in Ohio.

Bernadette inhales sharply. "Rikki, this is gorgeous. How did you find this place?"

"Victoria."

"Oh," she says succinctly. It's as if she can't imagine associating Victoria with a place as beautiful as this.

"She came to see me this week," I say.

"Hmm," she says without commitment. She faces away from me and flings out the blanket. It lands perfectly and is ready to receive our baskets and bodies. The rushing water of the stream is a soothing backdrop in this small clearing. I'm so glad I decided to share this space with her after our three days apart. I missed her more than I realized I would.

"Victoria wants to talk to you. She wants to apologize."

"She told you that?" She doesn't look at me. I know this is an extremely uncomfortable topic for her.

"Look up," I say softly. I could have gotten stern with her, but she is vulnerable right now.

She looks up and kneels with her hands face down on her thighs. I wonder if she knows how turned on it makes me to see her like this, wearing my collar, even if it is a day collar meant to placate the vanillas.

"Do you agree that people can make mistakes?" I ask her gently.

"Yes, Ma'am. I've made a lot in my life."

"We all have. And you'd agree that learning from mistakes is part of life, too, right?"

She nods. I usually like her to speak her responses, but this is a serious topic, so I don't interrupt with a protocol reprimand.

"Victoria is banned from the community for three months. Did you know that?"

She looks startled by this news. "No. No one talks to me about Victoria. Everyone knows what she did to me, is that it?"

"Yes."

"I'm so embarrassed." She hides her head in her hands.

"For what? You were the victim."

"For being so stupid that I didn't know she was trying to make me lactate without my permission."

"You're not stupid," I say. "And you are never allowed to say that again about my property. It's insulting to me."

"I'm sorry, Ma'am," she says.

"I will set up a date and time. I can be there with you if you wish."

She nods once, but this time, I demand words. "Yes, Ma'am," she says. "Thank you for setting it up." She says the words, but I can tell she is not happy about it.

"All right," I say. "Let's eat."

Bernadette visibly cheers up and unpacks the subs I got from the Queen City Sub Shop this morning. She has come to love Queen City subs as much as I do. She gleefully spreads out a paper towel for each of us as a placemat and then divvies up the subs, potato chips, and brownies. Her eyes light up at the brownies, as I knew they would. She knows to wait for permission to eat it, though. My heart is full as she takes care of us. I told Shasti once that Bernadette is not a passive partner. I was referring to the bedroom, but it's true in all aspects of life, as evidenced by the way she is taking care of me right now.

We eat, sitting side by side, watching the stream, and looking for birds. She unquestionably knows a lot about birds, and I find myself looking for them, too. She gets frustrated when she can't identify a few and takes mental notes about their wings, beaks, and size. Maybe I should get her a bird book or an app for her phone or something. Jaleesa and her submissives do a lot of hiking. Maybe they're into birds. It's not a question I ever thought to ask.

"How did your assignments go while you were on your own?" I ask.

"So good. I felt close to you."

"Perfect."

"The pain ones, in particular, were, mmm, divine. I liked the belt. A lot. Can I keep it?"

"Yes, of course. Make sure you thank Madison."

"Awkward much?" Bernadette says with a laugh. "I will, though." She pauses for a moment and adds, "I liked that you made me kneel before going to bed."

"Kneeling calms you."

"Yes, Ma'am. It's like meditation."

"Good. That's exactly what I wanted for you."

"I missed you so much, Rikki." She looks down as if embarrassed.

"I missed you too, little bee. But sometimes, life gets in the way, and we have to be apart. Just for a short while, you know?"

She nods but looks sad, so I say, "Are you still wanting to have Cinco de Mayo at your house?"

She brightens up. "Yes, kind of a small housewarming dinner with Shasti and Madison. Too bad Brittany's in England. I wanted to have that whole initial gang together."

"We can Skype with her," I say. "We'll have to check the time difference."

"And make sure her Domme isn't, err, sewing things shut." She laughs, and it is the most amazing sound. It comes straight from the depths of her belly and fills the trees. It fills my heart, too.

"I will help you cook," I say, not sure if I'll be any help at all.

"Deal," she says. "I just have to figure out how to make enchiladas and tacos and margaritas."

"Virgin for the kid."

"Absolutely," she says. "Shasti would not like an impaired *little* after that whole gummy-gate thing."

"Exactly," I say. I pick up the frisbee and suggest we play. Although it's warmer than usual this time of year, it's still April, and I need to get some blood flowing. I guess she likes the idea because she leaps to her feet and then helps me up.

It takes me a minute to get the wrist snap again, mainly because my muscles have been overworked from snapping whips and floggers and paddles and canes at willing submissives over the past few days. Most of Dominique's clients are male, but a woman in her mid-twenties sheepishly came in on my second evening there. She said she'd never done anything like this before but wanted to try a spanking. I typically drape Dominique's clients over a spanking bench for this, but not this time. I made the nervous woman lay over my lap on the couch and ran my hands over her ass and back to soothe her. Nudity is not permitted at Dominique's, but I used a commanding voice and had her strip down to her panties and sports bra to help her feel more vulnerable. She seemed to relax a bit once she lay face down in my lap, and I started slowly. She jumped at the first few smacks, but we soon got into a rhythm. It wasn't a hard spanking, not by any means, and my voice held only light Dominance, but she landed in a quasi-subspace, nonetheless. I held her in my arms for a long time while she floated. She seemed to need the aftercare. When she came down, she cried embarrassed tears and hid her face. I told her she was beautiful and that she obviously needed this release. I don't usually, but I invited her to the coffee shop for the Monday night darts tourney to be among other BDSMers. I hinted that I already had a submissive and was monogamous so that she wouldn't get her hopes up about me. We'll see if she's brave enough to show. Her one-hundred-dollar tip surprised me but made me understand how healing BDSM can be.

Thoughts of my three-night stint as Mistress Rikki fall away from my mind as I watch my girl run and jump. She is such an athlete. She leaps for my errant throws and catches them. She runs them down like a wide receiver. She was a college athlete, after all. She's good at everything she does. I rub my sore shoulder, my whipping shoulder, when she's not looking. I'll have to get some ice on it later. I think it is inflamed. I can't tell Bernadette why my shoulder is sore, so I just try to ignore it.

"Rikki," she says, running back over to me with the frisbee she just caught. "I'm getting tired." Oh, she is lying. I don't know how I know, but I can tell. "Can we maybe have dessert now?"

"Is your name Madison?" I tease her.

She smiles and pulls me toward the blanket by my good arm. Once we sit, she doesn't reach for the brownies. Instead, she sits behind me and asks if she can rub my neck and shoulders. I love that she asks before diving in. She wants to serve, but she also wants my permission. She is perfect.

I give her the go-ahead, and her hands feel wonderful on my neck, smoothing down my tight and tense muscles. She kisses the back of my neck and then helps me shrug off my sweatshirt. She kisses my sore shoulder and gently massages it. She checks in now and then, asking if her touch is okay. I murmur my approval, and she continues for a while on the one side before moving to the other.

"Rikki?" she says as her hands slow.

"Mmm? Yes, love?"

"I think you should be kissing me right now."

Great idea. I spin around on my ass, put both hands on her shoulders, and push her to the blanket. I lay my full length on her, my thigh insinuating nicely between her jeans-covered legs. I look her in the eye, and she moans at my dominant expression, which conveys that she is about to be devoured. I dip my head down and kiss her gently, a feather-light touch on her lips. I smirk at her. *Yes, I am teasing you, Bernadette.*

She is having none of it and pulls me down into a crushing kiss. My passion matches hers as we explore each other's mouths as if for the first time. She pulls me tighter to her, if that's even possible. She likes my body weight on her. She's missed that. It isn't long before she sucks my offered tongue. I fuck her mouth while she squirms underneath me. She opens her legs and arches up against my thigh. She bucks her pelvis rhythmically against me. I move down a bit, kiss her throat, and strategically press my hip bone against her clit.

"Rikki," she screeches as I hit pay dirt. "Yes, yes, yes."

I rock against her, kissing her neck, finding all the sensitive spots, and delight at the low moans I elicit from her. She is so expressive when she's turned on. I kiss her collarbone and trace her lips with my fingers. I push my index finger into her mouth, and she sucks it like she's starving. I push two fingers in and press down on her tongue, opening her jaw a little. I don't want her to suck them. I just want her to feel my passive possession of her. She seems to understand and relaxes. I stop kissing her and whisper in her ear, "You are mine."

"Ohhhh," she moans as if I've just entered her with a dildo. I love that my words have that effect on her.

It empowers me to take control, especially someone's pleasure. I gauge Bernadette's moans and facial expressions, the arching of her pelvis, her body movements. These are signs that I read and interpret. I pull my fingers out of her mouth and sear her with another kiss.

I put my hands on either side of her body and do a pushup. I move off to the side. She groans at my sudden departure. I look her in the eyes. They are full blown with arousal. Yes, I believe I've read the signs correctly.

"Ten," I say. She sighs in frustration. "Nine."

"Rikki," she whines breathlessly.

"Eight."

"Not here. Ohhh," she moans.

"Seven." Her pelvis lifts.

"Six." Her eyes roll back. "Five. Look at me," I command. "Four." Her eyes open one at a time. "Three." Her breathing is heavy. "Two."

"Oh, Rikki," her voice is high and tight.

"One!" I say. "Cum for me, my good girl. Cum now."

Her entire body shakes as the orgasm hits with full force. "Rikki," she screeches. She reaches for me, but I stay just out of reach. Sadistic, I know.

"That's my girl," I encourage. "You're mine. No one can have you. You are my property."

"Property," she echoes. Her back arches, and she screeches as another wave hits her. Oh, how I wish I had a strap-on. As soon as I entered her, I would cum instantly, I think.

When her aftershocks finally slow, and she catches her breath, I let her pull me into a passionate embrace. She kisses my face and lips and falls back exhausted.

"When you do that—" she pauses to take a big breath. "When you do that, it is the ultimate control. Knowing you can countdown and make me cum. I don't have anything to do with it. My body simply opens up or something, and the spark of orgasm starts. It starts way deep inside in a place I've never been. Every number moves it forward until it just blossoms out of me."

Bernadette is not the first woman I've done this with, but I've never had anyone explain it so perfectly.

"It's like you're actually touching me," she continues, "but you're not. I seriously don't understand, but it makes me feel kind of vulnerable that you could start a countdown, and I'd have no choice but to cum. It's like I have no control over my body. You do. Like my body belongs to you. It's your plaything."

I look at her, and sweet, devious plans form in my head. She sits up and then gets on her knees in front of me. She lowers herself and kisses my hands.

I stroke her face and make her look into my eyes, "You're a good, good girl, my Bernadette. I love you."

"I love you, too," she says and then adds, "Mistress."

I cock my head at her and narrow my eyes at the word. She is making a request. It is a request that will need some thought. She may not truly understand that she is asking to be my slave. I'm not sure that's what I want.

I clear my throat and say, "Let's pack up. I want to get you home and fuck you properly."

Bernadette leaps to her feet, and my usually meticulous and orderly submissive throws our food and wrappers in the food basket and the drinks in the cooler and then tugs at the blanket, requesting that I step off so she can fold it.

I laugh at her fervor, but she is already heading back down the path carrying everything except the frisbee.

Chapter 11
Drop That!

Sunday should be a day to sleep in, but I wake up in Bernadette's bed aroused almost to the point of orgasm. I leap out of bed and throw on the strap-on she is required to keep ready for me. I am overwhelmed by my urge to possess her right now. I rip the covers off of her, and she protests the sudden cold. I yank her legs apart and mount her. She blinks her eyes open in confused sleepiness. I thrust my lubed dildo inside her. She groans in protest yet automatically arches her pelvis to give me better access. I grip her hips harshly and practically pull her body onto my thrusting dildo. I pound her hard and fast. I am relentless.

My orgasm builds. This endearing woman I'm dominating is the reason. She moans as I thrust. The slapping of my flesh against hers fills the room. She wraps her legs around me and begins to buck her hips in rhythm.

"Yes," I hiss. "My little fucktoy loves when I possess her."

"Yesssss," she hisses back.

She's close, so am I. I cum first and moan my release but keep thrusting. I grab her ankles and lift her legs in the air, spread in a V shape. She moans at this move.

"Cum, my love," I say softly.

Wait. No. Sunday mornings usually warrant softness, but not today. Not for me. I ramp it up. "Cum for me, my fucking slut. You live for me to use you, to make you squeal."

"Yes, yes, yes." She arches her pelvis toward the ceiling. "Fuck, Rikki." She cums with such force that I can't thrust smoothly. Her pussy grips my phallus tightly. I push through and continue to fuck her until her cries die down. She is breathless when I pull out of her. I throw her legs down on the bed and then fall onto my back.

"Take this off me," I command. I know she has not yet recovered, yet I command her anyway.

"Yes, Ma'am." She reaches over and undoes the straps.

"Clean it up." I gesture toward the bathroom.

"Yes, Ma'am."

When she comes back out with the clean dildo, I tell her to go back in and freshen herself up. She knows that this includes shaving and also cleaning her tiny hole. Who knows? I may decide to use that hole this morning.

"Inspection," I say when she comes out of the bathroom. I lay in the bed, inspecting her from afar. Usually, I would compliment her on something like her perky breasts or erect nipples. Instead, I want her to feel what it is like to be a slave. "Stand up straight. Robert was right. You are a sloppy slut." Okay, Robert didn't call her a slut, but I'm using a little artistic license here. She straightens up, lifting her head higher. "Make sure I don't see your sloppiness again, slave." I see her sharp intake of breath. Ahh, now she understands what's happening. I am not a slave owner and don't want to be, but an occasional foray into something different keeps things interesting.

"Go make my coffee. And then cook me a four-egg omelet. Ham and pepper jack cheese. A large fruit cup on the side."

"Yes, Ma'am." She hesitates for a moment but then turns to leave.

"Get back here," I roar and leap out of bed. I grab her by the hair and pull her back into the bedroom. "How do you leave a room respectfully?"

She whimpers at my sudden aggressiveness.

"I apologize, Mistress."

"No excuses." I let go and stand back. "Show me respect, slave, or you'll be chained up naked tonight for the Dommes to use."

She makes a fearful sound in the back of her throat.

"Don't think I won't," I threaten. "Now, show me."

She takes three steps back before turning around.

"Such outright disrespect will no longer be tolerated," I call after her. I get no response, but don't expect one.

I do my morning routine and get dressed to open the coffee shop. It is currently 4:45 a.m., and I should be there in plenty of time to help Lydia open. I must make sure to swap her and Mark tomorrow so that she will be there during the darts league tournament. I am going to charge Lydia with taking care of the young newb from Mistress Dominique's dungeon if the woman shows, that is. Lydia is a switch who has been in submissive mode for far too long, and if I am reading things correctly, her Domme instincts should kick in once she meets her. And who knows? I won't force it, but Aunt Tilda always said that nudging people toward each other never hurt anybody. And now that I think of it, that's precisely what that sly young Madison did to Bernadette and me last December. She is a *little*, but she is not a child. Why did I not see it before? Oh, wow. Shasti most definitely has her hands full with that one.

I smell the coffee, and its aroma beckons me downstairs like a cartoon finger. Bernadette has my coffee ready and turns down the stove on my omelet she has just started cooking. She has yet to put my fruit cup together. I am pleased that she didn't put on an apron because she would have gotten reprimanded for that.

"Ma'am?" she says and gestures to the coffee.

I nod and sit down at the kitchen table, my phone in hand, reading my text messages, pretending to ignore her. She stands before me, patiently holding the cup. I look up after a bit. "Kiss the side of the cup and present it to me." Her eyes are down as she does so. I take it from her and then dismiss her to get my food. She takes three steps back and then turns.

Bernadette places the omelet in front of me with the cup of fruit on the side. Silverware and a napkin are laid out for me. Instead of thanking her, I tell her to get the silicon spaghetti server. She looks perplexed but does as I ask. "Bend over the table. Ass lifted high." I smack the server in my hand. "This is for your blatant disrespect upstairs." She knows not to respond, and I smack her ass hard with the flat side of the server. It's not as bad as a cold caning, but she is not warmed up, and I know it stings like crazy. I redden up her ass and the backs of her legs. She is stoic at first but eventually cries out with each whack. I turn the server over and, with less strength, hit her with the rounded prongs.

What turns me on is her obvious acquiescence to the pain I am giving her. I puff up at her acceptance of my desire to hurt her body. Despite her obvious discomfort, her legs spread slightly. I whack her five times in succession on the sensitive lower part of her ass toward her inner thighs and then switch to the other side.

I reach into my pocket and pull out a condom. I roll it over the server's handle and apply lube to it and her tiny hole. My finger enters her hole first to widen her canal, getting her ready to receive. She tenses up. She knows what's about to happen. I should reprimand her, but having a serving utensil shoved in your ass for your Mistress's enjoyment is torture enough.

I tease her opening and then gently slide the server handle inside. I fuck her ass with it and then leave it embedded so I have a pleasing appendage to look at while I eat. I wash my hands and then sit down to enjoy my coffee and delicious breakfast. Bernadette is truly becoming a good cook. Normally, I would thank her and tell her how good the food is. Not today. Slaves don't get thanked; they get used. Maybe I'll have her take cooking lessons from someone. Jaleesa's Tina feeds their whole crew, so maybe Jaleesa can loan her to me for a few days to teach Bernadette. We could have some fun together during that time, too. I'll feel Jaleesa out this evening.

I eat half of my food and place the plate with the remaining food on the floor. I take the silverware to the sink and drop it in with a clatter. I make a to-go mug of coffee, taking my time to make sure the sugar to creamer ratio is perfect. I lean back against the counter, observing Bernadette so obviously subjugated. She looks lovely with her reddened ass and legs. Her spaghetti server tail is a perfect reminder that I am in charge of her body and what happens to it. This is making me wet, and I clench my pussy. I accidentally moan, and I know she hears it. Good. That lets her know that I like seeing her enslaved this way.

I push off the counter and walk over to her. I lift her chin and snap on her leash. I kiss her slowly and passionately. She receives my kisses well and moans her arousal. Too bad I need to get to the shop to open. I need a little tension relief – the kind only a slave's tongue can give. She will be servicing me later before the Dommes arrive this evening, that is for sure.

"Slave will eat on the floor as soon as she no longer hears my car engine after I leave. No utensils may be used. Slave may take out her new tail when she is finished eating." She nods her understanding. "Slave may also have coffee." I debate whether to make her wear a plug in her ass all day but decide against it. This morning's events should be enough to carry her through the day. "Slave will attach the leash to her desk upstairs and grade exams or do other schoolwork. Slave may use the restroom only when necessary. Slave will do yoga at ten o'clock, eat lunch at noon, and nap at two."

She nods her understanding.

"Slave will be at the coffee shop by five o'clock ready to strip and kneel until her Mistress wishes to be serviced."

She visibly shudders at this. Good. I want her to think about pleasuring me later.

As I push her head away, I see the devotion in her eyes. My heart fills. She is dedicated to me even when I treat her like this. Yes, life has gotten good, hasn't it? I grab my coffee and keys and head out the door.

I leave Mark in charge of the shop, head into my office, and lock the door. Bernadette is kneeling, wearing only her leather collar and attached leash. The leash is wrapped around the leg of the couch. She straightens up when I enter, and without acknowledging her, I unwrap the leash and tug her up. Pulling a slave by a leash is a recipe for injury, so I simply tug in the direction I want her to go. I gesture for her to get on all fours on the floor. Slaves should crawl anyway, right? I sit in my desk chair and push my pants and panties down. I tug her leash toward me, and she wordlessly services me until I smash her face against my sex and cum against it. She gasps for air, and I allow her this small necessity. She cleans me up first with her tongue and then with a warm washcloth and mild soap. I wish I had time to throw her down and fuck her. After the meeting. Definitely.

"Slave will get dressed and grade final exams at this desk. You will be watching the *littles* while the Dommes have our meeting upstairs."

She nods her understanding and then leans down to kiss my shoes. She lays her forehead on the top of one of my shoes, and I hear her crying softly. I'm not sure what emotions this day has brought up for her, so I command her to speak.

"I love you, Mistress," she answers and kisses my feet again. "Thank you for using me."

Ahh, she is feeling gratitude. I wonder if she senses the gratitude that I also have for her today and every day. "Get dressed," I say instead of pulling her into my arms like I really want to.

She stands, steps back three times, and then puts her clothes back on. I wish I could keep her vulnerable, but the Dommes are expected soon. I had almost hoped Jaleesa had gotten here early and barged in on us while

Bernadette was going down on me. *Almost.* I don't want to press Bernadette too hard today. She's had difficult experiences with abusive Dommes, and there must be some post-traumatic stress associated with it. I reason that she has used her safewords before, so I'm confident she would throw in a cautionary yellow if things got to be too much for her.

"Inspection," I say to her quietly, even though she is now fully clothed. I remove her leather collar and replace it with her day collar. I will put the leather one back on later to get us both into the right head spaces after the meeting.

"Shanice and Madison will be here. Jaleesa's new puppy will be taken care of by one of her subs at home." Bernadette nods, and I can tell that she is hoping I will kiss her. I want to back her up against the wall and sear her with a kiss. But I don't. She is in deep submission, and I want her to stay there a while longer. "Go," I say to her instead. "Get set up at my desk and be ready to greet my guests as they come in." She picks up her school briefcase and places it on my desk. The boxes of exams are on the floor, ready for her to dive into.

I can tell she feels dejected. Aww, I'll make it up to her after the meeting. I turn my back on her and, without saying another word, head up the stairs to my apartment where the meeting will be held. Oh, yes. After everyone leaves later, I'll kiss her senseless and then let her feel my whip. She hasn't experienced it yet. Obviously, it'll have to be the small whip since I can't wield the big one in the apartment. I will redden her ass and back and legs. I'll spin her around and do the front of her legs, getting as close to her pussy as possible without striking her there. Sometimes, I miss and make a direct hit. Oh, well. Such is life in the whipping business. One or more of us will cum, and then I will cuddle the fuck out of her, letting her know how much I love her.

It isn't long before the gaggle of Dommes arrives. I hear Madison's voice downstairs in the office, and she is chattering excitedly to Bernadette about how well she thinks her Calculus Two exam went. Shanice is quieter, but I hear Marta give Bernadette instructions about caring for Shanice and getting her in and out of the wheelchair.

Once the Dommes gather in my small living room upstairs, I call the meeting to order and indicate that this evening's meeting is strictly for shoring up the plans for the masquerade ball. A few of us will meet up with representatives from the men's group closer to the event.

Each person gives her report, and although it takes us an hour and a half to get through it all, we cover everything. This is my third spring ball and my fifth party overall as lead Domme for our community, and I have an organized checklist that we plow through thoroughly. I am pleased to hear that we now have an overabundance of volunteers and a great lineup of demonstrations after dinner. Jaleesa reports that the venue is allowing us to come in the night before to decorate and set up a changing room. Many folks drive to these events in vanilla clothes and then change at the venue. This makes perfect sense to me. Bernadette and I, however, will be dressed beforehand. It's game on the moment I walk in there. The printing of the tickets has been delayed for some reason, and I put it on my list to handle tomorrow morning first thing.

"Sounds quiet down there," Shasti says as we break up the meeting.

"It does," Marta agrees, but she doesn't sound concerned.

I follow everyone down the stairs, and we all melt at the sight we come upon. Both Shanice and Madison are asleep on the couch under one blanket. Bernadette is grading papers on her lap and facing them. She puts her current paper down when we invade their submissive space.

Jaleesa, Hayley, and Rowena say their goodbyes. Oh, shoot, I never did get a chance to ask Jaleesa about cooking lessons or bird apps. Darn it. I'll text her tomorrow.

Bernadette reaches for some papers on my desk and shows Marta and Shasti the coloring pages the *littles* did for their Dommes. The two Mommy Dommes in our group gush their thank yous to Bernadette. Apparently, my girl is a *little* whisperer. Who knew?

Marta reaches down and picks up the sleepy Shanice and then lowers her toward the wheelchair. "No, no, no, Mama," Shanice protests sleepily and wraps her arms around Marta's neck tightly.

Marta sighs and asks, "Can one of you follow us out with the chair?"

"I've got it," Bernadette says and stands up.

"No," I say to Bernadette. "Stay here and finish that one exam." She has had her hands full this evening with the *littles*, I'm sure.

"Yes, Ma'am," she says. Ahh, she didn't call me Mistress in front of Shasti and Marta. I will have to correct that later.

They all bid Bernadette goodnight, including the uber-sleepy Madison. Shasti always says Madison has two speeds—turbo and off.

I hate that Marta has to park on the street. Wrestling that wheelchair has got to be tiring. She's saving up to get a handicapped-equipped van that Shanice can learn to drive with hand controls. I'm just sorry that I can't give her a raise to help out with that.

I repeat my goodnights out on the street and give hugs all around. Madison's return hug is perfunctory, but I'll let it slide because she is so sleepy. We often let *littles* get away with things we would never dream of allowing other subs to get away with.

I whistle as I head back to my office, thinking about my plans for my slave this evening. Is she finished with that exam? Is she kneeling, waiting for me?

I open the door and see that she is still at my desk. I am confused. She doesn't have her exams in front of her. What is that? A knife? No, it's a letter opener. She's opening my mail.

I rush at her. "Drop that! What are you doing?"

She drops the letter opener and the envelope in her hands and stands up, backing away several steps. "I was just—"

"Why were you touching these?" I rush past her to see that she has opened practically all of the mail on my desk. "Show me your hands."

She holds up her hands and then starts crying. I've scared her. It can't be helped.

"Empty your pockets."

"Why?" she asks but does as she's told. "What's happening, Rikki?"

"Your phone." My voice is shrill. I hold out my hand. She gives it to me, and I scroll through her photos. Nothing. Good. Wait, what about email? I check her outgoing and incoming emails, and again, there is nothing. Just because she wasn't successful this time doesn't mean she won't try again.

I hand back the phone.

"Rikki, I was just trying to—"

I cut her off with a hand gesture. My brain is buzzing with static. Those were the exact same words Eileen said to me when she lied to my face about what she was doing. I'm trying not to panic. I look at Bernadette, wondering if I had her all wrong. Is she another parasite, and I didn't recognize it? Did my libido and ego blind me to reality? Again?

She looks from me to the door behind me. I didn't mean to, but I have her cornered in my office. She rushes past me as if her feet finally figure out how to move. The outside door is locked. She cries in scared frustration and pounds on the door until her brain engages and she remembers how to unlock it.

I shouldn't let her leave. What if she has enough information to do what Eileen did? I don't move fast enough, and Bernadette is out the door. I storm after her. She turns and sees me and bolts around the corner. She is sobbing.

I take a few steps in pursuit but stop when dizziness overtakes me. I reach for the brick building to steady myself. I take several deep breaths and release them slowly. I am about to hyperventilate. The last time I did that, Shasti made me go to the hospital. An anxiety attack, they'd said. Well, it sucked, and I don't want another one.

I hear Bernadette's hybrid start up and then drive away. Fuck, fuck, fuck. What the fuck just happened?

Chapter 12
The Porch

"What the fuck happened?" Shasti says before I even have a chance to say hello.

I take a deep breath and sigh into the phone.

"Seriously, Rikki," her voice softens. "What happened? Madison came home from school crying today. You know how sensitive she is. She said the professor was crying in her office and refused to talk about it."

"I lost my shit last night."

"Go on." I recognize her Mommy Domme tone.

"She was opening my mail."

"And?"

"I freaked out. Flashbacks of Eileen."

"Mm hmm," Shasti says. Her tone tells me she understands the dangerous ground we are now treading on. "Are you okay?"

"I checked her phone, her emails, her pockets," I say, not answering her question. I can't answer because, no, I don't think I'm okay. "I even went through her boxes of exams and her briefcase after she fled last night."

"'Fled?'" Shasti says. She sighs and asks me, "Did you find anything?"

"No."

"Did you call her last night? Did you talk about it?"

"Yes, I called her, but she didn't pick up. I left a voice mail and, like, twenty texts." I sit down on the couch in my office, unable to bring myself to sit at the desk. "I said we needed to talk. I told her I needed to explain some things."

"And?"

"She hasn't gotten back to me."

"Oh, Rikki." She clucks her anguish. "You must pursue this. I mean, do you think she was truly going after your personal information?"

"I didn't sleep last night, Shasti. I went over it in my mind over and over and over. I mean, if she were stealing my identity, she wouldn't have been so blatant about it. I came to realize what she was doing. Do you know what that was?"

"What?"

"Organizing my desk, tidying it. That's all. I flipped out like an idiot, and now—" I can't help the flood of tears. "I fucked it up, Shasti. Oh, my fucking God. The best thing that's ever happened to me, and I fucked it up. Can't I ever get past this Eileen shit?"

"I'll be right there," Shasti says. "Stay on the line with me."

"No. I'll be alright."

"I'll be there in ten minutes."

She arrives in nine. She lets me cry and even holds me while I go through a million different emotions. Extreme anger at Eileen. Shame at accusing Bernadette. Regret at scaring her. Utter despair because she is going to walk out on me. Like they all do. Once I'm cried out, Shasti makes me promise to call her if I want to talk or vent or just have someone close by.

It isn't long after Shasti leaves that a text comes in. It's from Bernadette.

BERNADETTE: Meet me on the porch. 6:00 pm

That's it. That's all she gives me. It's a breadcrumb, but I'll take it.

At precisely six o'clock, I pull the Subaru up the long drive, past the thick trees blocking the house from the road, and park next to her car. I swallow hard when I see her sitting on the top step of her front porch. Her arms are folded over her chest, and her knees and legs are pressed tightly together. She is wearing her comfort clothes – a flannel shirt, jeans, and sneakers. She has never looked more beautiful to me. My heart sings with hope when I see the collar. She is still wearing it. This is not a done deal, though. She might make a big show of removing the collar and unceremoniously placing it on the porch between us as she tells me to go fuck myself. My hope is fading now.

I get out of the car and reach into the backseat for her box of exams and briefcase. She makes no move to help me. That's fine. I don't deserve it, anyway. Should I have kept the exams hostage? No. Stop that. This is

Bernadette, not Eileen.

"Thank you," she says as I place the box and briefcase on the porch next to her. She makes no move to hug me. That's ... fine.

"May I sit?" I ask, letting her know I will follow her lead.

"Yes," she says succinctly. "I'm leaving for California tomorrow."

I exhale as if punched in the stomach. Tears choke my throat, but I do my best to shake them away. "Okay."

"I'll be back in a week to teach the summer session."

"I see." I say the words, but I don't see. What is she telling me? "Bernadette, I'm sorry about my reaction last night. I had a bad moment."

She doesn't let me continue and blurts, "I don't understand what happened. I just want to be with someone who loves me. Someone who respects and trusts me. I thought I had a place in your life." She swallows down her emotions. Is it anger? Sadness? Both? "I thought I had finally gotten past the 'toss-Bernadette-to-the-curb' point in relationships. This always happens to me. I thought we had something. I thought we were turning a corner into something else, something stronger. Am I important to you, Rikki?" She looks over at me. Her red-rimmed eyes tell me she has been crying as much as I have. "Or am I just another one of your, I don't know, conquests?"

"No, no, no. I love you." I reach a hand toward her. She recoils as if I am a snake. "I am not infallible. I completely destroyed the trust you had in me. Honesty is one of the basic tenets between us. It's not that I have been dishonest with you, or maybe I have by not telling you *why* I don't want you or anyone touching my mail or my paperwork." A rush of longing sweeps over me. I may have lost the best thing to ever happen in my life. A sob involuntarily escapes. I have to get this right. What I say next might make or break our relationship.

Bernadette makes no move to comfort me, making it hurt all the more.

"I am the victim of identity theft." I look toward the trees and not at her. "They call it familial fraud when someone close to you does it."

"Eileen," she says.

"Yes. She stole my mail and looked through my files. She set up a post office box in my name and opened up new credit cards. She filled out those stupid credit card applications that come unsolicited in the mail. She signed up for one of those credit monitoring services, made a list of all my inactive credit cards, and reported them lost so she could have new ones sent to the PO box. She changed my usernames and my passwords. I trusted her. She knew my birthdate and my social security number. She took out loan after loan in my name." I look from the trees directly at Bernadette. "She has taken me for over half a million dollars."

Bernadette's jaw drops open. Her expression softens.

I continue. "She did a lot of this shit while we were still together."

"No fucking way," Bernadette says. She is mad. So am I.

I nod. "I finally figured it out when a car dealership called to tell me they were not going to approve a loan application to finance over $65,000 for a new car. At first, I didn't know it was her until they told me the make and model of the car. It was the car she had been lusting after."

"Oh, my God," Bernadette says.

"But then I did a stupid thing. I confronted her before going to the police. She disappeared that night. She cleaned out all of my bank accounts. Checking, savings, business. All of them."

Bernadette groans her disgust.

I haven't told this story to many people. To tell it is to relive it. Eileen's betrayal is like a tangible thing, cutting me over and over again. Trust does not come easy, and that is why I hadn't even considered a new relationship after Eileen. Until Bernadette walked into my life. I glance up at her and then back to the pines.

"They haven't found her. I'm not sure anyone is looking anymore."

"I am so sorry that happened, Rikki." Out of the corner of my eye, I see her uncross her arms. She puts her hands in her pockets.

"Oh, I'm not done," I say. "I had just inherited Aunt Tilda's house at that point, her money, her possessions, all of it. I think that was the catalyst that made Eileen ramp up the fraud. "I have credit services working to stop it. I canceled all, and I mean *all*, of the credit cards, but the damage had already been done. There were many loans to deal with—loans that weren't mine, remember. There were and still are threats of liens against the shop and against my car. I sold the house to pay off some of the loans. Victoria helped me out by buying a lot of Aunt Tilda's dungeon equipment. A Cincinnati Mistress bought the rest. I used the money to pay off enough debts so they wouldn't take my business. It helped for a little while, but it hasn't been enough."

We sit in silence for a few moments. I gather my thoughts, hoping Bernadette will say something, but she does not.

"You know," I continue, "Aunt Tilda always said that you have to master yourself before you can master another. I guess I have not been successful at either." I turn toward her, facing her. "Bernadette, I made a mistake. I let my panic get in the way of my ears. I couldn't hear you last night. You are not Eileen. You are nothing like her. And I'm sorry I was so aggressive and distrustful. I knee-jerked. I know now that you were not snooping through my personal stuff."

"I was trying to help you," Bernadette said matter-of-factly. "I have mild OCD if that's even a thing. I like my environment neat and orderly. You told me not to touch your papers when I mentioned the messy desk in the past. And I left your desk alone for a long time. Months, but I just couldn't take it anymore. Even Shanice commented on the messiness last night. She said her Mama would put her in timeout if her room were like that. Maybe that's what tipped me over. I don't know. But the long and short of it is I made a mistake. I disobeyed your command." She looks up at me, wiping away tears from both cheeks. "I thought you would be pleased, that you would see how much better it looked, and…" She looks away, wiping her eyes again. "And I thought you would praise me."

"Oh, Bernadette. And then I went and lost my freaking mind."

"You scared me, Rikki. I keep reliving the frenzy in your eyes, the aggressive way you spoke to me, the complete and utter distrust and disdain you had for me. At that moment, I wasn't special to you. I wasn't worth honest communication. You made an assumption about me and what I was doing." She turns to face me. "Do you seriously think I am the kind of person that would do something like that? Do you not know me at all? That's the thing that hurts most of all." She clears her throat several times as if trying to hold back her rage. Her face is red with anger. No, this is fury.

"I wish you had been honest with me about your financial troubles, Rikki. I have eyes, you know. I figured your pride kept you from saying anything about it. I see the disrepair in the shop. It's not something that everyone would notice, but I did. The shop clearly needs a new furnace. I froze my ass off this winter because you can't afford to replace it. The sinks in both customer bathrooms are in sore need of replacing, and the plumbing needs to be redone, not to mention the peeling wallpaper.

"The overhead lights, the ones that make your place so quaint – I am about to lose my mind over how many of the bulbs are out. Fourteen at last count. I even went looking in the supply closet for replacements to change them myself, but there was not a single one. I have been tempted to buy the bulbs myself and take care of it, but I didn't want to upset you. I didn't want to point out your neglect of the place because I knew that would rub salt in the wound of your financial issues. But that's not what I should have been worried about." Her voice is loud and hard as she says, "Oh, no. Slitting open the envelopes to your fucking mail and stacking them neatly sent you into a tailspin. Mail that I didn't even look at." She groans and smacks a fist against her thigh. "All I wanted to do, Rikki," she says with a sigh, "was help you. I wanted to please you. That's it. Nothing more than that."

I can tell that she's not finished. She stands up, looks down at me, and says, "You're right. I am *not* Eileen." She lifts her head high. "I just wish you understood who I am. I thought you did." She sets her jaw and says, "I am going to take a moment—a time out, if you will. I need to reevaluate. Everything. My plane leaves tomorrow morning, and I will be back next Tuesday, May fourth."

Her words kick me in the chest. I close my eyes, take a deep breath, and let it out slowly. My entire body is dizzy. I reach into my pocket and feel for the key to her house she gave me the day she moved back in. I don't want to give it back, but I will if she asks for it. I stand up, the key now clenched in my fist. If she takes off her collar and hands it to me, I will throw in the towel. I will be done with my life as a Domme, and I will be done with any and all attempts to find happiness. Thank you, Eileen. You win.

Bernadette folds her arms across her chest and looks off in the distance. She has said her peace.

"I'll just go then," I say. I know she can hear the dejected tone in my voice. It's impossible *not* to hear it. I stand up and walk down the three steps to the ground below. "Just know that I do love you, Bernadette, and I'm sorry that I was triggered so badly last night. Again, I know you didn't do what she did. I know that. I acted irrationally."

"But it could happen again," she spats. "Will I need to walk on eggshells around you, never knowing when you'll freak out at something or get angry? I can't. I can't …" She covers her mouth with her hand as she begins to cry again. She recovers long enough to say, "You should go." She points toward my car.

"If that's what you want," I say with much more calm than I feel. I take two steps toward the car and then turn back around and ask, "Can we talk when you get back? Or while you're away?"

"I don't know," she says and then looks at me. She raises her head high and says again, "I don't know."

I nod and press my lips together so I don't out and out sob right there in front of her. I'll do that in the car.

Chapter 13
Hollow

I am in a daze. I am empty. I'm going through the motions. Even my staff has figured out they need to go to Lydia or Mark for help because I am more apt to pat their forearm and walk away without addressing their needs. I know everyone is worried about me. In one instant, I completely shattered the only good thing that had come into my life. Maybe I'll sell the business or just let the fucking bank take it. I'll work for Mistress Dominique until I can't stand that anymore. I already can't stand it and have no clue why I agreed to work there again this week.

The one bright spot was Monday night. The spanking girl, whose name I found out is Pam, hit it off with Lydia, as I suspected. Maybe I have that match-making gene Aunt Tilda seemed to have. I wish I had listened to her warnings about Eileen.

"Aunt Tilda, what should I do?" I say out loud as I drive home from the dungeon and another oh-so-fun evening dominating men. "Everyone says I need to keep asking Bernadette for forgiveness. And I do. Every day. Twice a day. My texts are always different, but they basically say the same thing. I fucked up. I'm sorry. I'm not that kind of person. It won't ever happen again. I know she reads them, Aunt Tilda. I see the little dancing dots. I hold my breath at those moments, hoping beyond hope that she will respond. I dread it too because she might actually respond and tell me to fuck off and leave her alone."

I turn onto Market Street. Almost home. "Home," I say out loud. "What is that?" A bed, now cold. I have things, but they have no meaning. Who the fuck cares about any of it if I don't have her to share it with? I want a new beginning with her. A fresh start. One with complete and open honesty. I kept insisting that she adhere to all those things, but I did not. "I am a fucking hypocrite," I yell and bang the steering wheel. For the billionth time, I start crying. I can't see clearly through my tears, but I am almost home anyway. I turn into the alley next to the shop and swipe at my eyes. Someone is sitting in the entryway. Is it her?

No, it's not. Bernadette isn't a tall Black woman. I wave at Jaleesa as I drive past to park. I almost consider turning around and leaving. I don't know if I'm ready for yet another friend intervention. Shasti, Marta, and Rowena have all come by to offer their unique advice. Even Victoria called me. I guess it's Jaleesa's turn. I park the car and dab at the tears in my eyes. Oh, fuck. Who cares? The mascara is smeared anyway, and I need to get out of this corset and tight mini-skirt.

I walk back around the building, my whips in hand, and Jaleesa turns toward me. Before she can say anything, I say, "Your turn for the pep talk?"

She closes her mouth and nods. "This is an, uh, interesting look for you, Rikki." She points to my Dominatrix ensemble.

I know she wants to know where I've been, what I've been doing, and if I've lost my mind. But I can't answer her on that last one. The jury's still out.

"C'mon in," I say and unlock the door. "Let's get this over with."

Jaleesa is uncharacteristically quiet as she follows me up the stairs to the apartment. "Let me, uh, get out of this." I point to my outfit and ruined makeup and head to the bathroom. I take a quick shower, trying not to remember the first time Bernadette and I showered together here. Her soft skin pressed against mine. She took my scrubby and insisted on washing me. That was an incredibly bold move. I remember how genuinely submissive she was because she expected me to shove my pussy in her face. I did not. She was too classy for a move like that right from the start. My tears come fast and hard. I smack a hand over my mouth so Jaleesa won't hear me sobbing.

I do my best to make it look like I haven't been crying in the shower and throw on my robe. I run a hand over Bernadette's robe. Will she ever wear it again?

"I'm sorry," I say to Jaleesa when I come out of the bathroom. I head to the fridge, grab two bottles of water, and hand her one. "My manners have disappeared."

"No worries," Jaleesa says and scoots forward in the chair. Ironically, it's the same chair that Bernadette pleasured her in a couple of weeks ago.

"Where's your head?"

"Get right to the point, why don't you," I say and then sigh.

"Shasti confided the whole Eileen thing to me."

I hang my head and growl.

"It's kind of already out there, Rikki," she says gently. "We all know there is something, but we respect your privacy."

"I feel like an idiot letting Eileen take advantage of me," I say.

"These identity thieves are good at what they do. Don't blame yourself."

"Right under my nose." I stare at the blinds covering the window as if trying to find an escape route.

"Are you, uh, going to Cincinnati at night?"

"Yes. Dominque's. I need the money, as you now know. As everyone now knows."

"You need to ask your friends for help." Jaleesa is gentle, but it doesn't dent the barrier that is my pride. "We're here for you, woman." She smiles, trying to reassure me.

I don't say anything. I just stare at the blinds. The only reason they are clean is that Bernadette cleaned them.

"You scared her," Jaleesa says simply.

"Bernadette?"

"Yeah." She takes a sip of water and places the bottle on the coffee table. She folds her hands in her lap. "She told me—"

"You talked to her? What did she say? Is she okay?" I'm desperate. Anything. Please.

"I did. This morning. She's coming back tomorrow, as I'm sure you know."

"Is she okay?"

"She told me she was enjoying her visit with her father and brother and his wife. Apparently, her brother and sister-in-law are trying to have a baby."

"They are?" I didn't know that. I'm missing everything. She's keeping it from me. She can talk to everyone else but not me. Talking to me is not allowed. I'm the enemy, and she doesn't want anything to do with me. She'll tell Jaleesa and probably everyone else things before she tells me anything. Ever again.

"Hey," Jaleesa says, "stay with me. Bernadette confided something to me if you want to hear it."

"Do I?"

Jaleesa nods. "She told me she had become so comfortable with you, trusting you to the max, that your outburst scared her 'to the core.'" Jaleesa uses air quotes around the last three words.

"I don't know how to make it up to her, Jaleesa. I don't know how to make this go away."

"Ahh, that's the thing, my friend. You don't make it go away. You have to face this." She clears her throat and says, "Your big thing is honesty and communication, right?" She points to the sign I hung up after Bernadette's collaring ceremony. The sign I've been avoiding.

"Yeah."

"Well, you can't demand honesty and communication from your subs and not reciprocate, Rikki. You have to be open and honest and not just with Bernadette. You have to be open with all things. Look, I'm not saying you have to blab your personal shit all over the place, but none of us knew exactly how deeply Eileen had cut you. We didn't know the extent that you were hurting. You can't heal if you deny that you're wounded. Let us help you."

I nod. I hate that she's making sense.

"Rikki, Bernadette counts on you to take care of her, to take care of both of you."

"That should be past tense. Used to take care of," I say.

"You don't know that," she reminds me.

"I'm not hopeful." I inhale raggedly, trying not to cry in front of my friend.

"Submissives often imprint on us. I'm not sure that's the right word, but they thrive when we set rules and create boundaries. They flourish when they think we have it all together and can manage everything. And when we show even the smallest chink in our armor, sometimes they get confused and don't know what to do with that."

"Is that what happened to Bernadette?"

"Could be," Jaleesa says. "Shasti told me Bernadette was still wearing your collar the night you had your, what did she call it? Your porch talk?"

"She did."

Jaleesa shrugs. "A good sign, maybe?"

I shrug.

"Rikki, it's taken me years, and I mean years, for Tina and me to become a team."

"You two are a well-oiled machine," I say, and mean it.

"We are. We clearly understand and provide for each other's needs. Together, we've created that, but it took a long time with many mistakes—mostly on my part."

"Tina has infinite patience," I say with a chuckle.

"That she does. How long have you and Bernadette been together?"

I want to correct her present-tense question and make it past tense, but I'm sure she's done with my pity party for one at this point.

"Three months. Last Friday." Not that I am counting the days, but I am.

"Ahh. Okay. Because Tina and I have put in hard and purposeful work, we have several subs together. You know how much she wanted to have a pet of her own. Surprised the hell out of me when she said she wanted a *boy* pet."

"Bailey is the cutest," I say.

"I know. I'm smitten with him, too. We're considering having him move in."

"Really? He's under consideration, though, isn't he?"

Jaleesa nods. "Tina is still my submissive, and she knows it, but I guess you'd call her my alpha sub."

"I won't take more subs, even if Bernadette doesn't take me back. I'm done putting my heart out there."

"You say that now, friend." Jaleesa raises a disbelieving eyebrow. She sighs loudly when I don't respond and adds, "Look, I've seen you two together. Everyone has. You two are what we all want. That easy intimacy. That mutual respect. That intuitive knowing. I've seen the two of you have entire conversations with each other without either of you uttering a single word."

I nod. "I took that for granted."

"No, I don't think you did," Jaleesa says. "Here's what happened. This thing you were trying to handle all by yourself blew up in your face. Bernadette took the brunt of the shrapnel. Your biggest mistake, my dear friend, is thinking that you can handle this by yourself."

"A Domme trait, I'm afraid."

"It is. Tina beat that out of me quickly." We both chuckle and for the first time, I feel my shoulders relax a little.

"Did Shasti send you over here?"

Jaleesa shook her head. "No. When I dropped Kari off this morning, you were a veritable shell of yourself. A walking, empty, hollow woman. I came by this evening, but Lydia said you had gone to Cincinnati. I figured that could only mean one thing—Dominique's."

"So, nothing I do is private anymore," I grumble.

"All eyes are on you and Bernadette, Rikki," she says. "You know that, don't you? Seamus calls me twice a day for updates. You and Bernadette are like royalty around here."

I roll my eyes and shake my head at her royalty analogy. I might be the royal shit shoveler, but I am not a monarch.

"Obviously, you'll accept whatever decision Bernadette makes?" Jaleesa asks.

I nod. Of course, I will, and I already know what her decision will be. But I don't say this out loud.

Jaleesa stands up with a sigh. "Okay, I'll check in with you tomorrow, my friend."

"Thanks," I say and stand to walk her to the door. "I appreciate you all checking in on me. I truly do. I'll be okay." And I one hundred percent don't believe my last statement at all.

~~~

Bernadette is flying back today, but I don't know any of her flight information. I check my phone constantly. I know Marta and Mark and Lydia all see it, but I don't care. I eventually hole up in my office and decide that it's probably over between Bernadette and me, so I might as well face my demons and deal with the mail. Even though it's hopeless, I prop up the phone open to our text chat. I look at the framed photo of my mom on my desk and silently ask her for strength.

Sorting out the bills from the junk is not soothing at all, but it must be done. And the sooner I get them off my desk, it will be one less reminder of my idiocy. Oddly, no one knocks on the office door, an infrequent occurrence. They must know that I am well in the middle of my nervous breakdown at this point.

"Shouldn't kid about that," I say out loud, "because it might just happen for real." I stand up, weary of just sitting and waiting. Maybe I'll go for a drive and get fast food or do something else equally reckless, foolhardy, and irresponsible. I reach for my phone, and my heart stops. The three little dots are moving in the chat. She's reading my last text, my latest desperate plea I made an hour ago.

A message pops up.

> BERNADETTE: I'm home safe. I'm planning on having that Cinco de Mayo dinner tomorrow evening if you still wish to come. 5:30 for dinner. If you would like to contribute, you may bring a dessert of some kind.

I read it seventeen times. At least she isn't kicking me to the curb yet. I don't allow myself to get too overjoyed because she could still kick me to the curb tomorrow night in front of witnesses. I hustle to the kitchen and show Marta the text. She hugs me and has tears in her eyes.

"Rikki," she says after pulling out of our hug, "this is a good sign. Shanice said Bernadette was in a good mood the other day."

"Shanice talked to Bernadette?"

"Yes. Shanice called her two days ago. Saturday, I think."

"Am I the only one who hasn't talked to her?"

Marta pats my arm. "Probably."

"Did you call her, too?"

She nods and says, "We're all worried about you two."

I am a bit floored knowing that all of my friends have called Bernadette. They've been counseling me, too. Shit, is this a group intervention or something?

"Shanice and Bernadette bonded that night when Bernadette was *little-sitting*," Marta says. "Shanice said Bernadette asked intelligent questions about the car accident and the amputations. She didn't show pity but had sympathy. Bernadette genuinely listened. Shanice has been going through something lately," Marta said, sounding a little lost. "Something she won't talk to me about. I think Bernadette is helping her make sense of whatever it is. Personally, I think Shanice is happy to have made a new friend."

My heart fills. "Bernadette is such a great listener," I say. "I was lucky to have her for the time I did, wasn't I? Maybe she was sent to me for a short while to teach me a lesson or something. I just have to figure out what that is."

"You're an idiot, Boss. You don't know that it's over." Marta rolls up her dish towel.

"You know, you're the only one I let get away with calling me an idiot."

She ignores me and says, "Whatever you do tomorrow, do not fuck this up again." She snaps the towel at me. "Now it's time for you to get out. Out." She snaps the towel again, this time connecting. "You have one whole day to figure out how to get yourself together."

Easier said than done.

Chapter 14
No Words

My nerves are barely under control the following evening as I pull into Bernadette's drive. The last time I left this property, I wasn't sure I'd ever be welcomed back. And I wouldn't say I have gotten myself "together" as Marta suggested, but I have successfully not cried since lunchtime, so that's an accomplishment, I guess.

Ahh, Shasti and Madison are here already. Okay, good. They will be a nice buffer. I step out of the car and grab the tray of brownies from the backseat. Yes, I made them all by myself from a box in my tiny apartment oven. Both Bernadette and Madison love brownies, so it was an easy choice.

I stop dead in my tracks at the foot of the steps when the door opens. It's her. I reach for the railing to steady myself. She is more fucking beautiful than I remembered. Is she wearing the collar? I can't tell. Damn it. She's wearing a hooded sweatshirt. The hood is down, but I can't see her neck.

Her expression is neutral as she says, "Thanks for coming."

"Hi," I say back. It's all very formal. Okay, I can go with that. I have to. I have no choice.

Madison comes bursting out the front door. "Miss Rikki," she cries and flies at me, almost knocking me over with her hug.

"Hey, little one." I hug her back with one arm and then hand her the tray of brownies. "Will you take this inside for me?"

Her eyes widen. "Yesssss," she says with reverence as if I have just handed her a treasure. "Brownies, brownies, brownies," she chants as she walks up the steps toward the front door. Bernadette holds the screen door open for her to walk through.

"Thanks for coming," she says again.

"Of course," I say coolly as if I haven't been dying a thousand deaths while she was away. "Thanks for the invitation."

She holds the door open for me, and I walk right by her. Oh, God, how I want to push her against that door and kiss her and tell her that I love her and how sorry I am.

"Hey, Rikki," Shasti says. She is in the kitchen setting the table.

"It smells so good in here." I say this mainly for Bernadette's benefit.

"It absolutely does," Shasti says. "I'm famished."

"That would be the chicken enchiladas in the oven and the beef taco mix on the stove," Bernadette says right behind me. "C'mon in." She walks past me into the kitchen.

I take my sweater off and lay it on the arm of the oversized chair where I used to sit. This is where Bernadette would cuddle in my lap and then slide down and kneel at my feet, looking up at me expectantly. I stroke the back of the chair and cough, trying to clear the growing lump in my throat.

"Miss Rikki," Madison calls excitedly. "Hurry up. We have to eat so we can have brownies."

"Ahh," I say and head into the kitchen. "You are such a sugar monster." I bug out my eyes, making her laugh. I look over at Shasti, and she sighs that resigned sigh I've heard so many times when it comes to her little one.

Bernadette's back is to us, and I shoot Shasti a desperate look. She gives me an I-have-no-idea gesture, and I nod. No one except Bernadette knows how this is going to go. Madison, witnessing our exchange, lowers her head and pouts. She reaches over and squeezes my hand to give me comfort.

Madison releases my hand and then leaps up to help Bernadette without being asked. Shasti's eyebrows hit the roof. "Will you look at that?"

"Can I help?" I ask from where I stand behind my usual seat at the kitchen table.

A quick "nope" from the hostess has me rooted where I stand. She tells me to sit, so I do.

Once the food and beverages are laid out and Bernadette thanks everyone for coming, we dig in.

"Professor," Madison says, "guess what."

"What, kiddo?" Bernadette leans closer and smiles at her former student.

"I'm eating dinner at Professor Garneau's house."

Bernadette tilts her head back and laughs. We all do. It is a great stress reliever.

"Guess what, Madison," Bernadette says right back.

"What?" Madison's eyes sparkle.

"I'm eating at Professor Garneau's house, too."

Madison screeches her delight at the comeback.

Once the laughter dies down, I say, "These enchiladas are amazing. Just the right amount of heat."

"I called Tina," Bernadette admits. "She offered to come over and help, but I wanted to do them on my own." She lifts the dish of sour cream. "Anyone need?"

Shasti takes a bit and says, "You'll either have to share your recipes or come over and make them at our house because I have never seen this." She nods toward Madison, happily eating everything on her plate.

"I think there are brownies she's rushing to get to," I say.

"Brownies, brownies, brownies," Madison chants happily.

Both the food and the company are wonderful. When we are finished eating, Madison helps Bernadette clear off the table, cut the brownies, and serve them. Coffee is also served all around, and I notice that the new coffee setup has arrived. I comment on it.

"The box was waiting for me when I got back yesterday," Bernadette says. "It took me a minute or two to figure it out, but it makes great coffee."

"Mm hmm," Shasti says and holds up her cup.

"Ahh, but it's also the time and attention the barista puts into it that makes a difference, too," I say. I know it was a cheesy thing to say since Bernadette made the coffee, but I'm dying here. If I ever wanted to know what limbo felt like, I know now.

"Madison," Shasti says, "I think it's time we head out. You have to finish cleaning your room, you know."

"I know," she says. "Thanks for dinner, Professor."

Whoa, what is going on? Madison isn't squawking about having to leave or having to clean her room? Oh, I get it. This is their previously agreed-upon exit strategy.

Madison stands up and then bows dramatically toward Bernadette. "Good lady, may I help you clear the table again?"

"No, my fine young knight," Bernadette answers playfully. "You have, err, served the castle well and must now ensure your lady knight arrives home safely."

"Your wish is my command," Madison says and bows again. She straightens up and is Madison again. "Bye, Miss Rikki. See you tomorrow at the shop."

"Okay, sounds like a plan." I stand up to hug them both and stay behind as Bernadette walks them out. I clear the table and finish filling up the dishwasher. I have no idea if I'm about to grab my sweater and be sent home or if we're going to have a chance to talk. I have to try. I can't go another hour without knowing where her head is.

"You didn't have to do that," Bernadette says, gesturing to the dishwasher. "But thank you." She leans against the doorframe.

"I wanted to help." I hear Shasti's car drive off, and now we're alone. I dry my hands with the dishtowel and lean back against the countertop.

"Is it warm in here?" Bernadette asks.

I start to reply, but my words get caught in my throat as she takes a step closer to me. My heart, which was already running fast, is now pounding.

She grabs the hem of her sweatshirt and tugs it upward. Her hands then reach behind her neck, and she pulls the entire sweatshirt off.

I gasp when I see it. "Your collar." I put a hand over my mouth. My tears start to flow. "You're still wearing it."

She takes another step closer. "You told me collared submissives aren't allowed to take off their collars. I'm just following protocol." She reaches for the edge of the counter, grabs it with one hand for balance, and squats down to her knees in front of me. She looks up.

"Are you—" The words get caught in my throat. "Are you still a collared submissive?" I need to hear her say it. I swipe at the annoying tears on my cheeks.

"Yes," she says, her own voice breaking up.

I grab the counter myself and go down to my knees in front of her. "Really?" My gaze sweeps her face. Is it true? Is this real?

She nods. "But I'll be honest. Your outburst that night shocked me. It threw me off balance. I went home to be alone and breathe, but my phone did not stop ringing and dinging. Rikki, you wouldn't believe how many friends you have. Everybody called me to tell me that you aren't like that. They all told me what a good person you are. They were so happy for you when you'd collared me. They said you've never abused a sub. It went on and on." She pauses for a moment, and I let her have the space. "I just had to get over the initial shock of it, that's all."

"I've been dying."

"I heard," she says. "From everybody. Did you know that even Victoria texted me?"

"For real?"

"Yes. I was shocked, but it was fine. It felt like she was giving you a recommendation or something. 'Good, hardworking, conscientious Domme. Never had an outburst like that before. Blah, blah, blah.' Victoria is a faithful friend to you."

"She is." And for some reason, it calms my soul that she does not refer to Victoria as Daddy Vic.

Bernadette reaches up to touch my face. "I have been dying, too, Rikki. My poor family didn't know what to do with me. I cried the whole time. My sister-in-law finally took me out for a hike one day and asked me point blank if I loved you. I didn't hesitate and said, 'Yes, yes, yes.' She laughed at my exuberance and told me just to call you and talk about what happened. But I wasn't ready yet." She drops her hand and looks me right in the eyes. "Rikki, I think we both needed this week to regroup."

I hold up my hand as if taking an oath. "Honesty about everything from now on," I say. "Everything."

"Domme Rikki," Bernadette says formally. "Your humble submissive would like to suggest we save the formal discussion about the, err, incident until tomorrow morning." She pauses for a moment. "Because I think you should be kissing me now."

"Submissive Bernadette, that is a fucking amazing suggestion."

She leans forward, and I close the distance instantly. Her lips are soft yet insistent. She puts her hand behind my head and pulls me to her. I kiss her like I'm hungry. No, I'm starving. Judging by her ardor, she has also been hungry for me. She breaks off the kiss breathless and stands up, offering a hand to help me up. She doesn't let go of my hand and leads me through the living room. She pauses at the bottom of the stairs to look at me over her shoulder as if asking permission to proceed to her bedroom.

I melt at her obvious need. It is not necessarily a lustful need. It's more like a yearning for love and affection. Her needs match my own, and my heart wraps itself around her as I take a step forward in answer. Her smile lights up—God, how I've missed that.

She runs up the stairs, practically dragging me behind her. We shower together slowly, savoring each other's bodies. Oh, how I love kissing her. When the water turns cold, we get out, and I dry her thoroughly. I don't rush. I take my time to let her know that I am one hundred percent tuned into her.

She dries me as well, and then I ask, "Do you want to put on your play collar?"

She doesn't move or answer me, but I see the physical effect my words have. She tilts her head back as a wave of arousal shudders through her. Her breathing is a bit labored. "Yes, Ma'am," she says finally.

I move into the bedroom and gesture for her to kneel on the pillow on the floor. I take off her day collar and buckle on the sturdier leather one. She shudders again as I do this. I lift one leg and place my foot on the edge of the bed. Instinctively, I understand that she needs me to take charge. She needs me to Dominate her. Maybe I know this because of that intuition thing Jaleesa says Bernadette and I have with each other.

I hook two fingers into the D-ring on the front of the collar and pull her toward my body. She looks up at me and then darts forward, hugging my leg. "I missed you so much, Rikki," she says, her voice choked with emotion. "I love you. Oh, God, I've dreamed of this moment."

"I didn't dare dream of it," I answer softly.

She groans into my leg at my words, communicating that she understands my anguish over the past week. She kisses my inner thighs. She thrusts her tongue into my folds. I am wetter than I realized. I lace my fingers in her hair gently. "That's it, little bee. You're a good girl, aren't you?"

She moans at my words.

"Such a good little bee."

She slips her fingers inside and explores me like she's never been there before. Her movements are slow and deliberate, and the best word I can think of is loving. Her lips find my clit. She knows just how to tease me. She circles me lightly and then increases the pressure. My fingers tighten their grip in her hair, and I press her mouth where I need her. She understands and gives me what I crave.

Her touch triggers something deep inside me. I relax and let it come. My moans spur her on. She thrusts two fingers inside and fucks me gently. I grunt my approval. Her fingers speed up. My hips undulate on their own.

"Oh, fucking yes," I moan as the white ball of light hits me, and I release a week's worth of tension into her eager mouth, soaking her. She draws out my orgasm as only she can. I am dizzy with my release and have nothing to hold onto except her head. She seems to understand and wraps an arm around my hip as if to steady me and keep me from falling out of the white-water raft we're in.

Once my breathing slows, I pull her away from my center. I nudge her up to a standing position and kiss her like I've never kissed her before.

"I love you, Bernadette," I say into her mouth.

"I love you, too, Rikki."

She pulls me onto the bed, and we lay facing each other. She strokes my face. I stroke her breasts and stomach.

"Kneeling wasn't enough," Bernadette says softly. "At home. In California."

"No?"

"You told me once that I needed a little bit of pain to settle myself when I'm alone."

"Yes," I say. "The homemade belt I gave you."

"I brought it with me."

"And you used it." It wasn't a question.

"Yes," she says simply. "It helped."

"But?"

"It wasn't enough. It wasn't from your hand," she says as if she finally realizes something.

"I see," I say. And I do see. I sit up and command her to drape herself over my lap on the bed. I see her eyes filled with equal parts lust and relief. "Lift your ass. Spread your legs a bit. Yes, that's it."

I stroke her smooth, exquisite ass, and she arches up into my touch. I stroke the backs of her legs as far as I can reach and then move to her inner thighs. I am surprised, yet not surprised, to discover that my girl's wetness has trailed down her legs. I moan involuntarily at my discovery, causing her to lift her ass again. She's inviting me to explore further, and I do. I circle her labia with two fingers, ignoring her greedy clit. Her legs open further. She is a good girl, and I tell her so. She knows what I want. I plunge my fingers inside and thrust several times. I pull out slowly and then split my fingers around her hooded clit, effectively taking down the hood. Ahh, she is swollen. I'd love to suck her pearl into my mouth and run my tongue over it. Soon. Maybe. Who knows? At some point this evening, maybe I will.

When her hips buck, I realize that I have lost my focus. Normally, I would swat her ass or thighs for moving like that, but I don't. This is my fault. I pull my hand away abruptly, much to her dismay. Her frustrated exhale almost makes me chuckle, but I don't. I rub her back and then her ass again and then tap it lightly.

I feel her shiver as I touch her. She has also dreamt of this moment, I think. She dreamt of the moment I claim her body as mine. The moment I remind her who gives the pain that lights up her body—the pain that turns to gold. The pain she needs to anchor herself.

"Did you fuck yourself when you were away?" I ask and lightly smack her ass. It's barely anything, and yet she moans, almost like she's climaxing. It must have been my words.

"No, Ma'am," she says. Her breathing is a bit labored. "You are the giver of pleasure. I only gave myself pain."

"Excellent," I tell her and rub her cheeks lovingly. "Now, you know I believe spankings are rewards. They are not punishments. My little bee did absolutely nothing wrong by taking a time out. And, if I might be selfish, she did everything right by taking me back."

"And you did, too," she says, turning her head to look up at me, "by taking me back."

"There was no question of that," I say, continuing to stroke her. "And now it's time my little bee got some relief from all that stress and tension."

"Oh, yes, Ma'am." She lifts her ass, inviting me to begin.

My hand comes down and leaves a delicious red handprint. She jumps and cries out at the suddenness of it. I smack her again and again and again. There is no anger in my impact. There is only love. I wish her a cathartic release of healing. And the fact that it comes from my hand is important.

I keep a slow yet steady rhythm, and it isn't long before she is writhing on my lap. Her legs spread more. Yes, I had sensed she was getting close. "Ten more." I tell her to countdown out loud, and she does. My last three smacks are done with all my strength. I let her soak in the pain. Her ass must be throbbing. I run my hands over her red and pulsing skin. She squirms so much that I can't delay any longer. I thrust inside her and pump my fingers. My other hand reaches up to her face, and I insert my fingers into her mouth. She moans as I fuck her from both ends. She lifts her ass and bucks back against me.

My core swells with Dominance. I am making her feel my possession of her body. I am playing her like a violin. And it will be me that makes her cum.

I pull my fingers out of her vagina and swirl them around her clit. I continue to fuck her mouth. She seems grateful that I am giving her so many sensations all at once.

"Rikki," she says around my fingers. "Let me see you."

I take my fingers out of her mouth and move a little so she can see me with her head turned.

"I'm going to cum, Rikki," she says. "It's there. It's been there. Waiting for you to release it." She arches up and moans as a pre-orgasmic pulse hits her. "Yes, Rikki. There's a spark inside that only you can—" Another wave hits, and she rides it. I used to think my expert skill made her ride the edge like this, but now I know it's a combined effort.

Her body becomes rigid. This is my favorite moment—the calm before the storm. She releases, bucking her hips against my still-working fingers. Her entire body shakes. Fantastic. She is having a full-body orgasm. "Yes, little bee," I encourage her. "Cum for me. Cum for your lover. Cum for your Domme. Such a good girl."

My words have the effect I was going for. She tenses and raises her body with another aftershock. She is swimming in sensation. As she often does, she goes still. Her deep breathing is the only way I know that she is all right. I let her be. She will rouse shortly.

A few minutes pass while Bernadette floats in whatever submissive space she has found herself in. It gives me a moment to breathe and settle myself. I dodged a bullet. I know this. It's not that I distrusted Bernadette—it wasn't that at all. When it comes down to it, Jaleesa was right. My pride got in the way and almost cost me the best thing that's ever happened to me. I shouldn't have kept all that Eileen shit to myself. I should have let my friends and Bernadette know what was happening. I arrogantly thought it was my problem to solve and that I didn't need any help.

Bernadette rouses, and I pull her up to kiss her gently. "I love you, my little bee."

"Me, too," she mumbles.

"You, too?" I tease. "You love yourself, too?"

"Ha ha ha," she says dryly and snuggles against me. "Can I keep you forever?"

Her question catches me by surprise. "Umm, yes. Yes, I think I can arrange that."

"Good." She sighs the most contented sigh I think I've ever heard and then pulls at me. "Rest. Round two. Soon."

"Oh, yes, Ma'am," I say to her and earn a light smack on my leg for it.

I lay by her side and pull her into a tight snuggle. She rolls over, and we become one spoon. I reach over for her Pooh bear and give it to her. She makes a happy noise and hugs him along with my arms.

My sigh is a relieved one. I honestly thought I had blown it and didn't dare picture this strong, amazing woman in my arms ever again. I can't contain my tears and cry softly behind her. I have so much trust to rebuild. I hope I'm capable.

She hugs my arms tighter, letting me know she hears my emotion and that it's okay for me to let it out. She's letting me know that she has me, even though my arms are holding her. I squeeze her back and relax into her, my tears slowing. No words are needed between us.

Chapter 15
Will You?

It's been the most amazing two weeks since my girl took me back. We've talked a lot about what happened, and it has brought us closer. Communication is open and honest between us now. I mean, I thought we had that before, but now we seem to be discovering each other all over again at a deeper level.

"Rikki," Bernadette says, "would you help me, please?" Bernadette is decked out in one of the summer outfits I ordered for her from Robert's Menswear, Inc shop. She has on a sleeveless lowcut button-down shirt with a lightweight vest over the top and tight-fitting ass-enhancing khaki shorts to match. I'd made enough money moonlighting at Mistress Dominique's to pay for the entire order. Bernadette fussed, but I would not allow her to contribute a single dime. I told her it was my choice to enhance my property. She didn't fuss after that. Her leather collar matches the ensemble perfectly, as I knew it would.

"What do you need, little bee?" I hug her from behind.

"Will you please put the veggie trays out on the table?"

"Belay that order," comes a voice from the living room. Ahh, Jaleesa is here with her gaggle of subs. "Give me a minute to give out assignments."

Bernadette wraps an arm around my waist as we watch from the kitchen doorway. It's almost as if she needs to anchor herself. My little bee is nervous today.

Jaleesa snaps her fingers, and three of her submissives gracefully go to their knees in front of her. She is not putting on a show for us. This is how things work in Jaleesa's house. Each one looks up at her adoringly. She says a few soft words to them collectively and then signals for the petite Dana, who is in her late twenties, to stand up. Jaleesa places both hands on either side of

Dana's face and pulls her into a sensual kiss that almost melts my own face off. Bernadette sighs at the sight.

"You are in charge of the *littles*," Jaleesa says to Dana. "Do a good job, and I might allow you to suck my pussy when we get home."

"Oh, yes, Ma'am," Dana says, obviously excited by this prospect.

Jaleesa turns her head and asks Bernadette, "*Littles* are where?"

"Down the hall, first room on the left, Ma'am," Bernadette says respectfully.

"Thank you." Jaleesa turns back to her sub, turns her physically around, and pats her ass as she leaves.

Jaleesa signals the remaining two to stand. DeShawn is a male sub in his early thirties or so. The other is a white, retired art teacher named Harriet, slightly graying, in her mid-fifties. She is primarily a service sub who lives with them in exchange for room and board, regular flogging maintenance, and Dominance from Jaleesa. She doesn't say much, but it's obvious that she adores her Mistress.

"Since Kari's coming later with the coffee shop crew, you two are the only ones serving for now. You will follow Miss Bernadette's or Miss Rikki's orders. Whatever they say, goes."

"Yes, Ma'am," they say in unison.

She nods her head toward the kitchen, and they head that way.

"Oh, oh," Bernadette says. She seems a bit flustered, so I take charge and give them short- and long-term tasks concerning the appetizers, the lunch buffet, drinks, and other protocols. She throws me a relieved look.

Jaleesa comes into the kitchen to check on her subs.

"That was some kiss you gave Dana," I say.

"Yeah," Jaleesa says. "She's been a little out of sorts ever since we got the new puppy. I'm giving her a little extra attention."

"Thank you for the help, Ma'am," Bernadette gestures to DeShawn and Harriet, who are working in the kitchen. "You didn't have to do that."

"Isn't this a housewarming party?"

"Yes?" Bernadette answers tentatively.

"Happy housewarming," Jaleesa says. "But that's only part of your gift," she adds cryptically and winks at me. I'm in on the second part, but I won't spoil the surprise.

"Speaking of puppies," Jaleesa says. "You haven't met Bailey yet, have you?"

Bernadette and I both shake our heads.

"Does this door lead outside?" Jaleesa asks, heading toward the backdoor in the kitchen.

"Mm hmm," Bernadette says. There is a long pause, and then she quickly amends, "Yes, Ma'am. It does."

Jaleesa nods, but her expression is serious. She shoots me a glance. Ahh, she caught the misstep from my submissive. I nod quickly, letting her know that I will be sure to talk that over with my sub later.

Jaleesa opens the back door and says, "C'mon out and watch this." She heads down the back steps, and we follow behind.

Bernadette gasps when she sees Tina throwing a tennis ball and a grown man chasing after it. He has gripping gloves on his hands and sturdy shoes on his feet and runs on all fours to get the ball. He reaches down and snatches it up in his mouth.

"Hello, Miss Rikki," Tina greets me and then calls to her puppy, "C'mon, Bailey." He perks his head up and comes running back to his Mistress. He drops the ball at her feet and nuzzles against her leg. She scratches him behind the ears, and he makes a happy, contented sound.

"That is so cute," Bernadette gushes.

Jaleesa embraces Tina from behind and kisses her on the top of her head. It is easy to do since Jaleesa is tall and Tina is a tiny thing, about five feet. In addition to the height gap, there is a slight age gap between them as well. Jaleesa just turned forty, and Tina is Bernadette's age, early thirties.

"I'm going back in," Jaleesa says.

"Okay, babe." Tina squeezes the arms holding her. Jaleesa lets her go and heads back to the house. "Do you want to throw it?" Tina asks Bernadette.

"Oh, sure. Thank you." Bernadette takes the tennis ball that has seen better days. She says to Bailey, "Ready to get it, boy? Ready?"

Bailey leaps up and jumps around. Yes, apparently, he is ready. Bernadette reaches back and launches the ball clear across the yard and into the stand of trees at the back of the property.

"Holy shit, little bee," I say and look at her with new eyes. "You've got a rocket launcher."

"That felt good." She waggles her eyes at me. "College softball player. Remember?"

"You play softball?" Tina asks almost reverently.

"Oooh," Bernadette says as Bailey skids in the leaves. "Umm, yes, four years. Pacific Coast League champions my junior and senior years."

"Position?"

"Shortstop."

Tina seems to melt. "Jaleesa wants to put together a team for the Denton Heights summer league. We need infielders. Will you play?"

"I would love to," Bernadette says. I can hear the excited lilt in her voice. "I'll have to check with my Domme, of course." She reaches for my hand and squeezes it. There is no doubt I will say yes.

"Of course," Tina agrees.

Bernadette shifts her weight from side to side. She is getting antsy. "I should get back inside. More guests could be arriving."

"Wait," Tina says urgently, "I just want you to see one more thing." She cups a hand around her mouth and yells, "Bailey, come." He picks his head up, and we all break down laughing. He has a big stick in his mouth and not the tennis ball. He starts running toward us, drops the stick, picks it up with his mouth, and repeats this several times. Tina and I both know why he is doing this, but Bernadette does not.

"It's okay," I whisper to Bernadette. "Jaleesa is inside. She'll take care of things."

"It's almost time for—"

"It'll be fine," I say. This time, more seriously.

"Yes, Ma'am," she says. Ahh, good. She heard the tone in my voice and seems to settle down.

Bailey finally makes it over to us, and he is winded, so naturally, Tina gives him a moment to catch his breath before showing Bernadette his tricks. Rolling over, begging, treat balancing on his nose. The last one he hasn't quite yet worked out, but we laugh watching him try.

"Tina," Jaleesa calls from the kitchen door. "Clean up that puppy and help out in here."

"Yes, Ma'am." Tina wipes him down with a towel.

"Let's go back in," I say to Bernadette, and she lets out a relieved sigh.

Once we go back inside, we see that Shasti and Madison have arrived, as well as Victoria and her official new sub, Alyssa. Alyssa has barely any fabric on her body, but all essential parts are covered. Victoria can't seem to keep her eyes off her new sub. I have high hopes for this union, but I'm not holding my breath.

Seamus and a few of his boys are here, and he sends two of them in to help the kitchen crew manage the buffet spread and one of them to the *littles'* room to play. Hopefully, Dana won't be overwhelmed.

"Any sign of them, Madison?" I ask. She has set up a sentry spot at the living room window and is peeking through the sheer curtains.

"Not yet, Miss Rikki." She turns back to the window but then sees Bernadette and turns back around. "Hi, Professor."

"Hi, kiddo," Bernadette says. "You're on a reconnaissance mission?"

"Yes, Professor."

"Well done, Private Madison," Bernadette says and salutes. I shake my head. She is so quick to catch on to Madison's headspace and invite herself in to play. Madison loves it and adores my girl for it. I should be jealous. But I'm not. This is what family is all about.

"Thank you, Captain," Madison answers, her eyes sparkling.

"Carry on, soldier."

"Yes, Ma'am," Madison salutes and then turns back around and peaks through the curtain. She circles her fingers and puts them up to her eyes as if they were binoculars. "Miss Rowena and Minjung are here," Madison announces.

Victoria sends Alyssa out to help Minjung carry in a large box. Apparently, it contains a housewarming gift for Bernadette. I didn't know about this one, but that's okay. I can't control everything.

In true Rowena fashion, she finds the most comfortable seat in the living room and commandeers it. Minjung fetches a hassock for her Domme's feet and then gets a raspberry lemonade for her, taking nothing for herself. Rowena pats her submissive on the head.

Bernadette puts on soft jazz music and triple checks the appetizers and beverages, even though Shasti has already taken over the kitchen.

Bernadette is getting a bit restless, so I call her to me. I wrap my arms around her waist and say, "Breathe." She takes a breath, but I can tell she is only doing it because I asked her to. "Look at me," I say. She looks up guilty. She knows I caught her. "I'll let that go. Now breathe, please." This time, she does and then lays her head on my chest for a moment.

"Thank you," she says. "I wish Miss Olga and her foxy husband could have made it."

"I know, but we'll see them next weekend at the ball. Do you hear the chatter in here? All these people in your home?"

"Yes, Ma'am."

"They're having a good time, so please stop worrying. I want you to enjoy yourself. Be present."

She looks up at me with gratitude. "You're right. I'm missing my own party, aren't I?"

I nod. "Go on outside. The coffee shop crew should be here any moment."

"They're here. They're here," Madison announces from the window. "The eagles have landed." She leaps away from the window, not wanting to get caught spying. She rushes to Shasti and grabs her hand for comfort.

Bernadette heads outside to the front porch, and I go with her. The entire human contents of the house, including the puppy, follow us out.

"What did you do?" Marta directs her question to Bernadette. Shanice sits in her wheelchair in front of Marta. Behind her, Lydia and Pam stand with their eyes wide. Kari is also with them, but in true brat form, she looks bored.

"This is a housewarming, Ma'am," Bernadette says to Marta. "I want *all* of my new friends to feel welcomed here."

"Thank you, Miss Bernadette," Shanice says. There are tears in her eyes.

"Give it a try," Bernadette urges.

"Okay." Shanice turns to look at Marta behind her wheelchair.

Marta grabs the chair's handles and turns it toward the newly constructed ramp leading up to Bernadette's porch.

"Wait, Mama," Shanice says. "I want to do it by myself, okay?"

"Go for it, baby girl," Marta says.

"Watch me."

"I'll be right behind in case you get tired."

"I won't."

"Perfect," Bernadette murmurs under her breath.

"What?" I ask her quietly.

"Shanice confided that Miss Marta helps too much. She wants her Domme to see that she can do things."

With a determined face, Shanice maneuvers the wheelchair to the foot of the ramp. She seamlessly wheels herself over the transition from the concrete driveway to the wooden ramp. Marta hovers nervously behind as they make their way up the first leg of the ramp. Despite the gloves, one of Shanice's hands slips, and Marta grabs the chair from behind.

"I have it, Mama," Shanice says quietly, but we all hear it.

A few "awws" go up in the crowd, me included.

Marta lets go and turns to us with a shrug. She dutifully follows behind and looks terrified when Shanice hurls the chair around the turn and speeds up the second leg of the ramp.

The crowd cheers and claps at Shanice's accomplishment, Bernadette the loudest. After Bernadette hugs Shanice, everyone heads back into the house.

There is never a shortage of things to talk about whenever this group gets together. Next weekend's masquerade ball is paramount on everyone's mind, but at one point, I hear someone ask Bernadette how her new summer course is going. I'm impressed that anyone even knew that. Ah, well, our community is small, and everyone seems to know everyone else's business.

Jaleesa sidles up to me as I lean against the kitchen doorframe.

"I'm glad you two figured things out."

I scoff. "You and me both."

"It feels like our family is finally complete," she says, sweeping her hand over the room and everyone in it. "And that Pammy is adorable."

"Lydia's new sub?" I ask. "She is. And who knew she was a *little*. Madison and Shanice are stoked to have another."

"Bailey's back there with them. They are a little confused that a puppy can color, though."

I laugh. "That is a bit confusing, even to me."

"Yeah," she says with a chuckle. Shasti joins our group, and Jaleesa says, "Madison seems okay with Alyssa now, yes?"

"She is," Shasti says. "The other day, Victoria asked if she could bring Alyssa by, and I hesitated but figured it would be good for both of them. They had a good chat. I think Madison will think twice before taking candy from strangers."

Jaleesa and I chuckle, and then Shasti excuses herself to check on Madison. Earlier, there had been a heated disagreement about which movie to put on. Madison wanted *Trolls,* and Shanice wanted *Frozen.* Apparently, Pammy suggested they watch the movie *Up* because it has dogs in it that Bailey might like. Happily, they all agreed on that, but I don't blame Shasti for wanting to check up on them.

Jaleesa nudges me in the arm. "We need to, uh, schedule another evening together. If that's something you two want."

"Yes, I think Bernadette would like that. Sometime after the ball. And let's hold off adding Tina, though. Let their friendship grow first."

"Yes, I agree," Jaleesa says. "Trust must be established. So, what d'ya think? Time for the unveiling?"

"As good a time as any," I say. "Go on up and get ready. I'll bring her up in a few minutes."

I head over to Bernadette and politely extract her from the conversation she's having with Seamus. I lead her to the foot of the stairs and tap a glass with a spoon to get everyone's attention. The conversations die down, and I say, "There is a special gift from Jaleesa and her family to Bernadette. It's upstairs." I feel Bernadette's confusion next to me. "Follow me for the unveiling."

"Rikki?" Bernadette asks. "What's happening?"

"You'll see."

We head up the stairs to the master bedroom, followed by the partygoers. Jaleesa and Tina are standing on one side of the gift. DeShawn, Harriet, Dana, Kari, and Bailey are kneeling on the other. A large sheet covers the gift.

"What is this?" Bernadette says to me. "How did this get in here?"

"When you were playing with the puppy," I tell her. Ahh, the jig is up.

"Sneaky," she says.

"Ready?" Jaleesa asks me, and I nod.

"Bernadette," Jaleesa says, "you've inspired my subs. They wanted to give you something special. DeShawn designed it, and everyone had a hand in it. Harriet painted it. She pulls the sheet off to reveal a large, long box. It spans the width of the king-size bed.

"Wow," Bernadette says. She goes up to it and runs her hand across the top. This is beautiful. "Is this a storage bench?

"Sure," Jaleesa says.

"It's gorgeous," Bernadette gushes. She is true grace. She is one of those people you like to give presents to because she genuinely appreciates anything you do for her. "Harriet, I recognize your artwork. The flowers and vines. Just beautiful. DeShawn and everybody, the craftsmanship is amazing." Her sweeping gaze takes in Jaleesa and all six of her subs. "Thank you all so much." Every single one of them, including Kari, beams at her praise.

Jaleesa opens the top and sweeps her hand through the empty space. "You can store comforters and blankets or sheets in here. All of the sides are mesh, as you can see. This way, you know, anything inside can breathe."

A twitter of laughter goes up behind us. Bernadette turns, and it is clear that she doesn't understand the joke.

Jaleesa closes the top and then makes a show of putting a lock on the outside and locking it with a key. She then hands the key to me.

Bernadette's eyes grow big. Ahh, she gets it now. She covers her mouth with her hand and turns toward me. I hold up the key, taunting her. The crowd "awws" again when Bernadette's face turns pink, her embarrassment clear.

"Thank you, Miss Jaleesa," Bernadette says. "Thanks to your entire family." She turns to the crowd and says, "Thank you for welcoming me into your family. I finally feel—" She stops, obviously choked up. She clears her throat and continues. "I finally feel like I belong somewhere. Thank you all. Thank you so much."

It is an odd place to do so, but everyone comes up to Bernadette one by one, giving their good wishes on her new home. Some of them include me in their good wishes, even though I am not the one living here. It's a bit awkward, but that's okay. This is my girl's day.

Bernadette opens more gifts downstairs, and I have never seen her turn so many shades of pink and purple. Almost all the gifts are sexual in nature. Edible panties, labia spreaders, clit jewelry, spreader bars, a ton of lube, dildos galore, vibrators, a gorgeous deerskin flogger from Seamus, clamps of every description, wax play items, toy cleaner, and more. The soft leather cuffs from

Madison get some awws from the crowd because she said she didn't want Bernadette's scars to hurt. Rowena's low stool is incredibly thoughtful. I had once confided in her that I worried about Bernadette's old "softball knees," as she referred to them.

Although Bernadette is sufficiently embarrassed by all the sex paraphernalia, we have an amazing day with our friends. Bernadette agrees with me when I say that her house has been sufficiently warmed.

Once everyone is gone, Jaleesa hangs back in the house, her family waiting in the van. As previously arranged, she looks at me and asks, "May I?"

"Yes, please," I say.

She lifts Bernadette's chin using a bent knuckle and leans down to kiss her. Bernadette wraps her arms around Jaleesa's neck and moans into her mouth. The kiss heats up until Jaleesa pulls back. Bernadette seemed woozy.

"Knees, please," I say. "In front of Miss Jaleesa."

Jaleesa graciously offers a hand as Bernadette lowers herself down. Bernadette kisses the hand.

"You need to apologize, Bernadette," I say.

"Yes, Ma'am." Her face is already flushed but turns an even darker shade of pink. "Miss Jaleesa, I apologize for being too colloquial with you earlier. I was, uh. I, umm. I have no excuse, Ma'am." She hangs her head.

Jaleesa lifts Bernadette's chin again and says, "I'm glad you recognized your mistake. We are a community, Bernadette. A group of people with specific rules and protocols. When the lines blur, then it gets confusing for everyone. Your Domme and I expect you to be more mindful from now on."

"Yes, Ma'am," she says to Jaleesa and then again to me.

"Domme Rikki," Jaleesa says, "although it is your prerogative, I recommend thirty minutes in the cage."

I nod my understanding.

When Jaleesa leaves, I lock the door behind her and close the curtains. I plop in the oversized chair and pat my lap. Bernadette crawls in, and I cradle her gently. It's amazing how well she fits in my lap. "You do understand that you represent me, right?"

"Mm hmm, Ma'am," she says quietly.

"You will do your time in the cage tomorrow. Understood?"

"Yes, Ma'am."

"Jaleesa has requested another liaison with you. How do you feel about that?"

"I would like that, Ma'am, but only if you're there and participating." She snuggles against me.

"I'll arrange it. Maybe a few weeks after the ball."

"Yes, Ma'am. Thank you."

Bernadette picks at my shirt, removing imaginary lint. She's done this before. She has something on her mind.

"Three strikes?" I ask.

She nods against my chest.

"I'll ask you questions, and if you answer 'no' for three of them, then that's three strikes, and I'm out. Then you have to tell me."

She nods again.

"Let's see," I say. "Are you nervous about anything having to do with Jaleesa?"

She shakes her head.

"Dang it. Strike one." I'm not surprised. I didn't think that was the issue, but Jaleesa was the last one to leave.

"Are you afraid Shanice will give up?"

She shakes her head again.

"Strike two," I warn myself. Hmm. I thought that might be on her mind. Well, it probably is, but something bigger is going on. It can't be her summer course. She's loving it and said her students are very enthusiastic.

"I'm down to my last question. If the answer is no, then you have to tell me."

"Okay," she says softly.

I kiss the top of her head. "Do you have something you want to tell me?" She nods.

"Oh, I got one right, finally."

She squirms a bit.

"Is it something difficult?"

She nods.

"Does it have anything to do with the housewarming today?"

Another nod.

142

It can't be that people didn't wipe their feet. I know that bugged her, but she put it aside and focused on other things. The new human cage at the foot of her bed might be causing her some fear, but she knows we'll talk about it before she goes in tomorrow.

"Upstairs, when people were congratulating you on the house. Did something bother you then?"

She nods.

"I am getting so good at this," I say, hoping she'll smile. She does, but I can tell her angst is still very present. "Is there something you want to discuss with me?"

She nods three times. Oh, okay. This is big. I could totally just give up this game and command her to tell me, but she is vulnerable right now. I've been learning to read her moods, and I'm positive she needs me to continue this soft approach.

"Is it something about this house?" She nods. "And about me in it?" I add quickly.

She doesn't answer but sits up and kisses me. Before it heats up too much, she says, "Rikki, will you move in here with me? Will you? I hate it when you have to leave. It's lonely and makes no sense without you here." She looks down and won't meet my gaze with her own. "I mean," she continues, "you could move out of the apartment. Rent it out or something. Lydia said she and Pammy have no privacy with their current living situations. Maybe Lydia could rent it, and then someone you trust would be at the shop all the time. And then you could be here with me."

"My turn?" I say when she finally stops for air.

"Yes, Ma'am."

"Bernadette Garneau, I would be honored to move in with you."

"You would?" The look of relief on her face melts my heart.

"Yes, but we'll have to talk more about it. We're not just going to be roommates."

"Yes, Ma'am," she says. "I'm so happy, Rikki. I thought maybe you'd want to keep things like they are."

"We're ready for the next step."

"Mm hmm," she says enthusiastically. "And you can finally get your stuff out of Shasti and Madison's basement."

"It would be nice to see my things again. I don't have much, actually. I, uh, had to sell off most of it. But you're right. I'm sure Shasti and Madison would be more than happy to get that space back."

"I have ideas about the shop, Rikki," Bernadette says, her eyes brightening. "But not tonight."

"All right. That sounds fair."

"But I do, err, have ideas about tonight."

"Oh, is that right?" I run my thumb along her lips. She kisses my thumb and then opens her lips slightly. I don't know if it's an invitation, but I slide my thumb inside. She sucks on it, even as I move it in and out. One hand goes to one of her own breasts and squeezes.

"Feeling frisky?"

She moans her reply and reaches down to unbutton her new shorts. Without asking permission, she slides her hand inside. By her undulating hips and her moans, it is clear that she is stroking herself.

"Are you allowed to cum without my permission?"

She shakes her head but doesn't stop stroking. Her legs open slightly wider. She pulls my thumb out of her mouth with her free hand and then pushes two of my fingers in. She fucks her mouth with them in time with her strokes down below. Her breathing gets heavy, but she doesn't once break eye contact. She writhes in my lap. Her breathing changes. This little dickens is going to cum, and I am going to let her. Her pelvis rises. She arches her back. Her hips buck against her working hand, and she goes rigid. She shoves my fingers in her mouth as far as they will go and then explodes. Her entire body shakes in my lap. Her eyes roll back as she cums. She finally quiets down and pulls my fingers out of her mouth.

The room is filled with her natural scent.

She will be punished for this extremely blatant act of defiance, but for now, I push her off my lap, pull my skirt up, and tell her to yank my panties off with her teeth. She does so, growling like Bailey in the backyard.

I move forward on the chair and say, "You know what to do, you bad girl."

Chapter 16
The Next Phase

I wake up in my chair, blinking my eyes to the late Sunday morning sun streaming into my apartment. Where is Bernadette? Oh, right. I fell asleep on her again. It's so easy to do because her foot massages are so soothing. I sit up and rub my eyes to wake up. Packing to move in with Bernadette—that's the order for the day, but where is my girl?

From the office downstairs, I hear Bernadette say, "She's sleeping."

"How are things going?" a strange voice with a southern accent asks. Ahh, this must be the famous Lisa I keep hearing about. I shouldn't listen in. That's not fair, but I'm going to anyway. There is still so much to my little bee that I haven't uncovered, and maybe this unguarded moment will reveal some things to me.

"Lisa," Bernadette says, "life is amazing. She's moving in with me."

A high-pitched squeal erupts from the speakerphone downstairs, and I chuckle. I'm glad my Bernadette has a friend outside of our local community. I get up from the chair quietly and start emptying my dresser drawers and making piles to go in the boxes we'd picked up early this morning on the way over here from her house. Today is day one of packing to move in with my girl. I think we're both ready for this step, but I know I'll miss this apartment.

"Okay, so wait," Lisa asks incredulously. "*After* your housewarming, you two decide to move in together?"

"I know. The timing was off, but I didn't know how to ask her. I mean, I wasn't sure I could take the rejection if she said no."

"I get that," Lisa says. "If you're like me, you rely on your Domme to make decisions for the both of you."

"Yes, that's exactly it," Bernadette says with a sigh. "I'm learning that I need to step up and ask for what I want, too."

"B, that's awesome."

I chuckle when I hear the nickname. Bernadette has known Lisa longer than she's known me. They discovered each other on *Kinks.com*, but they've never met. My wheels start turning, and I wonder if it might just be time for a road trip so Bernadette can finally meet her friend.

"Tell me more about the dungeon," Lisa says, her voice lit with excitement.

Bernadette laughs. "We don't have one yet, but Rikki has it pretty much mapped out in the basement. She's even set up this whole schedule for us to clean and paint. And she wants better flooring down there."

"Oh, is it a dry basement?"

"Mm hmm. She wants the laundry moved up to the second floor, too. That'll make laundry so much easier for me."

"Ahh," Lisa says, "another Domme that doesn't do laundry. I think sometimes that's why they want us subs."

"It's not like that," Bernadette says. Wow, it sounds like she's defending me. "She never required it. I just, you know, wanted to."

"I get that, B. You want to thank her for taking you to those amazing headspaces she takes you to, and this is one way to do it."

"You get it," Bernadette says. "Of course you do. I mean, how do you thank someone for taking such good care of me that I don't have to worry about anything. And, Lisa, the sex. Oh, my God, she knows my body so well. She knows how to edge me until I detonate."

"Aww, B, that's so awesome. I'm so happy for you." Lisa is positively gushing. "So, c'mon, tell me more about this dungeon."

"Oh, yeah," Bernadette says. "There will be a St. Andrew's cross, a spanking bench, and cabinets along one wall for storing her implements of impact. Did you know she wields a whip?"

"Whoa," Lisa says, clearly impressed. "Has she used it on you yet?"

"No," Bernadette says succinctly.

"Why not?"

"She says I'm not ready."

"But you think you are?"

"Yes," Bernadette says.

Ahh, see? She clearly wants this, yet is waiting for me to make the decision. She is *not* ready for all that my whip can bring her. Soon. But not now.

"B, if she thinks you're not ready, then guess what? You're not ready."

"Fine, take her side," Bernadette says with a chuckle, letting her friend know that she is teasing. "I think I want her to have a queening chair."

"Love those. So zen for me," Lisa says. "Laying underneath. Slowly satisfying her until she either cums or yanks me off the floor and throws me on the bed to have her way with me."

"I love that," Bernadette gushes. "Check, one queening chair for certain. She also talked about a fucking machine, but I'm not sure."

"Ever since that whole Daddy Vic thing?"

"Yeah," Bernadette says simply. I hear my office chair squeak as she adjusts her body in it.

Hmm, she is obviously still bothered by that whole Victoria situation. Maybe it's time for another talk with Victoria.

"Oh," Bernadette adds, "Rikki wants to create a bank account with me where we both put equal amounts of money in for household expenses."

"Ahh, so she is definitely not a findomme."

"Not at all. And on the flip side, I do *not* want her to think I am a scab."

Lisa scoffs. "Oh, darlin', even I can tell you're not a sponge. But it sounds like you're doing well under her leadership."

"Oh, yes. I trust her. I trust that she won't ever take me further than I can cope with."

"Which is why she says you're not ready to take the whip."

"Oh, hush," Bernadette says. "Stop making sense."

Lisa laughs, and Bernadette adds, "She makes me feel safe and well cared for. She is teaching me to trust that my body knows what it likes, even when my mind is screaming otherwise. My body likes pain, Lisa. Not extreme, but more than I ever thought possible. I mean, I trust her implicitly. If I didn't, I couldn't let her do those things to me. I used to crash hard and drop after every play session with those fake Dommes. But I don't drop with her, only once in a while."

"Drink lots of water before you play, B. That helps."

"She tells me that, too," Bernadette says. "I just have to listen, I guess. You know, Lisa, when she wraps me in her arms, the whole world fades away.

Sometimes, I get to wear one of her t-shirts. You know, after sex, and it makes me feel like I've crawled inside her. It's so comforting. And she respects me. She actively listens to what I have to say. And even if we have different opinions, like when to change the oil on her old car, she listens and doesn't just discount me. Even continuing to disagree is okay."

"She treats you like an equal," Lisa says. "Rachel and I pretty much have the same agreement."

"I love Rikki so much, Lisa," Bernadette says. "It's kind of scary. And, you know what? Degradation is not really part of her MO. We sometimes play at it, but it's not a regular thing. I don't like it most of the time, but if it's part of playtime, it's okay."

"Same," Lisa says.

"She is calm but firm. She gives me structure, guides me with rules. She pushes my limits and boundaries and has total control. She has expectations of me, and she says I'm strong. But pfft. I don't know about that."

"You are strong," Lisa says. "You couldn't have survived those wanna-be Dommes if you weren't."

I nod my head, thoroughly agreeing with Lisa. I must have made a noise or something because Bernadette says, "I'd better get back upstairs. I think she's awake now."

"Great talking to you, B," Lisa says. "Let's do this more often."

"Absolutely. The next phone call will be all about you. I monopolized this one. Sorry about that."

Lisa scoffs. "Are you kidding? I love hearing about your love life."

"You're sweet," Bernadette says. "Okay, I'll send you a text tomorrow, and we'll pin down a phone date and time."

I hear them say their goodbyes and then hear Bernadette's soft footsteps coming up the stairs.

Wordlessly, I wrap her in my arms and kiss her.

She is smiling big when I release her. "Thank you for that hug, Rikki," she says. "I love your kisses."

"I love yours, too, and I wish we had more time, but we have a busy week, don't we?" I ask, not waiting for an answer. "I need you to put together those boxes. Use the packing tape on the bottom and then pack up all these clothes I've laid out. After that, you can also start on the bathroom stuff, too."

"Yes, Ma'am," she says. Ahh, I've put her in submissive mode. "I'm sorry I wasn't here when you woke up."

"No, no, no, little bee," I say and stroke her cheek. "It is okay. You needed your time with your friend."

"Thank you," she says simply.

I can tell she is genuinely grateful. I pull her into a hug and then kiss her forehead upon releasing her. "I have some work to do downstairs—at least two hours' worth. You are not to come down or interrupt me until at least 1:00 when my work is done. Is that understood?"

She nods and says, "Yes, Ma'am. There is plenty to do up here." She looks around, and I agree with her overwhelmed expression. The apartment may be small, but there is still a lot to pack.

"Good girl," I say and smack her ass. "And why do you have clothes on?"

"Oh, I'm sorry. I went down to the office, and I was nervous about someone coming in from the shop."

"Understandable, but the door is locked."

"Yes, Ma'am." She hangs her head as if I've caught her in a lie. "I will rectify that now." She strips off her clothes and lays them neatly on the chair.

"Better." I stroke her ass, and she sighs softly. "Get to work." I turn away abruptly and head down the stairs.

Knowing Bernadette is handling things upstairs, I can relax and do my work down here. After a quick survey of the Sunday morning activity in the shop, I am satisfied that Mark and Marta have things well in hand and lock myself in my office for the dreaded paperwork, emails, and phone calls. There is the inventory to look over and then the ordering. And let's not forget about payroll. I had to fire my payroll company when I couldn't afford them anymore. I also need to shore up the contract I will be signing with Lydia later this week to rent the apartment. She was ecstatic at my offer and jumped at the opportunity. I want to put in a no candles or open flame clause so that she doesn't accidentally burn down my business. So, unfortunately, that means no wax play or fire cupping for her and Pammy. Lydia and Pammy are on a strict gag rule at this point because I've asked them not to say anything about me moving in with Bernadette yet. It's partly due to my need to control things and partly because I want to savor our little secret for a bit longer.

I work diligently at my tasks and am satisfied with my productivity. If I weren't so paranoid about identity theft, I would give some of these jobs to my assistant managers. But I'm not there yet and may never be. When I finally finish with the must-do list, I am ready to call Miss Dominique. I punch in her number, and it goes right to voicemail. Fine, I probably shouldn't be calling on a Sunday anyway. I look up at the clock Bernadette installed near the stairs—my girl has a thing about clocks. She needs a visible clock in every room. She has her quirks, but so do I, I suppose. It's 12:45, and I have about fifteen more minutes before heading back upstairs. Or maybe I'll summon her down here. Yes, yes. She said she is uncomfortable being nude in my office, so perhaps we'll work on that.

The voicemail asks me to leave a message, and so I do. "Thanks for the donation, Dominique. You are very generous. I'll come around sometime this week and pick up the certificates. If there's a—" I stop mid-sentence when I see movement out of the corner of my eye. Bernadette is sitting at the top of the stairs, looking down at me. I raise my eyebrow and look at the clock again. It's clearly not yet 1:00. "Umm, if there's a good day for me to stop by, let me know, but I'll need them before the ball on Saturday. Thanks." I hang up and raise my eyebrow at my girl. I am not smiling. She drops her gaze.

I sneak a peek at the office door. Yes, it's locked tight. I look back up. Her cheeks are bright pink. Yes, she understands that there are rules, and she has broken one. "Come down here," I say gruffly. "Stand in your spot." She moves quickly and catlike. Her nipples are erect. My girl is excited. "No, your back to me. Bad girls have to look at the cinderblock wall until I'm done working and can figure out your punishment."

She makes a slight noise that I'm not sure how to interpret. She knows I don't mix punishment with play. So perhaps she is regretting pushing my rule this morning. Let's up this ante. "Hands over your head. Palms touching the wall." She complies quickly. "Keep your eyes to the wall. Do not look at me while I work."

She nods once but doesn't speak. I open my emails and sort through the junk, making sure none of the emails are suspicious. I do not doubt that Eileen has started dabbling in cybercrimes. Happily, nothing looks like phishing or causes my gut to question the authenticity. I deal with a late payment notice on a credit card that is not mine and add this to the list I have for my lawyer to pursue. Next, I hit up the postal service website to officially change my address to Bernadette's. Wow, you would think packing my shit upstairs would have made moving in with Bernadette seem official, but actually, changing my address makes me tremble. This is real, isn't it?

I sigh contentedly and sneak a peek at my girl. Her ass is lovely in this light. With her arms raised, the curve of her breast from the side is positively delicious. I love the proportions of her body. She doesn't think so, but she has a beautiful body. Her body and her subservient pose turn me on a little. No, a lot. Mmm, I want to caress her skin. Ahh, but that would be a reward for her, wouldn't it? She turns her head as if feeling my gaze stroking her body.

She smiles at me in direct opposition to the second rule I'd given her this afternoon.

"Are you supposed to be looking at me while I'm working?"

"You're not working."

I raise both of my eyebrows to the sky. I mean, technically, she is correct. I was ogling her body, not working, but still. I made the rule, and she broke it. "You already did thirty minutes in the box this morning. Did you like it that much?"

"No, Ma'am," she says. "I did not."

I power down my laptop and stand up. I walk behind her and rub my fingertips across her bare back and ass. "That's two broken rules now," I say this as if to myself. "What will I do now?"

Bernadette moans in response to my words. I step closer and run both hands around her body, caress her breasts briefly, and then make my way down her torso. I pull her to me, so we are spooning standing up. She lays her head back against my shoulder. She likes being touched gently this way. I reach lower with one hand and feel her core tighten with the other. I dip into her center. "You're wet. Just for me. As always. I love that about you, Bernadette. Never a need for lube here." I stroke her lower lips, grazing her clit now and then. I turn to kiss her neck, and her moans are music to my ears.

I laugh and then push her back up against the wall, instructing her to resume the pose she was in. She groans but does as I ask. "Do not move."

I practically spring up the stairs for the nearest strap-on. Thank goodness she hadn't packed them up yet. I strip down to a t-shirt and panties and grab the harness and a couple of waters. One of them is room

151

temperature.

I know she hears me come back down the stairs, but she doesn't turn. Excellent. That's my good girl. Oh, yes, she will be rewarded. I move my office chair close to her and ask her to turn. Her expression makes my heart leap. She is aroused, yes, but she is also as content as I am. She practically glows with happiness. "My god, you are a beautiful woman," I tell her.

She clamps her lips tighter and tinges pink.

"Take these off me." I lift the band to my panties and let them snap back in place.

She smiles knowingly and races to her knees in front of me. I hold her chin and look deeply into her eyes as she completes her task. She places my panties on the arm of the couch.

I sit in the chair. "I need your lips on me, but only lips. No hands. No other touching. Just your lips and tongue."

She nods as I move to the edge of the chair. She grasps the front chair legs, one in each hand, and moves toward me. I arch my pelvis toward her as she teases me with a kiss. She looks up at me adoringly and then licks my labia agonizingly slowly. "Oh, yes," I say in encouragement. She knows how to please me. I snake my fingers in her hair but do not apply pressure or guide her in any way. She has the reins, but holding her head this way reminds her of who has the power.

I can't help bucking my hips to her rhythm, and she picks up speed. Her tongue darts into me, and she moves her entire face around, covering herself with my wetness. She truly does love giving girl-head. At one point, a hand reaches up, but then she remembers and groans. She wants to finger fuck me and can't. Maybe this is part of her punishment.

I release her head and slide my ass toward her and open my legs wider. "C'mon, baby," I say breathlessly. She pulls her tongue out and then lightly sucks on my clit. The suction increases, and then my thighs slam shut on her head as I cum. "Yes, yes, yes," I screech. She doesn't stop sucking until I push her away. Her satisfied smile makes me chuckle. I moan in bliss for a few moments while she kneels, waiting for further instructions. "Clean me," I finally manage to get out. Her tongue and lips lap up my spendings until I push her away again.

I lean forward and kiss her on the forehead. I give her the room temperature water, and she takes a hefty swig. I do the same with my cold water. I stand up and grab the strap-on. "Put this on me."

She puts the harness on me with a practiced hand and then opens her mouth wide. She knows what's coming. I nod, and without a word, she rakes her hands down my t-shirt and then wraps one arm around my leg for purchase. She swallows my phallus in two pushes. One day, she'll do it in one, but that's *her* goal, not mine. I fuck her throat for several strokes and then pull out. "Go lay on your stomach on the couch. Pussy up and spread open for me." Her gaze doesn't leave mine until she lays down on the couch.

I move in behind her and let the tip of the dildo play around her dripping wet opening. She moans impatiently. I lean down and say in her ear, "You cum when I say you can." She groans, and I laugh out loud at her impatience.

I slowly enter her body. All I can think about is fucking her. Being inside her, having this control while she takes it from me. I push deep, holding her hips. I thrust slowly, getting her used to being occupied. I slide a hand up her spine and then reach around to pinch her nipples. She gasps at the sudden pain and rocks her body back to meet my thrusts. She wants it harder and deeper.

"Mmm," she moans. "Touch my clit, Rikki. Please? I want to cum for you."

"For me?" I laugh. "I'm sure you've got that backward. You want to cum for you."

She nods and continues rocking back against my dildo.

"No, not yet, little bee," I say and tighten my grip on her hips.

Her moans reach a higher pitch. I want us to cum together, and I'm not quite there yet. I reach for her hair, which is so much easier to grab now that it has grown out a little. I pull her head back. I pull her body up toward me using my other hand so her back touches my front. She is breathing hard. Pumping my hips into her, I reach around her body and run my hand down to her clit. I move my fingers in small circles, the way she loves. She exhales in frustrated satisfaction and bucks her hips against my fingers. My other hand holds first one breast and then the other, tweaking each nipple in turn. I push her back down to the couch in order to sink my dildo deep inside.

"Rikki," she says as her entire body tightens.

"Cum, baby. Cum for me, my good girl."

She stops bucking, clamps her hand over her own mouth, and screams her release. One day, I'll tell her the door to the shop is double-insulated, and no one can hear a thing. I get in the perfect rhythm, and the harness hits my clit just right. I moan low as I cum and then drop my weight on her, my phallus still inside. I am so spent I can't hold myself up.

"Rikki," she says, rousing me from a doze. "I can't, um, you're heavy."

"Hmm?" I realize what the problem is and sit up. I pull out of her slowly.

Bernadette swivels on the couch and kisses me deeply. Lips to lips, she says, "Thank you for everything you do for me. You are so attentive and loving, and you take care of me. I can't wait for this next phase of our lives together."

Her words choke me up, so I clear my throat and say, "You take care of me too, little bee. I'm over the moon happy to be moving in with you. But, uh, there is something we do need to address."

"Oh?" She pulls back and hands me my water bottle and then reaches for hers.

"Two punishments."

"Oh," she says dejectedly. "Okay."

"Each punishment will be one-half hour in the new cage. So that's one hour in total. Tomorrow morning, you will get up with me at 4:30 a.m. and go right into the cage—no cell phone, no reading, no touching yourself. Oh, and no sleeping."

Bernadette groans. It's not that she loathes the small confining space. No, she told me this morning that losing time when she could be working or being in service to me aggravates the hell out of her. To be still and useless for that long is truly the perfect punishment for her.

Chapter 17

The Masquerade Ball

I grab our masks from the top of the stack of boxes that we'd moved from my apartment. I still have a few more things to move out, and then all of my worldly possessions will be in Bernadette's house. The house belongs to her, but I fully intend to make it *our* home.

We are both dressed for the ball, but now it is time for Bernadette to lower her pants. She kisses the paddle, and my body surges with power as I strike her ass with it. Her gasps and moans stoke my ego as she gives me her pain. I toss the paddle on the couch and grab the crop. It whistles in the air as I strike her. She jumps and reaches back to soothe herself. I strike the other cheek. She screeches in pain. It is brief but is music to my ears.

"Who do you belong to?" I ask and strike her again.

"You, Mistress," she grunts. "I belong to you."

I strike her one last time to even out the strokes on each cheek.

"That's right," I say and toss the crop next to the paddle. I squat down in front of her and whisper, "And I belong to you, little bee."

"Mmm," she moans. I tell her to get dressed and head to the car.

We arrive at the old firehouse early, and I am more than pleased to see the hired crew ready to receive our Denton Heights community. The caterer and hired servers are from a BDSM group in Cincinnati, so there will be no shock factor for them. We'll pay them, of course, but local groups helping each other out like this is common. Some in our community say our submissives should serve, but Aunt Tilda always insisted that the subs get a night off from serving and have a chance to simply enjoy the evening. And I agree.

Hayley and her submissive husband are taking the tickets near the door while Bernadette and I greet the arrivals as they come into the main room.

Bernadette has been charged with pointing out the changing rooms, the bar, and the numbered tables. And since it was a last-minute addition, she informs people about the silent auction in the back of the demonstration room.

During the week leading up to the ball, we talked about a way to help Marta and Shanice get a wheelchair-accessible van with hand controls, and Bernadette came up with the auction idea to raise money. It was entirely her idea, and she single-handedly called around for donations. Well, okay, I made a few calls, too, and Mistress Dominique was more than happy to donate a few gift certificates for sessions in her dungeon. As for the rest, it seems that no one can resist my beautiful Bernadette.

I rub Bernadette's ass over her tight dress pants as we wait to greet the next group of masquerade ball attendees. She groans when I squeeze. Her feminine masculinity is accented by the perfectly tailored outfit I put together for her. I combined the suit I picked out at Robert's shop with tasteful fetish wear for female subs. She is wearing a dress collar around her neck with a bowtie that hides the D-ring underneath. Trailing down her chest from the D-ring is a stranded leash that looks like a long necktie. It is made from the tails of a flogger, though, and fans out playing peek-a-boo with her cleavage. Her button-down shirt doesn't have many buttons and is open wide in the front, showing much more of her breasts than she would ever do on her own. Her black blazer matches the pants, and how Robert found purple dress shoes to match is beyond me. Even her masquerade mask matches her outfit. She is getting a lot of compliments on her attire, which pleases me greatly.

I also show a lot of skin, and Bernadette's expression when I came down the stairs at the house was priceless. If she'd had her way, we never would have made it to the ball. The bow tie on my halter dress matches hers, as does the color palette. My dress doesn't show any cleavage, but that's okay. I want the attention on my property, on her. This is her maiden voyage, her coming out ball, if you will. My dress is floor-length, but the slits up the sides reveal my hips and ass as I walk. The front panel covers the crucial parts, but one wrong gust of wind will reveal my black lace thong. Ahh, but I love the freedom this dress gives me. I can't wait to feel it move later during my whipping demo. I don't typically wear a lot of makeup, but tonight is an exception. Part of Bernadette's jaw-dropping must have been due to my bright red lipstick and thick mascara. My hair is piled on my head, and loose tendrils fall as they do despite my best efforts.

She cracked me up when she whispered, "Mine" in the living room before we left. Yep, I thought the same thing about her.

"Thank you for coming," Bernadette says to a couple walking into the main room. She blushes when they compliment her ensemble. That's what I love about my girl. She is humble through and through. She truly doesn't know how attractive she is. It almost makes me mad, though, that no one made her feel beautiful throughout her life because she is quite stunning. Her high cheekbones, her ready smile, her engaging blue eyes that tell you everything she's thinking. Well, almost everything. I'm still figuring out a few things about her.

"What?" she says to me. Ahh, she caught me staring.

"Just admiring my girl."

She smiles and reaches for my arm. It's interesting how she touches me for comfort. I like it. She is unique, my little bee.

"Miss Olga," Bernadette gushes and runs forward to hug her coworker. "So glad you could make it."

"We wouldn't miss this," Miss Olga says and tugs on a leash. There is a fox attached to the other end. This is her husband, Doug. She introduces him to Bernadette, but he simply bows without speaking. I guess we'll never know what the fox says, now will we? He is wearing a headpiece with ears and fluffy hair that disappears seamlessly into his collar. He wears no nosepiece but has theatrical makeup on that blends in well. And, yes, he is wearing the requisite foxtail, which Bernadette gushes over. His eyes sparkle. Ahh, yes, leave it to my girl to make everyone feel special. And to think I almost lost her.

The old firehouse is a perfect venue for the ball. The acoustics are good, there is plenty of room, and it is tastefully decorated by Hayley and her team of volunteers in the traditional black and white and red theme. I also like the novelty traffic lights they placed strategically around the room as a subtle, or maybe not-so-subtle, reminder about safe play and safewords. Well played, Hayley. I will add that to my opening speech, the one I am to make with Seamus. I'm not much of a public speaker, which is fine because Seamus is an attention whore and will be an amazing emcee, as usual.

Jaleesa and Tina relieve us at the door. Her family is decked out in black and white tuxedos, some of her subs showing more skin than others, but it is quite clear who they belong to. They have an entire table all to themselves. I'm disappointed to see that Kari looks like she's been dragged out unwillingly. Still, she looks cute in her short shorts and sleeveless tuxedo shirt. Although she is doing better at the coffee shop, there is still a restlessness about her that even Jaleesa hasn't seemed able to tame.

Bernadette goes back to check on the silent auction while I check in with Seamus.

"You look lovely as usual, my lady," he says, always a gentleman.

"You look lovely, too, fine sir." His silk shorts are always the hit of the ball. He and his boys sport light blue silk shorts piped with gaudy white faux fur. He has on a matching long-sleeve shirt, but his boys are wearing suspenders and ties on top. That's it. Where he finds these outfits is beyond me. They must be custom-made.

Seamus and I make our way to the podium as the hired servers ask everyone to find their seats. Bernadette sits bolt upright. Aww, she is nervous for me. She sits next to Shasti. Madison is next to Shanice, who is next to Marta at our table.

As predicted, Seamus hams it up for the crowd and gets them in a good mood. He points out the "fetishes screaming out loud for the world to see" and pokes fun at people he knows can take it. He even mentions my girl, "the first woman to successfully steal our very own Domme Rikki's heart." I nod and feel myself blush. He then introduces me as Bernadette's other half, which is fine by me. I go over the rules and protocols – no sex, which gets some good-natured booing, no nudity, no drugs. I thank each committee member and every single volunteer by name. It is a lengthy list, but I am all about rewarding and recognizing people for hard work and dedication. I compliment the decorations and the stoplight reminders and, lastly remind everyone about the silent auction, cautioning them not to outbid me on anything because I know how to wield a whip. That gets some laughs, but they know that I would actually love to be outbid on everything and say so.

Seamus reminds everyone that the servers will release each table one at a time for the buffet and then says a quasi-prayer, semi-grace, and declares that dinner is served.

"Baby, that was so good," Bernadette gushes when I get back to the table. She leans in and whispers, "I want to have your babies."

I burst out laughing but shake my head when our tablemates ask what was so funny. Bernadette puts her hand on my leg when I sit down.

"Thank you, little bee," I say. "We've kind of honed that act over the years. This is my last spring ball, though."

"Aww," Madison says. "That stinks."

"Nah," I say, looking from her to my Bernadette. "I'm looking forward to having more time to spend with my best girl." I raise my eyes in question, and she nods. Ahh, I have the green light. "We have an announcement," I tell my close friends at the table.

"Oh?" Shasti raises her Mommy Domme eyebrow. I am, however, unaffected by that eyebrow and have one of my own with equal power.

"We're, uh, moving in together."

A cheer goes up at our table. Heads turn toward us. No worries. The word will be all over the hall in moments.

"Yes," Bernadette says, "she's been moving her things in a little at a time."

"That is fantastic, Boss," Marta says.

Madison and Shanice are doing happy dances in their seats. *Littles* are so animated and cute, and the world is so much better with them in it.

"What about the apartment?" Shasti asks.

"Lydia did backflips when I offered to rent it to her," I say. "She's moving in on Tuesday."

"Is tomorrow, like, your official moving-in day?" Madison asks.

"Yep, it's our four-month anniversary tomorrow, so it just seems fitting."

"Isn't that poetic?" Bernadette gushes.

"Aww," Shanice says. "It really is. I'm so happy for you guys."

I lean over Bernadette to say to Shasti, "We'll be by sometime tomorrow to get my boxes."

"Sounds good," Shasti says. "Give us a heads up before you come over so that I can let someone out of her cage." Apparently, Jaleesa and her crew made a similar storage bench slash cage for Madison. Jaleesa said it was a reward for doing so well in school.

One of the servers approaches our table and says we are good to head to the buffet. Once seated again, we enjoy our meals and desserts. And, yes, all the subs and all the *littles* are allowed to have dessert. Dessert rules are traditionally suspended during community parties.

Soft music plays in the background as we eat, but soon enough, the DJ announces that demonstrations will begin in a few minutes in the back hall. She successfully changes the mood by putting on some upbeat dance music. The floor is filled almost instantly.

"You'll be fine," I say to Bernadette. I can feel her nervousness. "Do you want to go back and check your setup?"

"Oh, please, yes." She sounds so relieved that I have to laugh.

We excuse ourselves and head to the other room. Everything is as she left it.

"You get ready," I tell her, "and I'll check in on the silent auction."

"Thank you, Rikki."

I blow her an air kiss and walk away. I leave her on purpose so she can find her own inner strength. She teaches for a living, but I know that this will be vastly different. These people are becoming her family, and she doesn't want to "mess up" in front of them, as she called it earlier. She won't.

When I get back, her volunteer is already seated before her, and a small crowd has gathered. Bernadette sits on the low stool that Rowena had given her as a housewarming gift.

"There are certain techniques you can use when giving a foot massage," Bernadette says to the audience. I hear the nervous lilt in her voice, but I'm confident she will settle in quickly. "You can place your partner's feet on a hassock or stool or even on the edge of the bed. I prefer a more personal approach and like to place her feet on my thigh like this."

Bernadette looks up at Jaleesa and silently asks permission to touch her. Jaleesa nods and grins like the Cheshire cat. Bernadette returns the grin, but her cheeks turn pink. It is an open secret that my girl is smitten with Jaleesa, and I am okay with that. Bernadette knows who her Domme is, just as Jaleesa knows.

Bernadette places one of Jaleesa's feet on her thigh and begins rubbing down her calves.

"You have a great view, Bernadette," one of Seamus's subs calls to her.

Everyone chuckles, including Bernadette. She lowers her head and closes her eyes, embarrassed. Her position has her sitting between Jaleesa's open legs. She clears her throat dramatically for his benefit and then reaches for a bottle of oil. "You'll, uh, want to use a massaging oil or a favorite lotion, but I recommend you don't use strong fragrances. Keep it natural." She pours a small amount into her hand and explains how she wants to warm up her partner by slowly massaging Jaleesa's calf.

"Next, use a long pulling technique on the top of the foot. Cup your hands on either side with your thumbs on top and fingers on the bottom. Run your hands up and press along her sole. Gently. You're relaxing the foot and relaxing your partner."

I have to admit, watching my girl touch Jaleesa so intimately is turning me on. And, yes, I have to admit that I am human, and a tiny kernel of jealousy has settled somewhere inside. I let it sit there but refuse to let it grow.

"And now," Bernadette says, "this is called a stripping technique."

"Take it off, Bernadette," a male voice calls. I didn't see who, but Bernadette simply chuckles. I'm glad my girl is a good sport.

"Using your thumbs," she continues like a champion, "start at the top of the foot near the toes and glide up with slight pressure to the top of the ankle. The top of the foot is sensitive. There are a lot of bones here, so go easy." She demonstrates the technique as she speaks. "Move on either side of the foot, covering the whole area."

"How ya feeling there, Jaleesa?" Rowena asks suggestively.

"Like my entire family is going to take lessons from Bernadette starting tonight." A good-natured laugh goes around the crowd.

Bernadette nods at Jaleesa, indicating that she would be honored to do so.

"Now it's time for the toes. A little pinching and kneading. Not too hard now. You don't want your Domme's foot to fly up in your face suddenly. Unless that's your kink, then have at it."

The crowd laughs, and someone says quietly, "That Bernadette is delightful." Someone else says, "It's about time Rikki found an equal partner." I'm not sure if the two realize that I'm standing right here within earshot, but I pretend I didn't hear them.

"You may discover some ticklish spots you hadn't found before," Bernadette continues. "Please use this to your advantage for all those times she edged you for too long or, heaven forbid, denied your release."

The subs in the crowd clap loudly.

"Using a good firm pressure will avoid those ticklish spots. Massage the top, bottom, and sides of each toe. She will be putty in your hands. Next, glide the knuckles up and down the bottom of the feet. Dig into the arch, but always check in with your Dominant to make sure she's okay and not in any discomfort. Who knows, she may want more pressure. And Dommes, don't forget that you can safeword out at any time."

Jaleesa bursts out laughing, as do most of the other Dominants. "As if," she says.

"Is that a challenge, Miss Jaleesa?" Bernadette asks. The teasing expression on her face is priceless.

"Err, not tonight," Jaleesa says, wimping out.

"I thought so." Bernadette scrunches her face in a wordless cringe, apologizing to the Dominant whose foot she is holding.

"You're a good girl, Bernadette," Jaleesa says. "Who's your Domme?"

"Domme Rikki Carmichael."

"Your Domme is a fortunate woman."

Many hands clap me good-naturedly on my bare back.

Bernadette doesn't miss a beat in her demonstration. "Next, squeeze the foot from the sides, use a twisting motion with the thumbs underneath, gliding side to side. Finish off with the pulling technique we began with. Use more oil or lotion if you need to."

"Lube it up, people," Seamus calls from the back, causing a ripple of laughter.

"Repeat for the other foot, and then your Domme will either fall asleep or throw you down and have her way with you. Both have happened to me." Now, it is my turn to burst out laughing. Both are true.

As previously arranged, Jaleesa's sub, Dana, takes over and does the other foot while Victoria sits in the other chair with Alyssa in front of her. Bernadette asked my permission to invite Victoria to be part of the demonstration. She told me she thought it would be good for people to see that everything is okay between them. And, she added, it would also be good for people to see Alyssa's humanity and get to know her as well. The olive branches floored me. She has such a big heart. I called Victoria myself.

After two more D/s pairs get tutelage from Bernadette, I finally shut it down. There are many other demonstrations that people should see. I tell the crowd that Bernadette will be available by appointment for personalized instruction. Donations would go toward Shanice's wheelchair-accessible van.

Shasti comes up to us afterward and congratulates Bernadette on a wonderful presentation. "I now have proof positive that you are an amazing teacher, Bernadette."

"Thank you, Miss," Bernadette says humbly and then begins to clean up.

"I think I will be adding 'massage my feet' to Madison's daily chore list."

"Only if you're going to throw me down and ravage me like you did on the dining room table this morning," Madison says seriously.

Shasti grimaces. "No filter. None whatsoever."

Poor Shasti.

Madison tugs on Shasti's sleeve. "Mama, can we go look at the knives now?"

"'Mama?'" I ask. "This is new."

Shasti smiles as she nods. No, she's not smiling—she is beaming. She has been waiting for Madison to call her that for years. She turns her attention to Madison. "Yes, yes, sunshine. Let's go."

"Yaaaaay." Madison puts her arms out to her sides like an airplane and flies toward the gathering knife crowd.

Shasti shakes her head and then touches Bernadette lightly on the arm. "You were great, Bernadette." She heads off after her charge.

"You are a woman of many talents," Miss Olga says to Bernadette, who had begun cleaning up.

"Thank you, Miss Olga," Bernadette says. "I had to teach myself. Thank goodness for YouTube videos."

"She wanted to learn for me," I add and wrap my arm around her. "I never requested or required it."

"Good heart, this one," Miss Olga says, pointing to Bernadette. "Well, I must get back to my fox. The puppies and kitties sometimes pick fights with him, so I need to supervise. He stares at them. He brings it on himself."

"Good luck, Miss Olga," Bernadette says.

Jaleesa and Dana walk up arm in arm. It's nice to see Jaleesa's sub looking so happy. "Thank you, Miss Bernadette," Dana says. Jaleesa winks at her. Ahh, apparently, a certain sub had to be reminded to say thank you.

"Thank you, Bernadette," Jaleesa echoes. "I think someone is going to get thrown down and ravished when we get home." She squeezes Dana, who beams her love right back to her Dominant.

We walk around the hall, checking out some of the other demonstrations that are going on. The bootblacking demo has grabbed the attention of many of the leather folk. The knife experts are popular with the sadists. I only have a passing interest in that, so instead, we head over to support Tina and Harriet's demonstration about household management.

Bernadette whispers to me, "Doesn't Tina get jealous of Jaleesa, you know, being with other people?"

I shake my head.

"I'm being nosy. It's none of my business. I'm sorry, Ma'am."

"Oh, no, no. It's not that," I say quietly, making sure no one can overhear our conversation. "Tina encourages Jaleesa. Tina is an ace. A romantic asexual."

Bernadette looks stunned by this revelation. "Don't be so surprised, little bee. Asexuality is a thing and is highly prevalent in BDSM relationships."

"Oh," she says, but I can tell she wants to know more. That's my little bee, always inquisitive.

"From what I understand," I say, "asexuality is different for everyone. Tina explained it to me this way. She wants a romantic and bonding relationship with Jaleesa, but she has no sexual desire for her or anyone else."

"But didn't you tell me that you and Jaleesa and Tina had a threesome?"

I nod. "Tina enjoys giving others pleasure, Bernadette. She is very generous with her body, but she does not experience sexual arousal. She never has, she told me."

"She's never had an orgasm?" Bernadette whispers into her hand, but I hear it.

"Oh, she has. Jaleesa makes her masturbate with a vibrator to achieve self-release regularly as part of a self-care routine. And before you ask, the nerve endings are stimulated to orgasm."

"Wow." Bernadette seems to be focusing on the demonstration in front of us, but I can tell that her wheels are turning. "I have so many questions."

"Which you should probably ask Tina."

"Are you sure it was okay for you to tell me this?"

"It's not a secret. And, just so you know, Jaleesa gave me the green light at your housewarming party to tell you should you ever ask."

"That should have been *our* housewarming party."

"No worries, little bee." I wrap my arm around her waist. "Five secluded acres? I foresee many parties in our future."

"Good."

"And now, the way I see it, we have just enough time for a dance or two, and then I'll have to get ready for my whipping demonstration."

"I cannot wait," Bernadette gushes. "One day, when I work up to it, will you whip me?"

"It would be my pleasure, sweetie."

"And mine," she adds.

"Oh, we'll see about that," I say with a wink.

Chapter 18
Whipped!

The first Saturdays of every month are so much more special now that Bernadette is mine. Our monthly women's community brunches keep us bonded and up-to-date on each other's lives.

"More coffee, hun?" the waitress Marlene asks me.

"Yes, please. Thank you."

She refills my cup and then gestures over to Bernadette's cup. I nod, and she refills it. I don't think Marlene has ever been told explicitly what our group in the private backroom is all about, but she is intuitive and seems to have picked up on our protocols. It's not that Marlene couldn't get Bernadette's attention to ask about the coffee because she could have. No, Marlene instinctively understands that I am the one who makes decisions when it comes to Bernadette. I believe Marlene has all the couples figured out as far as our D/s relationships go. And, yes, Marlene gets tipped well by each of us because of her accepting approach. Today's group is wonderfully large and includes Shasti and Madison, Marta and Shanice, Victoria and Alyssa, Jaleesa and Tina, Rowena and Minjung, and finally Lydia and newcomer Pammy.

"Thank you, Marlene," Bernadette says with a smile. See? Bernadette was well aware of her favorite waitress nearby.

"You're welcome, Professor."

"So," Bernadette says, continuing her conversation with Pammy, whom I suspect Lydia purposely sat next to Bernadette, "you will eventually come to understand that our submission to our Dommes is a gift to them. Miss Lydia knows this. Miss Rikki knows this, too. They all do. But they also know this gift of ours is not all-encompassing. If something doesn't sit right with you, Pammy, please voice it to Domme Lydia. Before Miss Rikki owned me, I hadn't learned that lesson." She shows Pammy the scars on her wrists. Pammy frowns and reaches out to touch them. Bernadette wears them now like a badge of honor.

"I'm sorry that happened to you, Miss Bernadette," Pammy says. "Miss Lydia is always talking to me about honesty and trust and stuff. I will try to remember."

"Are you two all moved in?" Bernadette asks, the lecture over.

Pammy melts. "Oh, yes. It's wonderful. I mean, I still kind of live at home with my parents but spend most of my nights with Miss Lydia."

"The apartment came with its own St. Andrew's cross," Lydia interjects. "Imagine that."

Bernadette and I both laugh and then Bernadette says, "I'm well acquainted with it." She pats Pammy's forearm.

Jaleesa clears her throat and says, "Can I get some opinions, please?" Once the side conversations die down, she says, "I need help with Kari. I don't think she's happy."

Tina puts a comforting arm around her Domme.

"If I may," I say. "As her employer, she responds well to praise, but it's almost like she doesn't believe the praise. She's cautious. Maybe something in her past? She's a brat, that's for sure, but doesn't act like the classic brat." I shrug. "All I know is that she seems to need attention but doesn't like it when she gets it. This is one brat I have not been able to tame."

"Me, neither," Jaleesa says.

Bernadette makes a small noise next to me, and I know she wants to say something but is afraid to.

"Bernadette," I say, "do you have something to add?"

"Yes. Umm, well, I'm going to disagree, if that's okay." She pauses as if asking permission to disagree.

Jaleesa nods and gestures for her to continue.

"I don't think Kari is a brat," Bernadette says.

"No?" Jaleesa says.

"No. Well, I mean, some of her behavior is bratty, but I think it's a matter of trust," Bernadette says. "I'm not sure what her past is, but if you keep things consistent and steady when interacting with her, she'll know where the boundaries are. She'll come around. I think. Maybe. I don't know."

"You have good instincts," Jaleesa says, and Bernadette's cheeks pink up as if on cue.

"Also," Bernadette continues, "have you considered that she might be a *little*?"

"I had not," Jaleesa says.

"Baby," Tina says excitedly, "she has that Powerpuff Girls keychain. Maybe we can try to reach her that way."

Madison, in true *little* form, raises her hand.

Jaleesa chuckles and says, "Yes, bucko?"

"Kari is a *middle*, Miss Jaleesa. Around, hmm, fifteen or sixteen."

Tina gasps. "She's a teenager. Oh, my gosh. A twenty-five-year-old teenager."

"That's what we've been missing," Jaleesa says, her wheels clearly turning. "We've been forcing her to act grown up when she's not quite ready." Jaleesa grimaces. Thanks, you guys. I think we'll try to reach her with that angle. And I will get to know her past a bit better. I was running out of options."

Madison raises her hand again, and Jaleesa calls on her as if they are in class. Bernadette chuckles quietly beside me. Madison truly amuses her. She amuses all of us.

"Video games would be good," Madison says. "Not coloring books or crayons—that's for babies. Maybe a sketch pad and colored pencils or fancy markers. Nail polish."

Shanice raises her hand, and Jaleesa calls on her. "Trips to the mall, definitely. Oh, oh, oh. A journal. Yes, a private lockable journal."

"And maybe a safe with a combo lock to keep her exceptionally private things private," Madison adds.

"Brilliant, you two," Jaleesa says. "I didn't know you knew so much about *middles*."

Both Madison and Shanice shrug and exchange a glance.

"I think Madison may be moving into the *middle's* stage," Shasti says.

Madison hides her face in Shasti's shoulder.

"Aww," everyone says, even Pammy.

Shasti pats her *little* on the head and then gestures to the rest of us that she's not quite sure what's going on with her.

Once it's clear that the Kari conversation is finished, Bernadette says, "Um, can I ask for help from everyone?"

Following a general murmur of assent, Bernadette says, "Um," again and quickly gathers her thoughts. Public speaking is still not her favorite thing to do, but she gets over it quickly when she is passionate about something. "First of all, I have Rikki's blessing to talk this over with you. The shop needs new HVAC and coffee equipment and some general updating. You all know about the hardship Rikki's had ever since, well, you know. I have ideas to help and would love to hear yours.

"For one thing, I think we should find local pee wee baseball, softball, and soccer leagues to come in after games. They can have pizzas or whatever delivered there, and we can sell them drinks and desserts. When I was a kid—"

"You're still a kid," Jaleesa interrupts, causing everyone to laugh.

"Thank you, Ma'am," Bernadette says with a laugh. Her pink cheeks are so adorable. "Umm, in my younger days," she amends, "my coaches always had trouble finding a place where we could go after games. I don't know. We could try it and see what happens."

"I love that idea," Shasti says. "I'm sure Rikki's staff will be able to handle it, but maybe some of us can be on hand to help out."

"Thank you," Bernadette and I say at the same time.

"Oh, no," Jaleesa says dramatically. "They're clones now."

We are a jovial bunch, and I love that we are still having a good time even though my public humiliation is being laid out in front of everyone. Bernadette has given me many a pep talk about gracefully asking for and receiving help. Funny how she is the one with the microphone and not me. Somehow, it's okay and actually might be better received.

"The grownups might purchase coffee," Victoria offers. "There are a lot of coffee addicts out there." Everyone with coffee raises her cup in agreement.

"Perfect," Bernadette says. "We can invite groups outside of our community to use the dartboards. You know, vanilla darts? Charge them a nominal fee that will go to the shop, but also have 50-50 raffles to raise money for Shanice's van."

"And I thought Madison had energy to burn," Shasti says with a shake of her head, causing everyone to chuckle.

Bernadette continues, "I'm not sure if any of you knew this, but Rikki owns the empty lot next to the shop."

"You do?" Marta asks. Her expression is one of bewilderment.

"Yeah," I say sheepishly. "I figured the city was just going to take it from me, so I never told anyone. Bernadette accidentally found out by checking the public property records."

"I am not letting the city take it," Bernadette says, setting her mouth firm. "I'll buy it myself first. I want to get it paved and painted for a parking lot. Better parking means more convenience to customers, and it means a dedicated handicapped spot for Marta and Shanice."

I think everyone at the extended table melts at her amazing soul.

"We'll see if the city will let us charge for parking on a regular basis," Bernadette continues. "You know, parking meters like they have in the street, but the shop keeps the money. If not, they will hopefully let us charge for parking on Denton Heights festival days."

"Like ten dollars to park for the day," Lydia says. "I'll stand out there myself."

"A lot of visits to the city offices will have to happen, I imagine," I say and then realize I'm putting a damper on the enthusiasm. "But we'll figure it out, right?"

"Exactly," everyone says in one way or another.

"We're going to beat this," Jaleesa says. "No one messes with Domme Rikki and gets away with it."

I can't help thinking that is indeed what Eileen has done.

Despite the airing of my dirty laundry, it's an uplifting brunch, and I am grateful for my girl's enthusiasm and my friends' support. I never in a million years would have imagined such an outpouring of love and care.

~~~

"Mail should be here," Bernadette says and pulls her hybrid up to the mailbox. She uses her key to unlock it and then pulls out the mail. She hands it to me, and I see a bunch of it has the mail-forwarding stickers on it. I cringe when I see a letter from my lawyer. Now what? I decide it can wait and toss it in the mail bin once we get inside. I'll read it later, or maybe never. It's probably just another bill, even though there has been little progress finding Eileen or recovering the money she stole from me. But I am confident that all of my girl's ideas will help save the shop. Maybe Eileen doesn't get to win after all.

"Go get freshened up," I say to Bernadette as she hangs up her keys. Her soft, contented sigh fills my heart.

"Yes, Ma'am," she says, turning toward me. "Shall I come down clothed or un?

"Un. Bring your play collar."

"Yes, Ma'am." She heads up the stairs. She is not quite in submissive mode yet, nor am I in full Domme mode, but I will send us both there swiftly. Bernadette may be submissive by nature, but she is not passive.

While she is upstairs, I use the half-bath down here to freshen up as well. I grab a couple of condoms from the drawer and put them in my pocket. A plan is forming in my mind of what I want to do with my little bee this afternoon. During the week, we both work long and focused hours, so weekends are becoming sacred.

We have christened almost every room in the house. Actually, the dedicated *littles'* room here on the first floor is the only one left. The detached garage will be after that, and then I'll have to get creative when we make love outside on her beautiful five acres. Maybe one day this summer, I'll tie her to a tree and leave her there while I have coffee on the back porch where she can see me. Ahh, my long whip would be perfect out back. But not today.

As she walks down the stairs, I lecherously admire her beautiful naked body. She moves in front of me, bows her head, and offers me the play collar using both hands. It is a gesture of submission and also one of invitation. She is inviting me to use her body for my pleasure. And I will. I take off her day collar. She has several now in different colors and patterns, and I buckle on the sturdier leather play collar. She purrs. I think it is one of the rituals that puts her into submission. I know for a fact that the sternness of my voice is another.

"Wash our morning coffee cups," I command her.

"Yes, Ma'am." She heads to the kitchen, and I admire her ass as she leaves. Her bare feet make little sound on the hardwood floors.

From the living room, I listen to the running water and the clinking cups.

I stand and quietly make my way behind her. I press my front against her back and use my left hand to grip the back of her neck under her hair. She inhales quickly. This arouses her. Good. I like to assert my Dominance this way. It's subtle but effective. My right hand snakes around her side and strokes her belly, her breasts, her thighs. I release her neck, and her head falls back against my shoulder. I reach around using my left hand and run my thumb over her left nipple. I pinch the hardening nipple between my thumb and forefinger. She arches against me. *Yes, yes, that hurts, doesn't it, Bernadette?* My sadist has come out to play.

I circle my right hand against her stomach and then move lower. She tilts her pelvis toward my hand. *Your greedy little pussy wants attention, doesn't it?* Fine. I dip my middle finger through her folds and discover that she is wet. I don't require her to be wet 24/7, but she often is.

"Mmm," I purr in her ear softly. I want her to know that her wet state pleases me. I kiss her neck, and she shudders. She moans when I suck on her earlobe. Lovely.

I bring my middle finger up and over her growing clit. It hardens as I touch it. I stroke her until she squirms, and then I smack her hard on the ass, leaving a blossoming pink handprint.

"Go get Rocky," I tell her. "And the harness."

"Yes, Ma'am," she says enthusiastically.

I love how she looks over her shoulder to see if I've left a handprint. She smirks when she sees the bright pink mark, and she knows that I see her smirk.

She comes back with the biggest dildo we own. "Put it on me." She goes to her knees and straps on the harness and then inserts the dildo into the base. She adjusts the straps, checking in with me to make sure I am satisfied with the fit. I nod. I hand her a condom and say, "Rocky was a gift from Victoria and Alyssa. You will be sure to thank them at some point."

"Yes, of course, Ma'am." She opens the condom with her teeth and places it in her mouth. She gets the condom on about three inches or so and stops. I push her head away and roll it the rest of the way on. I know she wants to deepthroat Rocky, but I won't allow it. It's too big, and I do not want my property damaged.

"You are my plaything," I say to her, "and I am going to fuck you now."

She nods her agreement. Good. I know I already had her consent, the collar tells me that, but sometimes it's good to double-check.

I grab her by the hair and pull her to her feet. I march her over to the kitchen table and throw her toward it. "Bend over it." She places her hips against the table and holds on to the edges. Normally, I might place a towel or padding against the hard edge of the table so she doesn't bruise. Not today. She looks back at me over her shoulder. Her subtle smile tells me that she knows and understands that I am recreating her first-ever orgasm with her first-ever Domme—the infamous Mistress Ciara from Columbus. Yes, yes, it's time to replace that memory.

"Open," I say, and she reaches back to present herself to me. "Lovely." She has done an excellent job grooming today.

I run the tip of the monster through her wet labia, coating the tip. She sighs in anticipation. I place the tip at the entrance to her vagina and push in an inch. She adjusts herself underneath me. I pull out and push in again, steadily.

"Mmm," she moans. "So big, Ma'am." Ahh, she is heading into submissive land. Good.

"Grab the table." She lets her ass cheeks go and reaches up to hold on to the sides of the table. I grab her hips and push almost the entire length into her. Her legs open wider as if this will help her accommodate the massive girth. The lifelike veins and ribbing are scraping along her inner walls and g-spot as I pull out slowly and then thrust back in.

"Oh, God," she says. Wow, she's in pre-orgasm already. "Ma'am?"

I don't respond to her unasked question. I thrust in and out at a steady pace. As her body opens up, I finally bottom out, and she's taken the entire monstrous dildo inside her. I feel it bump against her cervix, and she cries out every time. "Don't cum," I say finally in answer to her question. I know she will anyway.

Her pussy squeezes the dildo, and I know she is having pre-orgasm spasms. "Don't cum," I say again.

"Ma'am," she says, her voice full of angst. Yeah, she's going to blow, but this is the game right now.

I pull her back toward my thrusting hips to maximize the sensations.

She screeches her orgasm and thrashes against the table. Her body shakes uncontrollably, and I wait until the intensity settles slightly before slowing down. I raise my hand and smack her ass three times in quick succession.

"How dare you defy me." I am not an actor, nor do I pretend to be one, but I think I made it sound authentic. "Get up."

She stands and is about to get on her knees, but I have other ideas. "Get the biggest butt plug and the lube. And the cuffs."

She is breathing hard and doesn't move quickly enough, so I get in her face and say, "Now." She moves like the devil is chasing her.

I pop the dildo out of the harness and toss it near the sink. Bernadette will wash it later. I keep the harness on, turn one of the kitchen chairs around, and sit in it. I pat my lap when she gets back. She drapes herself over me, and I adjust her so she is balanced. "Hands," I say simply. I hold her, and we rebalance once she successfully gets her hands behind her back. I put on the soft cuffs and remind her that Madison got her the cuffs, and she will be thanking her after we've used them.

"Why are you getting this punishment?"

"I came without permission," she says. She understands that I don't normally use impact as punishment, but we're recreating her experience in Columbus and that Domme did.

"Yes," I say. "Your white cunt spasmed out all on its own, disobeying my direct order. Now count." I smack her right cheek where my previous handprint is and reinforce it.

"Ow," she says first and then quickly adds, "One." Smack, smack, smack. "Two, three, four."

I smooth out the redness. Her ass must be burning. Although a spanking is a rather vanilla activity, it still hurts. I alternate cheeks, and she keeps up wonderfully. When we get to thirty, I stop and undo her cuffs. "Open." She arches up so she can reach her ass cheeks. She separates them. I use a liberal amount of lube on her rosebud and on the plug itself. We are going big today. Go big or go home, I always say.

I press it in, and she grunts. *Yes, I know. It's big. But you like to be filled, don't you?* I press gently, and the tip goes in. I pull out, and she groans her disapproval. I smack her burning ass, and she grunts. She opens her cheeks wider for me. Good girl. I press on and gain a bit more. I repeat this process until I have her hole opened as wide as it will go. She whimpers a bit. *I know, I know. It hurts.* I take pity on her and push the plug all the way in. She groans in relief. "Release." She lets her cheeks go and then puts her hand on the floor to hold her own weight.

"Living room. Stool." She gets off my lap, and I smack her one more time as she goes. Her ass has pinked up nicely. No, actually, it's more than pink. It's bright red.

I take a moment to get a couple of water bottles from the fridge. I lean on the kitchen doorframe and admire my exquisite submissive sitting on her low stool. Her eyes are down, and her palms are up, showing me she is open to and respects my Dominance. I hand her water, and we both take a silent moment to hydrate. There is always room for humanity in D/s.

Normally, I would tell my sub to get something for me, but I know what I want, so I open the toy drawer in the hutch beneath the television. You never know when a play session will erupt, so we keep supplies conveniently stashed all around the house. I grab a crop and one other item. I leave the drawer open because I know I will need something else.

I show her the crop. She inhales sharply enough for me to hear. Good. Anticipation is an incredible aphrodisiac. It is for me, too.

"Stand, please."

Once she does, I tap the crop lightly along her ass and the backs of her legs. I move up and tap her back and shoulders. It's light, not meant to hurt, just meant to make her aware of my presence and my power. I move to the front and tap her breasts. Okay, I may have put a bit more oomph when I tap her nipples, but I like hard nipples. I tap her thighs and then use my crop to silently request she spread her legs.

"Present your clit, please," I say simply.

She moans. It is a short exhale of breath. It is quick but very telling.

It is a lovely clit. Oh, yes, my girl is still aroused. I pull the clamps from my pants pocket. Her breathing increases. She continues to present her clit to me, but I ignore it for now. I flick the crop at her nipples again, hardening them and sending her little jolts of pain. It is my message to her that I am in charge of her body and will do what I wish.

I open one of the clamps wide and then let it snap closed on her erect nipple. Her body writhes as she groans through the pain. I let her feel it and then do the same to the other nipple. The pain is traveling to her sex. I can tell because she arches her pelvis toward me slightly. Again, she isn't entirely conscious that she does this, but I know that she does. Interpreting silent signals is the key to caring Dominance.

I tug on the ornate silver chain connecting the clamps, and she writhes again. She licks back a bit of drool. She thinks I don't notice, but I do. Ahh, yes, she will be hitting subspace today. She's probably halfway there already.

The third clamp now dangles between the other two but down between her legs. She knows where it is going. I dip my fingers in her center and coat her clit while keeping eye contact. She continues to present herself to me until I push her fingers aside and swiftly attach the clamp directly to her clit. Her body shakes as she groans. Her body flushes. I wait while she pulls in the pain. She lifts her head, which tells me she is now available and ready for more.

"The jewelry I've just put on you was a gift from Jaleesa. She wants you used to wearing it when she comes in a few weeks."

"You set a date, Ma'am?"

"Mm hmm." I know she wants to know when, but I am not going to tell her. Her anticipation will be part of the fun.

I pull up gently on the chain connected to her clit, and she groans. It is a curious mixture of pain and arousal. I like it. Thank you, Jaleesa.

"I want to hurt you, Bernadette." No, that sounds wrong to my ears, so I amend it. "I want to hurt your body, not *you*. I want nothing in this world to hurt you." I lean in and kiss her. Before it heats up, I pull back and add, "I want to hear you cry out the way Mark did when I whipped him at the ball." I run the crop over her body and move to stand behind her. I smack the crop against the meat of her ass.

She squirms minutely away from me. I smack her again.

"The audience liked when I coiled the bullwhip behind me, brought it over my head, and then snapped it at Mark. He jumped when the tail connected with his back. He yelled, didn't he?"

She is quiet, probably anticipating the next crop strike.

"Didn't he?" I ask again, punctuating my question with three quick strikes from the crop on the backs of her legs.

"Yes, Ma'am. Yes." Tears are building in her eyes.

"If you can't take these minuscule strikes, how are you going to stand my whip?"

She swallows back her tears and says, "I will try, Ma'am." And now she knows what else I have in store for her this fine Saturday afternoon.

"That's all I can ask." I circle her again. I whack her inner thighs, and her knees buckle slightly. I should have this girl bound to the wall—we installed braces for that purpose, but today, I feel like making her struggle a little. I get a power surge from it. Her submission and willingness to feed my desires make me feel alive, exceptionally alive.

I snap the crop, enjoying the thwack it makes against her skin. I enjoy her cries more. I grace her ass, legs, back, and breasts. I make sure to smack the end of the butt plug to remind her it's in there.

I switch out the crop for the geometric shapes stingers. They were a gift from Shasti. My girl loves them, but wow, do they sting. The plastic shapes are about a centimeter across and are attached to a bendable metal rod. I pull the rod back and then let it fly against her skin. A wonderful circle appears on her fiery red ass. I fill her back and ass with circles, squares, and triangles. The star seems to hurt the most, so I use that one on her inner thighs while making her watch.

"Shasti uses these on Madison," I remind her. "What's good for your student is good for her teacher, don't you think?" I don't give her time to answer as I strike her repeatedly with the stars. Oh, her thighs are turning a lovely shade of decorated red.

She can't help her grunts. That's okay. We're on five acres, and no one can hear her.

I hit the fleshy part of her mons three times and stop to rake my fingernails over her red and throbbing flesh. She has no ball gag, yet she is drooling anyway. "That high you have right now, Bernadette? I gave you that. Feel it." I tug on the nipple clamps, and she yelps. She wasn't expecting it. I laugh. I could get out the satin cloths or my faux rabbit furs to cool her aching flesh, but I don't. I am not interested in that right now.

"Look at me," I command.

She does. Her eyes have glazed over. Oh, yes, she has reached subspace. When her eyes finally semi-focus on mine, another emotion takes over. Her mouth opens slightly, and she chews on her bottom lip.

"Please, Ma'am," she whispers. "Can you? Will you? Oh, God, please fuck me."

I laugh. "I doubt that's on God's agenda for today."

"Ma'am," she groans the word.

I grab her chin and squeeze it in my hand. I lean in and kiss her hard. She slams her arms around me and kisses me back just as hard. She is swimming in a sea of endorphins. I am not, but we both pull away breathless. Her kisses always get my attention. They are a curious mixture of need and possibilities.

"Inspection," I bark. I need a minute to cool my own ardor. I pick up the crop and tap her pussy gently, careful not to hit the clit clamp. I flick the crop up and hit her square on the pussy near the back.

She yelps and hops away for a moment. I hit her again, and this time she stays put. I toss the crop and pull out my short bullwhip. It's perfect for the living room. I don't need a ton of space to wield it.

I show her the whip and then snake my fingers through the D-ring on her collar. I yank her over to the wall and attach her by the cuffs. These are not Velcro cuffs. No, my girl has graduated to big girl cuffs. She cannot get out of these without my help. And she knows it. So do I.

She groans in fear.

"You wanted this," I say and crack the whip behind her.

She jumps at the sound. "What makes the cracking sound, brainiac?"

"Tiny sonic boom," my brainiac says. "Waves traveling faster than the speed of sound, Ma'am."

"And did you say this out loud at the ball last weekend?"

"Yes, Ma'am. I'm sorry if I embarrassed you."

I laugh. "No, you didn't. But now everyone knows how smart my little bee is. Except that she is about to get whipped for the very first time, and she's not really ready for it."

"I'm ready, Ma'am."

Ha. I can hear how scared you are.

I crack the whip behind her a few more times. My next swing takes it right behind her back but doesn't touch her skin. She jumps and lets out a closed-mouth whimper. She is so tense she just might break something.

My next strike does touch her, but barely. It doesn't crack because I'm snapping it softly. I snap another soft one, and then I don't. *Crack* goes my whip against her back. She screams at the sudden pain. *Crack* goes another, and then a third.

"Yellow," she cries, and I am not disappointed. She should have called red, but I'll take yellow.

I toss the whip in the drawer and close it. She is breathing heavily when I walk up to her. I unhook her cuffs and pull her to me. I whisper in her ear, "Red."

She starts crying, and I know it's because she thinks she has disappointed me. She has not. Far from it, and I tell her just that.

I hold her tight and walk her to the full-length mirror in the *littles'* room. "Look how brave you've been," I say to her. There is genuine pride in my voice. I hope she hears it, too. She finally stops crying and turns around to look at her back and ass. "I love it," she says, admiring the red welts from the crop strikes, the geometry shapes, and the three whip marks. I know she feels them deeply. "You've marked me."

"You're mine. I can do that. Now go inside and grab the cock you want me to fuck your ass with."

"Really?"

"Go."

Chapter 19
Love the Sound

Bernadette looks back at me, her blue eyes filled with lust. The crayons, coloring books, and plastic action figures are scattered on the floor from her hand that swept them off the table in the *littles'* room. This is the last room in the house that needs christening.

I already removed the butt plug, and the lubed anal dildo she picked out is pressing against her back entrance.

"I need you inside, Rikki."

I comply and push in slowly but steadily. She is impatient because she has permission to cum at any time.

"Yes, yes, yes," she murmurs into the tabletop. Her lustful cries arouse me. Oh, yes, she will be servicing me later. Right now, it's her time. "Fill me, Rikki," she cries.

I push inside, and she shudders. I pull back and then pick up the pace, drilling her harder and harder. Banging my body into her backside enflames her already ravaged skin, I'm sure of it. I smack her sore ass with every other thrust making her shriek.

"Release it, lover," I tell her. "Release it."

I thrust in and out at a steady rhythm. My thrusts jam her hips against the table. She will have bruises. Good bruises.

"Cum, my good girl," I grab her hips and pull her ass upright to drill deeper. "Cum for me, Bernadette."

Her growl is low and long. She gasps and then holds her breath. She is going to have an assgasm. "That's my girl," I murmur.

"Ahh, ahh, ahh," she moans her orgasm at full volume over and over. I keep drilling her until she falls limp on the tabletop. I exit her body slowly and back up. I take off the harness and dildo and place both in the bag she had at the ready.

"Rikki," she says weakly.

"Oh, no, you're dropping, sweetie," I say. "C'mon." I pull her up and help her walk to our oversized chair in the living room. It's our favorite chair for cuddling and kissing. Occasionally, I fuck her here, and she often uses her very talented mouth on me as well. Yes, it's a very well-used chair.

Our waters from earlier still sit on the coffee table, so I grab them before pulling her naked form into my lap. She is putty, but I make her take a few sips of the water before she curls up small in my arms. I rock her gently and caress her.

I find myself humming as I hold her. I am so content. I have a beautiful, amazing girlfriend that I probably don't deserve. I always tell her that she represents me, but truth be told, I have recently become aware that I also represent her. I don't know why it's taken me so long to figure that part out, but what I do reflects on her as well. This is an extremely humbling discovery on my part and one I needed. I think Aunt Tilda would approve of Bernadette. No, I know she would.

"Rikki?" she says weakly.

"I'm here." I squeeze her gently. "I'm right here."

"Always?"

"Mm hmm. Always."

"Don't leave me. Don't you ever leave me."

"I won't." And don't you ever leave me. I want to say it out loud, but to do so would make me way too vulnerable.

She sleeps, and after a while, I cramp up a bit. Certain body parts are becoming numb, but I refuse to disturb her. Oh, great, now my bladder is rebelling.

Bernadette stirs and stretches. "Oh, hi," she says and blinks the sleepiness from her eyes.

"Hi, sweetie. How are you feeling?"

She groans. "Sore."

I chuckle. "I'm sure. You took a lot today."

"Mmm," she snuggles against me.

"Why don't you go clean up?"

"Okay." She gets up slowly from my lap.

I hide the agony of the blood now circulating back in my arms and move them subtly.

"You may put on a robe."

"Thank you, Ma'am." She takes three steps back before turning for the stairs.

As quietly as I can, I bolt to the bathroom to relieve myself. I wash up and laugh when my stomach growls. I'll have Bernadette start dinner, I guess. It's a little early, but I'm sure she's hungry, too.

I walk back into the living room and grab the mail from the inbox. I might as well organize the bills into "pay now" and "can wait" piles. Of course, my lawyer's bill is in there to pay. That'll probably go in the can-wait pile.

I set up on the kitchen table and smile at the memory of my girl draped over it, taking everything I gave her. I honestly don't want to deal with bills on a Saturday, but Bernadette has me convinced that sorting the bills will make them easier to pay on Monday morning. There is some logic to what she says, so I'm going for it.

I hear her pad down the stairs.

"Clean up this place," I say simply.

"Yes, Ma'am."

She understands that I mean for her to clean and sanitize the dildoes and plugs and clamps and whatever else I used on her body. She also knows she has to straighten up the *littles'* room.

"Come kiss me when you're finished," I call from the kitchen. Although she knows I love her, I find it's important to keep checking in after a heavy scene like today's. And besides, I like kissing her.

I hear her working, and it fills my heart. I am a mess financially, but I am on top of the world in every other category you can think of because of her. I sigh and grab the first envelope from the stack.

I want to toss the bills aside but instead make a neat and orderly pile. Bernadette will be pleased when she sees it. An odd feeling runs through me at that thought. I've always thought it was the sub's job to please *me*, but now I find that I want to please *her* more than anything.

I grab the envelope from my lawyer's office and open it. I scan the contents. Nope, not a bill. Good. I almost toss it aside, but my eye catches the name Eileen.

I close my eyes, take a deep breath, and start reading from the top. Is this a joke? I read on. No, it doesn't seem to be. My heart is pounding.

"Bernadette," I call. "Bernadette," I call louder.

"Yes, yes, yes, honey," she says as she races in the kitchen. "Here I am. Are you okay?"

I hand her the letter, and she reads it, saying some of it out loud. "Pleased to let you know … the funds will be sent to your account … the state considers this matter officially closed." She looks at me and shakes her head. "They found Eileen?"

I nod. I am in shock. "Apparently."

"And she didn't spend all the money?"

"No, apparently not. But where is she?" I wonder out loud. "And why now? Did she suddenly have a change of heart? I am so confused." I pick through the rest of the mail absently and find an envelope from a different lawyer's office. It looks official.

"Do you want me to read it?" Bernadette offers.

"Yes, please. My heart can't take much more of this."

She sits in the chair next to me and squeezes my hand. She opens the envelope, and her eyes widen. She looks from the contents to me and back again.

"What?" I ask her. "You're scaring me."

"Let me read it all first, and then I'll paraphrase for you." She reads the entire thing and then goes back to the beginning. "Okay, this letter is from the lawyer representing Eileen Donaghue's estate."

"Estate?"

Bernadette nods. "Apparently, she passed away."

"Oh." That's all the sympathy I can muster for the woman who ruined my life.

"She had a will with explicit instructions to give you everything left after expenses. Umm, this says that her possessions are in storage for you to pick up. Uh, wow. A two-year-old convertible Mercedes Benz is waiting at a towing company for you."

"Her dream car." I am in shock. "Bernadette, what's happening?"

She takes another piece of paper out of the envelope and hands it to me. It's a business card with a lawyer's name and number on it. "She's making amends, Rikki. The letter says she confessed to scamming you."

I look up at Bernadette, and a sob escapes from deep inside. Her arms are around me instantly. She rubs my back and shushes me quietly as I wipe at my eyes. She gets me a fresh water bottle, and I chug half of it. I am suddenly very thirsty.

"Rikki," she waves the letter in her hand, "this says Eileen left you over $350,000."

I sit back. "No way. That can't be." I reach for the letter and speed-read it until I see the dollar amount. "Holy crap. Finally, someone isn't asking me *for* money." My chuckle is one of relief. "It says here that she knew she was dying. Cancer." I put the letter down for a moment. This was her dying wish. To make amends. To make it right. I look up at Bernadette with tears in my eyes. "This was her last act here on earth. The very last thing she did."

"It's impressive," Bernadette says and rubs my shoulders.

"Did you read this part? About the sealed personal letter from her waiting for me in their offices in Cincinnati?"

She nods.

"I am floored." I rub at the tears in my eyes. "And more than a bit confused. And a lot of me is angry."

"You have every right to be," Bernadette says.

I tuck the letter and the business card in the envelope and push them aside. "I'll call that lawyer first thing Monday morning from the shop. I'm, like, in shock here. I am not even going to think about using that money for anything until I verify that it is real and legit and not one last joke played on me by an extremely manipulative woman."

"So, I assume we'll be keeping this under wraps until we know for sure?" Bernadette asks.

"Yes, little bee," I say. I realize my Bernadette is no longer in submissive mode. No, she is in full partnership mode, and I love her for it. "Are you done cleaning up?"

"No, I need to finish and then start the casserole." She steps back three times, and before she can turn, I leap to my feet and pull her into an embrace.

"I love you, Bernadette Garneau." I hold her tight.

"And I love you, too, Rikki Carmichael," she says into my neck.

"And you know who I also love?"

"Who?" she asks, her curiosity piqued.

"Madison."

"Madison? The *little* who stuck eighty-seven Trolls stickers on the back of the door in the *littles'* room? That Madison?"

"You counted? Never mind. I know you did." I pull back and kiss my girl on the lips. "I would never have found you if she hadn't set us up."

"I always wondered about that," Bernadette says. "She was so persistent that I come out for brunch." Her eyes narrow. "Little devil." She scoffs and adds, "And you know what? I love all of your friends."

"They're your friends, too."

"Yes, I guess they are, aren't they? I have you to thank for that because you were the one that attracted them to you in the first place."

I didn't think my heart could get any fuller. "Go get dressed, little bee. I'm taking you out to dinner. There's a celebratory spring roll with your name on it out there."

She steps back, and I stop her. "Just, just go. You don't have to do that anymore."

She cocks her head searching my face for meaning, trying to figure me out. A knowing smile lights her face as if she understands that I've had some kind of epiphany. She nods, spins on her heels, and heads toward the stairs.

I watch her go, knowing that I am the luckiest woman on the planet.

~~~

Late Wednesday morning finds us in Cincinnati in a cavernous conference room at the law firm's offices handling Eileen's estate. Bernadette graciously offered to come with me, understanding that this would be difficult. My leg is pressed against hers as she sits next to me in the swivel chairs at the formal mahogany table. I'm not used to relying on anyone for anything, but her touch is comforting and oddly grounding.

Two lawyers are handling Eileen's estate. Ms. Harris, the tall Black woman wearing the impeccably tailored suit, seems to be in charge, while the "junior team member," as she called him, hands her files when she puts out her hand. She sits at the head of the table, and he sits to her left. I can't help noticing the power differential between them and how they both accept their roles easily. I wonder if they've noticed the same with my girl and me. Ahh, it doesn't matter. I won't ever see these people again.

"Here are the keys to the storage unit that Ms. Donaghue willed to you," Ms. Harris says and slides an envelope over to me. "I have no idea what's in it, but Martin checked, and the unit is all paid up. You will be responsible for it from now on."

I nod and slide the envelope over to Bernadette, who had the foresight to bring a folder for "any and all paperwork."

"The only other tangible asset is the car," Ms. Harris says. She puts her hand out, and the junior lawyer hands her a printout with a business card stapled to it. "It is being stored here. There may be some storage expenses you'll have to pay." I glance at it and then slide it to Bernadette, who puts it in the folder.

"Here is the bank information for receiving your inheritance. I suggest you bring all of this paperwork with you. They will want proof of inheritance. And I'm sure there will be a long delay while the government investigates the money transfer. Generally, transactions over $10,000 are reported."

"Why is that?" Bernadette asks.

"The way I understand it, they want to make sure there is no money laundering or criminal activity involved."

"I see," Bernadette says and pats my thigh.

"And finally, this." She hands me a thin, sealed envelope. "This is the personal letter handwritten by Ms. Donaghue to you."

I recognize Eileen's handwriting on the front of the envelope. It reads, "For Rikki Carmichael."

"It was sealed by her own hand," Ms. Harris says. "As far as I know, no one has read it." She stands up. "Now, if you don't have any further questions, my colleague and I will let you have the room if you wish to stay here and read it."

"I, mmm," I say, gathering my thoughts. "I don't have any questions right at this very moment. I may after reading this." I wave the envelope as if fanning myself.

"That's understandable," she says. "I'll be in my office, and you have my card if you think of anything after you leave."

She puts out her hand, and I thank her as I shake it. She reaches over me and shakes Bernadette's hand as well. They leave and quietly shut the conference door behind them.

I blow out a sigh. "This is a bit overwhelming," I say to Bernadette.

"I know, sweetie." She rubs my thigh and then stands. "I'll wait in the lobby."

I grab her hand and pull her back down. "Oh, no," I say teasingly. "You're not leaving me alone with this."

The look on her face is one of pure compassion, and it's all I can do not to burst into tears.

"You're okay, sweetie," Bernadette says to me. "Everything will be okay. C'mere." She pulls me into a healing hug. "Just breathe."

I soak in her calm, her steadiness, and then do what she asks. I breathe for a few moments, content in her arms, and then lift my head. "It's now or never," I say and open the envelope.

Bernadette gives me privacy as I unfold the letter and begin to read.

Rikki – If you're reading this, then I'm dead.

These people in this damn hospital keep telling me I should save my strength and don't want me to write. Fuck that noise. I won't have any strength when I'm dead, right?

Okay, so … elephant in the room. It was really shitty what I did. I'm sorry. Yeah, yeah, I know. "Shitty" doesn't begin to describe it. I mean, it's not like I found Jesus or anything, but when the big C came knocking, it kind of made me reevaluate some shit.

It was so easy, you know—stealing your identity. You had blind trust in me and probably shouldn't have. You've probably noticed by now that I didn't spend too much of the money I took from you. Just enough to pay for my apartment, food, and the basics.

It's been a few days since I started this letter. Bear with me. I think these fucking treatments are killing me faster than the cancer.

Anyway, you're wondering why.

At first, I just wanted to get back at you. We had committed to each other. But it turned out that you were married to that damn coffee shop. And you spent more time with your Aunt Matilda than you did with me. I was sad when she passed away, and I naively thought you would fall into my loving arms for comfort. You even went to Victoria and Shasti before me. Why was that?

Sorry. I'm still bitter over your lack of affection toward me.

You told me you were in love with me. You know now that you weren't. We both know it. You were in love with the power you had over me, I think. You wanted your aunt and everyone else to see you as a legit Domme. At my expense.

I scoff. "What the fuck. Seriously? At *your* expense?" I put the letter down, close my eyes, and take a deep breath. Bernadette pours me a glass of water and hands it to me wordlessly.

"Relax your shoulders, please." She gently rubs the back of my neck. I pat her hand and smile at her. I twist my neck around until it cracks.

I take another sip of water before diving back in.

Do you remember that time—no, you probably don't—but that time I wanted us to go away for the weekend to Cedar Point? I had already booked us in the big hotel there. But you said, "No." As simple as that. No explanation. Just no. When I asked why you never answered me, you basically ignored me. Oh, I was fuming, Rikki (Yes, it's taken me this long to address you by name inside this letter). You didn't seem to care that I might have needs, too.

And then there was that fateful day a credit card application came in the mail in your name. It was my way of getting back at you. You never noticed. Honestly, I didn't intend to go beyond that first card, but then another one came, American Express, I think it was. It was so easy, and you were so oblivious to me or anything I did. When you wanted my body, you were attentive, but not really any time else.

And then, when your aunt died, you shared no emotions with me. That's when taking advantage and scamming you became my drug. The first time I took out a loan in your name – oh, my God. I was the fucking king of the world. I always thought you'd figure out what I was doing, but you didn't until I got too greedy. Then you pieced it together, didn't you? I'd already had an exit strategy if the time came. Too bad for you that I had already gone to another car dealer, and they gave me the loan and the car—no problem.

Why did I keep the money if I was only going to give it back to you? I ask myself that all the time. I should have taken a cruise or traveled through Europe. Do you know why I kept it? Well, I was slow to realize that although we were amazing sex partners, we weren't in love with each other. You hadn't yet learned how to open up and love someone. And as for me? Well, I realized that I was chasing a fetish dispenser, and you foot the bill nicely. The attention you gave me—yeah, I mistook it for love back then. I know now that it wasn't. <u>Taking</u> your money was my way of making you think about me. <u>Keeping</u> it was my way of thinking about *you*.

Why didn't I spend the money? This is the part where I get sappy – so please excuse a dying woman's emotions. I have no one, you know. But I'd had you for a while. And even though you weren't always emotionally available to me, you did defend me to your aunt (who hated me, I know). That told me that you saw some worth in me.

I didn't expect to be dying so young, Rikki, but I'm glad you'll be able to use this money and the car. Just sell or donate the rest of my shit. It's all crap. Sorry to burden you with it. I know you've been making payments on all those loans and credit cards I took out in your name, but I made sure to pay off all the balances. I kept accurate records. Weird, I know.

Rikki, I'm sorry to burden you with the shit I did to you. It wasn't fair.
You're a good person, Rikki Carmichael and if you ever find someone you can love, make sure she knows it. Open up to her. Take care of her. Pay

attention to her. Do little things like putting love notes on her steering wheel, bringing her coffee in bed, making her dinner. You deserve to be happy, Rikki.

Sorry I fucked things up for you. I hope your newfound inheritance helps. It's your money, after all. Take care of yourself.

Sincerely Yours,
Eileen Donoghue (as if you would have forgotten)

P.S. – You're still allowed to hate me.

P.P.S. – I'm sure your Aunt Tilda is on the other side waiting to give me a piece of her mind. I'm not looking forward to THAT, let me tell you, but hopefully, YOU can make peace with what I've done and forgive me a little bit. Again, I'm sorry for being such a vindictive asshole.

I blow out a sigh, emotion squeezing my chest. Bernadette rubs my back. "Are you okay?" she asks softly.

I nod. Surprisingly, I *am* okay. I mean, I'm going to have to reread this letter a few dozen more times, but yes, I think I'm okay.

"I'll let you read this when we get home," I tell Bernadette. "Home," I repeat, and the waterworks start up in earnest.

"Awww," Bernadette pulls me to her and lets me cry on her shoulder.

I get myself somewhat in check and swipe at the tears in my eyes.

"Are you happy, little bee?" I ask, my tears starting up again. "Are you happy with me?"

"Yes, of course I am. I love you." She is crying now, too. She taps my thigh and says, "Oh, how can you ask me that?"

My words come out between tearful breaths. "Tell me if you're not happy. Okay? I'll fix it. I'll do better."

"Sweetie, you're perfect." She slides off her chair and kneels at my feet. She lays her head in my lap, so I stroke her hair. "I am devoted to you, Rikki Carmichael. You and me? We fit together like two puzzle pieces. We're a team. A good one. Do you know why I love going to work?"

I sniff and grab a tissue from the box. I hand it to her and then take one for myself. "No, why do you like going to work?"

"Because then I get to come home to you. You're my partner, Rikki. And to answer your silly question, yes, I'm happy. Deeply happy."

I swipe at the tears in my eyes and pull her up off her knees. "I'm so happy with our life, Bernadette, that it scares me a little."

She smiles. "I'm not going anywhere. We had that one moment when we kind of lost our way, but we realized that this thing we have is too big to let go of. And personally, I think your mom and my mom somehow manipulated things from above so that we would find each other."

"That's a nice thought." I look up to the ceiling of the conference room and say, "Thanks, Mom. And Mrs. Garneau, I hope it's okay that I'm in love with your daughter. It will be my life's work to take care of her."

"Aww, Rikki," Bernadette says. "That is so sweet." Bernadette takes a turn looking up and says, "Mrs. Carmichael, I'm not sure how you and my mom set this up, but I'm grateful that you did. She is my heart and soul. And I, too, will take care of her. For my entire life."

I pull her into an embrace and say, "Baby, once my financial shit is taken care of, and I'm sure I won't be a burden on you, do you think you might want to get married? To me, I mean."

Bernadette bursts into tears. She nods, her face scrunching up as she cries.

"Is that a *yes*?"

"Yes, yes, yes. A thousand green lights." Bernadette pulls me into a kiss so powerful it makes me forget where we are and why.

When she pulls back, I say, "Thank you. You've made my life."

I stuff Eileen's letter in my pocket and gather up the other papers. "C'mon, little bee, let's go home. I'm making you dinner."

"Wait," Bernadette says as she opens the conference room door for me. "Who are you, and what have you done with my girlfriend?"

I waggle my eyebrows and say, "I turned her into your new and improved fiancée."

"Fiancée. I love the sound of that."

I link arms with Bernadette as we walk out of the building, ready to start the next phase of our life together.

~~~ THE END ~~~

Newsletter Signup

Sign up for Danielle Grainger's newsletter to stay on top of new releases. She also likes to provide recommendations for books to read (other than her own, of course).

Sign Up Here:

https://mailchi.mp/32c278368547/danielle-grainger-newsletter

Reviews

Reviews help get my books into the hands of readers who enjoy books like mine. It's often difficult for readers of certain, err, tastes to find books they enjoy. Would you consider writing a review? Let's get the word out. Thank you for at least thinking about it.

About the Author
Danielle Grainger

Dani is an instructor who currently resides in the southeastern USA and has several pampered fur babies. She has always been an avid reader and ventured into writing after reading several novels she felt didn't accurately represent the BDSM lifestyle. With so many rampant misconceptions, she took a chance and crafted admittedly idealized versions of possible experiences. Dani hopes not only to entertain her readers but to enlighten and educate them as well.

Dani's Amazon Author Page:
www.amazon.com/stores/Danielle-Grainger

Dani's Facebook:
facebook.com/danielle.grainger.7777

Dani's Instagram:
DaniGrainger84

Dani's Goodreads Page:
www.goodreads.com/author/show/19699760.Danielle_Grainger

Books by Danielle Grainger

THE DENTON HEIGHTS SERIES

The Denton Heights Series is the series that comes BEFORE the Bernadette Series. This group of books tells the stories of the beloved characters who populate the Bernadette Series world and live the BDSM lifestyle. We learn more about the origin stories of Madison and Shasti; Jaleesa, Tina, Harriet, Dana, DeShawn, and Kari; Rowena and Minjung; and Rikki. Victoria (AKA Daddy Vic), Lydia, and Brittany also feature in this series. The Denton Heights Series is basically the "Prequel Series" to the Bernadette Series.

Under Her Wing (Denton Heights Book 1)
(The Shasti and Madison Story)

An age-gap lesbian erotic romance with consensual light BDSM aspects featuring *littles*.

*** 2023 Finalist in the Golden Crown Literary Society Awards ***

Madison Kim finds herself on a bus headed to Denton Heights, Ohio, a suburb of Cincinnati. Her mother sent her there without notice to care for an elderly Korean woman Madison had never met. Madison is twenty-two-and-three-quarters years old and has a high school diploma, but she isn't smart enough to go to college...so they tell her. Now, she spends her time caring for Mrs. Park, going to the beloved Cincinnati Zoo, and watching movies on her outdated phone. She's not really sure why she's there, but she's taking it day by day. Then, she meets strong, nurturing Miss Shasti at a tea dance.

Shasti Balakrishnan has been looking for someone to call hers for more years than she cares to count. She wants a woman to love and care for in a nurturing Mommy Domme/*little-girl* scenario. She's thirty-two and already a partner in a thriving medical clinic in Denton Heights, but truth be told – she's lonely. She thought she'd found a companion in Amber back in D.C., but that fizzled out once they realized they weren't what each other wanted—or needed. And then she meets adorably precocious Madison at a tea dance.

ISBN: 978-1-953734-10-5 (e-Book)
ISBN: 978-1-953734-13-6 (Paperback)

In Her Cage (Denton Heights Book 2)
(The Jaleesa and Tina Story)
A lesbian interracial erotic romance with consensual light BDSM aspects.

Jaleesa Whitmore is a lesbian Domme in and out of fast relationships fueled by sex. She didn't understand addiction. Not yet, anyway. Although she had almost one full year sober, she was done with it. She was moments from heading down the familiar road of drinking that always made her feel good and filled that void. She was about to get her life back on its old track when a fateful encounter with a stranger, who would become a trusted friend, halted her downslide. She didn't know it then, but this encounter would not only lead her to a series of events and people that would change how she looked at life but how she approached it.

Tina Jenkins likes women but is asexual and afraid to try for another relationship. She does understand addiction. Just shy of eleven years clean of her opioid addiction following a dental procedure right out of high school, her parents carefully constructed and monitored everything in her world. It didn't matter that she was thirty-one years old and still living in the pink bedroom in her parents' house. It didn't matter that her mother now had to work from home, and her parents had to track her location and do routine searches of her bag, car, computer, phone, and room. None of it mattered because she was clean.

And then asexual Tina meets promiscuous Jaleesa. And everything changed for both of them.

ISBN: 978-1-953734-28-0 (e-Book)
ISBN: 978-1-953734-29-7 (Paperback)

Within Her Grasp (Denton Heights Book 3)
(The Marta and Shanice Story)
A lesbian age gap interracial erotic romance with consensual light BDSM aspects.

"Within Her Grasp" is an age-gap interracial lesbian romance that tells the tale of two women who had settled for unhappy lives. And then they meet.

White, thirty-something Marta Ingersoll was done with people. She just wanted to be left alone at work and at home, thank you. Her inside cat and the outside stray were all she needed. And her sister, Nora, too, of course. But that was it. And then, one fateful afternoon, her instincts to save a woman in obvious distress kicked in, and her life was shoved onto a strange new course.

Black, twenty-something Shanice Ward never got a break. Life had thrown challenge after challenge at the young woman, and this latest thing was too much, but it wouldn't stop. Woken up from a sound sleep by someone trying to remove her clothing, she shrieked for him to leave her alone. He didn't, but then, the most amazing thing happened. She discovered that superheroes were real, and one had just flown into her room to save her, and her life was shoved onto a strange new course.

ISBN: 978-1-953734-30-3 (e-Book)
ISBN: 978-1-953734-31-0 (Paperback)

By Her Command (Denton Heights Book 4)

(The Rowena and Minjung Story)

A lesbian interracial erotic romance with consensual BDSM aspects.

"By Her Command" is an erotic interracial lesbian romance containing consensual aspects of BDSM. It finds Rowena Tate in need of a submissive who can also manage her household. It's also the tale of Minjung Lee, who is desperate to find a Domme so she won't find herself homeless again. Trust does not come easily for either of them.

Rowena is a white Domme in her late thirties. Through experience, she has come to believe that most, if not all, submissives are selfish creatures who only want what she can provide without considering the person behind the flogger and the paycheck.

Minjung is an East Asian submissive in her mid-thirties. Through experience, she has come to believe that most, if not all, Dominants are selfish creatures who go well beyond contracted limits because there is no one to tell them not to.

Despite their reservations, both are told by members of the Denton Heights BDSM community that they are a good match and lucky to have found each other. Rowena isn't so sure. Neither is Minjung. Time will tell, won't it?

ISBN: 978-1-953734-32-7 (e-Book)
ISBN: 978-1-953734-33-4 (Paperback)

THE BERNADETTE SERIES

Dr. Bernadette Garneau holds a Ph.D. in Mathematics and has just gotten out of a four-year relationship. Shortly after the breakup, she began an exploration of her repressed sexual desires. One message from a beautiful and powerful online Mistress and Bernadette leaps into the world of BDSM. The Mistress takes charge, and Bernadette reels in the heady power this stranger has over her. She has gotten a taste of the life, and she wants more. She needs more. Several online and in-person experiences with BDSM and Power Exchange have led to cravings she doesn't quite understand. A brief sexual exchange with an online Goddess unleashes an incredible pain-to-pleasure connection that she hadn't understood before. As she sifts through the posers and one-night stands, she homes in on what her submissive nature needs from a Domme. The Bernadette Series follows Bernadette's journey into the world of BDSM and her search for love and sexual satisfaction. As she said, "I want a monogamous partner who wants to not only love and nurture me but who also wants to drape me over her lovely couch and have her way with me."

Wrecking Bernadette

(Book One in the Bernadette Series)
A lesbian's exploration of her sexuality with consensual aspects of BDSM.

Dr. Bernadette Garneau holds a Ph.D. in Mathematics and has been out of a four-year relationship for four months. One good thing about breaking up is that Bernadette is free to explore her repressed sexual desires. One message from a beautiful and powerful online Mistress, and Bernadette leaps into the world of BDSM. Mistress Ciara takes charge, and Bernadette reels in the heady power this stranger has over her. She has gotten a taste of the *life*, and she wants more. She *needs* more.

ISBN: 978-1-953734-00-6 (e-Book)
ISBN: 978-1-953734-14-3 (Paperback)

(S)mothering Bernadette

(Book Two in the Bernadette Series)

A lesbian's continuing exploration of her sexuality with aspects of BDSM.

Dr. Bernadette Garneau's universe is pushing her toward change. Her initial experiences with BDSM and Power Exchange have led to cravings she doesn't quite understand. A brief sexual exchange with an online Goddess unleashes an incredible pain-to-pleasure connection she hadn't understood until that encounter. But after sleeping on it, she clearly understands that this Goddess would never be the long-term relationship she sought.

Disappointed, she wonders if she should just give up and move back to California to be closer to her family. That is until she meets Mama_Luvs, an online Mommy Domme. The woman is nurturing yet stern from the start and is just ... perfect. And then Mama_Luvs wants to meet. Starry-eyed Bernadette packs for a New Year's Eve weekend, hoping that this time she's found *the one* – the one who wants to love and nurture her but who also wants to drape her over a couch and have her way with her.

ISBN: 978-1-953734-01-3 (e-Book)
ISBN: 978-1-953734-15-0 (Paperback)

Becoming Bernadette

(Book Three in the Bernadette Series)
A lesbian erotic romance with light consensual BDSM aspects.

University professor Dr. Bernadette Garneau has fallen in love with the world of BDSM. She has a nascent interest in the pain-to-pleasure connection, but she has yet to find partners interested in nurturing the soul within her body that they play with. Admittedly, she's had incredible sexual encounters with experienced Dommes, but all of them left her feeling cold for whatever reason. Most of them simply wanted a sadistic roll in the hay. Bernadette wants a strong Domme who will love and nurture her before flogging her on a St. Andrew's cross and afterward when her body is spent.

One afternoon, she finally musters the courage to venture out and meet some new friends in the local BDSM community. In walks a tall, handsome butch woman with fantastic hair and a confident stride. When this woman asks Bernadette, "Are you collared," Bernadette truthfully answers, "No," and accepts a dinner invitation for that very evening. She is walking on stars when she gets home at 2 a.m. after an ethereal sexual liaison. On the one hand, she wonders who she is becoming – she's never been this promiscuous. And on the other hand, she wonders if this strong butch woman could finally be the Domme of her dreams.

ISBN: 978-1-953734-02-0 (e-Book)
ISBN: 978-1-953734-12-9 (Paperback)

Desiring Bernadette

(Book Four in the Bernadette Series)
A lesbian erotic romance with light consensual BDSM aspects.

*** 2022 Finalist in the Golden Crown Literary Society Awards ***

Rikki Carmichael finally feels that deep D/s relationship she has been craving since her Aunt Tilda introduced her to *the life*. She embraced her dominant side early on, but finding a suitable submissive woman who wanted more than a quick roll in the dungeon proved elusive. That is until Professor Bernadette Garneau arrived on the scene. Now collared and committed to Rikki, will Bernadette prove to be different, or will she turn out like all the others — fickle and full of lies and deception?

And will this perfect sub stay with her when she realizes Rikki's ship is sinking? She'd almost lost the coffee shop she owns when creditors came knocking down her door en masse, seeking payment for debts that weren't hers. Rikki managed to keep her staff and most of her friends in the dark about it, but she has not been able to get out from under it. With high stakes all around, Rikki looks for the peace she is seeking within her relationship with Bernadette. If this one fails, it may be time to leave the life entirely and go live in a cabin somewhere isolated in the woods. But buying a cabin takes money – money she just doesn't have.

ISBN: 978-1-953734-03-7 (e-Book)
ISBN: 978-1-953734-09-9 (Paperback)

Loving Bernadette
(Book Five in the Bernadette Series)
A lesbian erotic romance with light consensual BDSM aspects.

Bernadette Garneau, a beloved professor of mathematics, is a natural submissive. She likes structure and rules and finally found a way of life and a woman who would provide those things for her. The BDSM community she stumbled upon in Denton Heights, Ohio, is where she found Rikki Carmichael, now her dominant partner and fiancée. Rikki is everything she's dreamed of. Yes, Bernadette found the captain of her ship. With Rikki's support and guidance, maybe other parts of her life can finally come together, too – like the respect she deserves but hasn't gotten at the university. Why won't anyone see that she deserves to teach those upper-level courses? And to move out of her closet of an office? What do they know that she does not?

Rikki Carmichael, the respected owner of Rikki's Coffee Shop in town, has finally found the woman of her dreams in super-smart and super-real Bernadette Garneau. Bernadette is a submissive who instinctively knows how to take care of Rikki and accepts Rikki's need to be in charge. Bernadette is the first submissive Rikki's ever had that wasn't solely out for her own gain. Once Rikki can climb out of the deep financial debt she's found herself in, she will finally make their engagement to be married public.

Miscommunication, faulty assumptions, and unmet expectations threaten this union seemingly made in heaven. When life comes at them hard and fast, they must rely on their bond and their loving, self-made family of friends.

ISBN: 978-1-953734-08-2 (e-Book)
ISBN: 978-1-953734-11-2 (Paperback)

www.ingramcontent.com/pod-product-compliance
Lightning Source LLC
Chambersburg PA
CBHW071158260626
47162CB00003B/1099